W9-BNV-034

THE LAMP OF DARKNESS

YOUNG READERS' EDITION

DAVE MASON
with MIKE FEUER

LIONSTAIL PRESS

Copyright © 2017 by David Mason

All Rights Reserved under International
and Pan-American Copyright Conventions.

Nevertheless, should you wish to take a small segment of the book for
quotation or teaching purposes, please feel free, since it is my hope that this
book will be used to stimulate thought and discussion. I just ask that you
don't abuse this privilege and certainly not to use it as a way of distributing
free or unauthorized copies, as I did work hard on it.

For further details on proper usage, please see
The Ten Commandments, Commandment 8
(I believe for some Christians it may be Commandment 7.
In any event, it's the one about stealing. I'm not so concerned about bearing
false witness, at least not in this context).

I feel like this is starting to ramble, but let's face it, none of you are reading
this page anyway. I'm certain my editor would
have cut this way back, but of course editors, like readers, never seem to care
about the copyright page. In fact, I think Amazon
programmed my Kindle to skip right over this page entirely.

For more details, visit TheAgeofProphecy.com.
Truthfully, you won't find any more copyright information there,
but it's a really cool site and I think you'll enjoy it.

For further permission requests, to place huge book orders, or just to say hi,
contact me at Dave@TheAgeofProphecy.com.

ISBN: 978-1-62393-008-0

Cover Design by the amazing Juan Hernaz.
Check out his other beautiful works at JuanHernaz.com.

Map by the fabulous Erika Givens.
Check out her site at Gleaux-Art-Design.com.

For Chana,
whose patience
was tried
many a time
by my six years of writing,
but who stuck by me
anyway
with undying support.
It wouldn't have happened without you.

Acknowledgements

As a reader, I always marveled at how many people were mentioned in the acknowledgements of books. After all, writing a book seems like such a lone undertaking. As a writer, I'm struck by the huge number of people who played a role in making this book come about. First of all, both Mike and I want to thank our wives Chana and Karen for supporting us throughout. My son Aryeh Lev, with his love of stories and desire to deepen his understanding, was a constant source of motivation. And of course our parents, without whom, none of this would have happened.

The origins of this book go back to when I was learning the books of the early prophets with Rabbi Aaron Liebowitz and studying the inner workings of prophecy with Rabbi Yaakov Moshe Pupko, both at Sulam Yaakov in Jerusalem. Most of this book was written within the walls of Sulam Yaakov, and I'd like to acknowledge the entire crew there, specifically Rabbi Daniel Kohn, whose teachings have been crucial to the development of our understanding of many key points in the book, and David Swidler, whose encyclopedic mind filled in many a random fact.

I'd like to thank Barnea Levi Selavan of Foundation Stone for helping us understand the historical context, Yigal Levin of Bar Ilan University for helping us identify the ancient city of Levonah, and Shoshana Harrari of Harrari Harps for teaching us about Biblical instruments.

Thank you to our editors, Shifrah Devorah Witt, who edited an early draft of the book, and Rebbetzin Yehudis Golshevsky who edited the final two drafts.

I'm incredibly indebted to the dozens of readers who offered comments, corrections, and direction over the years. I can't come close to mentioning them all. But I have to give special mention to: Rabbi Joshua Weisberg, Chaya Lester, Eliezer Israel, Michelle Cahn, Leia Weil, Beth Shapiro, Hadas and Gidon Melmed, Moshe Newman, David Shaffer, Jen Bell Hillel, Rachel Winner, Rabbi David Sperling, Rabbi David Fink, Eitan Press, Josh Fleet, Diana Maryon, and my uncle Sam Firestone.

Thank you all.

Two quick notes before you start reading:

1) We've created an introductory video for anyone who would like more background regarding the world you're about to enter, available at TheAgeofProphecy.com/video.

This video can be viewed at any time. It's not necessary to watch it before beginning. You'll also find both written and video notes on the website providing sources for ideas discussed in the book and deeper insights into key concepts.

2) We are constantly striving to improve the quality of our work as well as the readers' experience. The current publishing revolution not only provides authors previously unknown flexibility, but also allows readers to play a prominent role in the writing process. Accordingly, we've put a feedback form on our site at TheAgeofProphecy.com/feedback.

If there is a specific element for which you'd like us to provide an explanatory video, or if there's a passage that you find confusing, or if you find (heaven forbid) a typo, please let us know.

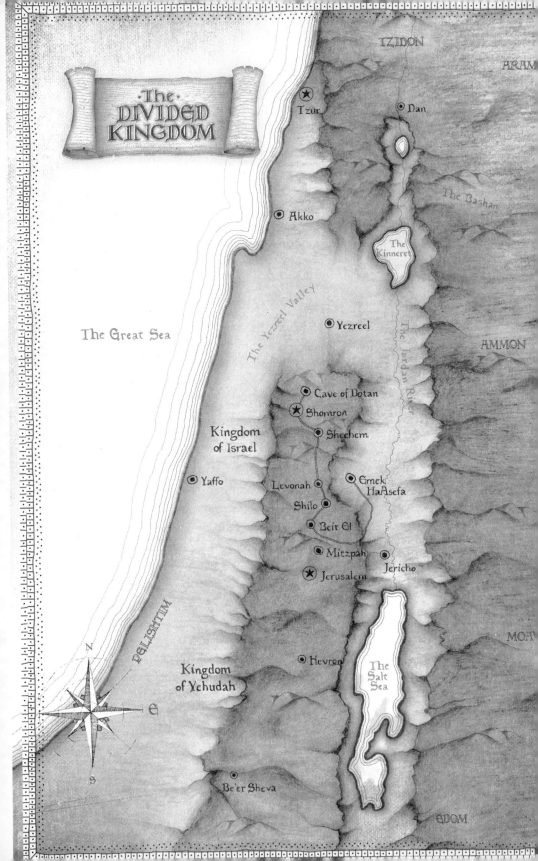

Hillel said: If I am not for myself, who will be for me? And when I am for myself, what am I? And if not now, when?

Pirkei Avot 1:14

1

A Shepherd's Inheritance

578 Years after the Exodus

The day before I was taken from my home, I grazed my uncle's flock on a hillside overlooking the path from the King's Road to the gates of Levonah. I sat under an old fig tree, taking shelter from the early summer heat while the sheep ate their fill. I strummed my kinnor, the small harp that was my only valuable possession, while keeping one eye on the sheep and the other on the travelers approaching the town gates for market day.

This was before the breakout of the war, when anyone could safely walk the King's Road, regardless of their loyalties. Many travelers passed me early that morning on their way to the city. Few spared even a glance for me, just a young shepherd boy, and none stopped to talk until my friend Seguv appeared late in the afternoon. The sheep bleated as Seguv drew his donkey off the road and climbed up to my perch. Seguv was only a few years older than me, yet he spent half his time traveling the Kingdom with his brothers. They came to Levonah three or four times a year to sell their father's dates. But this was the first time I ever saw Seguv traveling alone. He approached me with a bounce in his step that told of news.

The sheep scurried out of his way; strangers frightened them. Yet, Seguv barely noticed. He untied one of his saddlebags and searched through a thick cushion of flax until he pulled out a tiny clay bottle. His eyes sparkled.

"Is that it?" I asked.

Seguv nodded.

"Put just a drop on my hands. I want to feel it."

He gave a sly grin as he pulled the flask away. "A drop of this is worth more than one of your sheep, and it would be worth my head if the King found out. I'll let you smell it only."

I reached out to take the bottle, but Seguv tightened his grip. Only when I dropped my hands did he uncork it and hold it under my nose. The scent contained the sweetness of wildflowers. Then Seguv pulled the flask away and a hot breeze carried the sheep odor back under the fig tree. I opened my eyes, confused. "If it's so precious, why do you have it?"

Seguv's eyes widened, "My father wants the first batch to go directly to the King."

"But why are you taking it?" The roads were safe, and had been ever since the last civil war ended years ago. Even so, who would send a kingly gift with a boy selling dates?

I could tell from the way he smiled, with his tongue between his teeth, that he was just waiting for me to ask. "It's early," he said, raising his thick, dark eyebrows. "This is the first batch of afarsimon oil ever produced in the Kingdom. The King isn't even expecting a crop this year. My father says there's no better time for my first appearance at Court."

Only the most important men in Levonah ever went to the King's Court—I'd never heard of a fourteen-year-old going to Court on his own. But of course, no family in Levonah was as prominent as Seguv's. "So that's why you're making the trip alone?"

"Hmm?" Seguv was hardly listening, his attention focused on returning the bottle to his saddlebag.

"Is that why you're making the trip without your brothers? To win the favor of the Court?"

"Oh." Seguv closed the saddlebag, his hands fumbling with the straps. "I forgot you didn't know." His eyes fell to the ground. "We lost Aviram a few months ago, and now Onan is too sick to travel."

"What happened?" I couldn't help but ask. I pictured Aviram's laughing face. How could he be gone?

Seguv's teary eyes rose to meet mine. "It's the waters in Jericho. Many have died from them, but Father says it won't stop the rebuilding."

A Shepherd's Inheritance

Seguv tied off the last strap of the saddlebag. I wanted to comfort him, but I feared saying the wrong thing. I reached instead for my kinnor—music had soothed my own heart so many times. I closed my eyes and quieted my mind until my fingertips found a new melody, one that I hoped would contain all the compassion that I couldn't put into words.

Seguv's head dropped forward as one, two tears darkened the dry soil at his feet. Seguv mumbled, "Thank you," and then drew his donkey toward the town's gate.

"Go in peace," I called after him, then added, too quietly for him to hear, "and may the Holy One protect you from the waters of Jericho."

I played the melody louder now, eyes closed, soothing my own sorrow at Aviram's death. I only opened my eyes when I heard the approach of footsteps.

An old man approached me, with a young couple from Levonah trailing behind. The old man's leathery face broke into a smile as his gray-blue eyes met mine. He pointed to the trunk of the fig tree, silently asking if he could join me. I nodded in response; this was common land so I had no right to object.

The young couple stopped at the edge of the road. I didn't know them well, but I would never forget their wedding a month before. The bride's father had hired me as a musician, the first time I was ever paid for playing my kinnor. When they stood beneath their wedding canopy, their faces were filled with nervous, joyous energy. Now they stood like stone markers at the edge of the road, waiting as the old man approached me alone.

He sat down slowly but smoothly—not like the old men of Levonah, whose knees creaked and faces groaned as they lowered themselves to the ground. He leaned his back against the fig tree's trunk, pulled in his feet, and raised his knees before him. Were it not for the couple watching from below, I might have thought he sought out the shade for a late afternoon nap. His head sank between his bent knees. He sat perfectly still.

I still plucked away at my kinnor, even as I watched a butterfly land on his elbow. A moment later the butterfly took flight in a flash of orange as the old man shuddered. The hairs on the back of my neck stood up as a charge filled the air, like lightning during a storm. The old man's bent back trembled and his hands flapped against the ground. Was he having a fit? Should I stop playing? Yet, my fingers kept plucking until my fingernail caught on one of the strings, slicing it in two.

The trembling stopped just as abruptly as it began. The old man's back slowly straightened. Without a word, the stranger stood. He raised his aged hand and extended his hand toward the couple waiting by the side of the road.

"Come," he called to them.

The young man and woman rushed up the slope to meet him. Only once they stood beside him did I notice how very tall he was, standing a head above the younger man. The old man called out, "It rolled behind the wine barrel at the back of the house, and there it lies—dirty, but perfectly safe."

The woman put a hand to her chest, as a relieved smile came across her face. Her husband said, "Now I know you are truly a Seer. Shall we escort you back to the city?"

"I remain here with the boy. Go in peace with the blessings of the Holy One."

"Peace and blessings upon you, Master Uriel," the young man said, taking his wife's hand and starting back toward the town gates.

The old man turned his blue-gray eyes on mine. "It's time to water the sheep and lock them in for the evening. I will come home with you, Lev. I need to speak with your uncle."

I gathered my things, wondering, "How does he know my name?"

The King's tower, empty of soldiers during these times of peace, cast a shadow across our small farm by the time we returned home. My evening chores went slower than usual as I kept turning to watch the conversation between my uncle and the old man. I didn't finish filling the watering trough and securing the pen until darkness began to fall.

The rocky spring behind our farm was normally dry by early summer, but this year a trickle remained due to heavy, late winter storms. Farmers had cursed these late rains, which soaked the barley crop, causing much of it to spoil before it could be stored. But I felt only gratitude now as the stream of cool water ran over my curly brown hair and washed the sweat off my lean body.

It was nearly fully dark when I came inside. The evening meal was mostly over, and Aunt Leah had already taken her three youngest children up the ladder for bed. Only Uncle Menachem and his two oldest children, Dahlia and Eliav, remained at the table. I dipped my bread in salted cheese, chewing quickly because it was so late. My mind was still on the old man, but as my uncle said nothing, I didn't ask. When I finished eating, Dahlia rose to clean up while Eliav and I remained at the table for our nightly studies.

"And you shall sanctify the fiftieth year," Uncle Menachem began, chanting a verse from the Torah that he had memorized as a child, "and proclaim freedom in the land for all who dwell in it." Eliav and I echoed him, repeating not only the words but also the melody of his chant. "It will be a Yovel for you," my uncle continued. "You shall return each man to his ancestral land, and return each man to his family."

"It will be a Yovel for you," we repeated. "You shall return each man to his ancestral land..." Dahlia, cleaning in the kitchen, pushed a stubborn, red curl away from her eyes and coughed."...and return each man to his family." The cough was our signal. She had a question.

"Uncle?"

"Yes, Lev?"

The problem was, I never knew exactly what was bothering Dahlia. "When is the next Yovel?" Silence from the kitchen—I'd guessed right.

Uncle Menachem ran his fingers through his beard. "I asked my father the same question when he taught me this verse."

"And what did he tell you?"

"That he had never seen a Yovel."

"Have you seen one?"

"No, Lev."

I gripped the edge of the table to contain my excitement. "Then the next one must be coming soon!"

Uncle Menachem shifted on his stool. "No, Lev. My father was older than fifty when he died. Do not put your hope in the Yovel; it is not coming. The land will not be returned." He rose to his feet, though we had recited just one verse. "That's enough for tonight. It's already late. Lev, see that the flock is secure and then get to sleep."

I bit my lip hard enough to taste blood. I ought to know better than to get excited over the Yovel. It was just another silly daydream. I grabbed my kinnor on my way out. I tugged at the gate of the sheep pen, testing that it was well fastened, then walked around the edge of the wall, feeling for fallen stones.

I lifted a flat rock at the edge of the pen, withdrawing a leather pouch from the hole beneath. After a month in the cool earth, my new strings were ready. I sat on the ground with my back against the pen's low wall, and ran my hand across the top of the kinnor until I found the empty spot. I threaded one end of the sheep gut string through the hole in the olive wood frame and wound the bottom end around its groove at the base of the kinnor. I began to stretch and tune, stretch and tune, searching for the right sound to match the other strings. When the eight notes were in harmony, I ran my fingers lightly across all eight strings, letting the voice of the kinnor ripple out into the night.

This was my favorite time of day, when I could be alone with my music. But tonight the music had barely taken hold when a voice broke my focus.

"You must have questions about today," Uncle Menachem said, standing above me in the starlight.

I silenced the strings of the kinnor and stood up. "Yes, Uncle."

"Did you recognize that old man?"

"No, Uncle, but he knew my name."

"His name is Master Uriel. He is a navi, a prophet."

I recalled Uriel's trembling beneath the fig tree, and the couple with their missing item. Was that prophecy? Is that how he knew my name?

"Do you know why he has come?" my uncle asked.

My uncle had taught me that silence is a fence for wisdom, so I kept my mouth shut and shook my head.

"The prophets have called a gathering in Emek HaAsefa and they need musicians. Master Uriel would like to hire you."

"Hire me? How long is the gathering?"

"Two months."

"Two months?" I hadn't slept even a single night away from home since coming to live with my uncle. "I can't leave for that long—what about the flock?"

"Eliav can look after them. He's ten now, the same age you were when you first took them out alone."

My breath came short. "What did you tell him?"

"I won't refuse a navi, Lev. Not without reason."

I said nothing. If having me at home wasn't reason enough, what could I say?

"This will be good for you," Uncle Menachem said, speaking fast. "It won't be long until you're of age, and…" he reached beneath his cloak and pulled out a small pouch, tipping the contents into his hand, "…look here."

It was too dark to make out more than shadows, but I heard the unmistakable sound as my uncle emptied the pouch: the clink of copper. I reached out, my fingers finding the heap of cold metal—there must have been thirty pieces at least. "Whose are these?"

"These are mine, but I weighed them out according to Master Uriel's word. You will receive the same amount at the end of the gathering." He dropped the pieces back into the pouch one by one, each piece ringing in the dark as it fell.

"So many…"

"Enough for a ram and three ewes, with some left over." He tightened the leather strap at the top of the pouch, tying it shut. "It's a shepherd's inheritance."

I flinched as the word fell between us: inheritance. "Uncle, tell me again what happened to my father's land."

Uncle Menachem crossed his arms and sighed. "It's as I've told you, Lev. Your inheritance was lost to the King in the civil war. Do not dwell on what was lost. The Yovel is not coming. Your inheritance will not be returned." He put his hand on my shoulder. "The Land is wide enough for all of us, if we each find our place."

I nodded, but knew I had no place. My uncle cared for me like his own, but his land would pass to his sons, not his nephew. I didn't even know where my father's fields were. It had been foolish to get excited about the Yovel—just another false hope.

"When you return from the gathering, we can start building you a flock of your own." He held the sealed pouch of copper in the palm of his hand, as if weighing it. "If that's still what you'll want."

I strained my eyes to read his expression, but it was too dark. Shepherding was the best profession for one without land—my uncle had taught me this from my earliest memory. "Why wouldn't I want that?"

"I'm...I'm sure you will," he said, avoiding my eyes. "You should take that pouch of spare strings with you and get to bed. It's late and you have a long journey tomorrow." He squeezed my shoulder—which was as much affection as my uncle ever showed—and turned back toward the house.

I lifted the flat rock and retrieved the pouch again. When I stood straight, I found Dahlia sitting on the wall of the pen. "So what does the old man want?"

I sat down next to her. "Weren't you listening?"

"Just tell me."

"He needs a musician for a gathering."

"For how long?"

"Two months."

Dahlia let out a low whistle. "Are you going?"

"Yes."

"Now you won't have to stop travelers to tell me stories of the Kingdom. You can see it for yourself."

I slid away from Dahlia. "Those are other people's stories."

"They don't have to be." She touched me gently on the cheek, bringing my eyes to hers. Dahlia was the opposite of her father—too affectionate. It was fine when we were kids—we were raised like brother and sister—but now we were both nearly of age. Soon we'd be separated, and all her affection would only make it harder. "What's bothering you?"

Dahlia kept pushing me; she always did. "Your father didn't give me a choice."

"What did he say?"

"He said it would be good for me, but I know what he meant."

"What?"

I tapped my thumb against the frame of my kinnor, distracting myself enough to keep my voice calm. "That I have to find my place elsewhere because

I have no land and can't inherit from him."

Dahlia pulled her hair away from her eyes, tucking a particularly obstinate curl behind her ear. "Neither can I."

"It's different for you. Your father will marry you to Shelah or someone else with land."

Dahlia said nothing, just stared toward the property of our unmarried neighbor and shuddered. She was younger than me, but would come of age first, reaching her twelfth birthday in less than six months. There was no telling how long her father would wait before seeking a match for her.

"I'll be thirteen in less than a year," I continued, still not looking at her. "Without land, I'll have no choice but to become a shepherd, following the grasses from pasture to pasture."

"You won't have to leave here when you come of age."

"Not right away, but your father's already sending me away so I can earn enough copper to start a flock. It won't be more than three years until it's too big to keep here."

"Where will you go then?"

I stared at the hills to the east. "To the edge of the wilderness, away from the villages."

"That's so far. When would we see you?"

I shrugged. "A shepherd doesn't just leave his flock." That was true, but there were other truths that Dahlia, who clung to her dreams as if they were the morning sun, refused to accept. Even when I did visit, I might not see her, and we'd certainly never be allowed to be alone like this.

Dahlia tugged her knees to her chest. "You don't know what will be in three years' time."

A fire burned in my chest. "You think I'll inherit my father's land? Your father already told me it won't be returned—I don't even know where it is. What will be different in three years?"

"I..." Dahlia's eyes glistened in the starlight. "I don't know, but when you come home—"

"What's going to change when I come home?"

"Well, if the Yovel is not coming—"

"If the Yovel is not coming, my land will never be returned."

Dahlia shook her head. "If the Yovel is not coming, then any land you buy will be yours forever."

I gave a bitter laugh. "Do you know how many years I'd have to herd a flock just to buy a small piece of rocky hillside? It's better not to dream at all."

"Is it?" Dahlia also had a fire in her—we were of the same blood, after all.

"This morning you thought you were stuck in Levonah, and tomorrow you're leaving with the old man. You never know what can happen."

"His name is Master Uriel," I said. "There's something strange about him."

"He's a navi. My mother told me."

The memory of him saying my name on the hillside brought a feeling of dread. "There's something more."

Dahlia lowered her voice and leaned in. "Your eyes were so dark when you came home. What was bothering you?" That was the annoying part about Dahlia: she could always tell my moods so easily. She always said that my amber eyes would darken to match my thoughts. Yet, how could I tell her about my unease? She would only tell me to trust my heart.

I kept my voice low. "Your father knows more than he says."

Dahlia sighed and lay down on the broad, stone wall of the pen. "The stars are bright tonight."

"What do you think he's hiding?"

"Look at the stars, Lev. Aren't they beautiful?"

"Why don't you answer me?"

"I'm trying to." Dahlia pushed me lightly with her bare foot. "Look at the stars. Whatever's going to happen is already written there. It doesn't matter what my father's hiding; he didn't give you a choice."

I pushed her foot away, but turned my eyes upwards. "No, he didn't."

"Try to remember everything you see at the gathering. I want to hear all about it when you get back—it will give me something to look forward to."

I woke to the drumming of my heart. My forehead was clammy with sweat and my breath came fast. It was my old nightmare. How long had it been since the last time? A month? When I was younger, it woke me night after night. Yet, as hard as I tried, I could never remember even a single detail.

I pulled my tunic over my head in the faint dawn light—today wasn't a day to dwell on dreams. I arranged my few belongings on my sheepskin sleeping mat: the extra strings, my shepherd's pouch. Together with my kinnor, sandals, and tunic, this was all I owned. I started rolling them in a bundle when something heavy dropped on the mat.

"This was your father's knife," Uncle Menachem whispered, trying not to wake the younger children. "I intended to give it to you when you came of age, but it may serve you well on your journey."

My fingers trembled as I picked up the knife. The stone of the handle felt

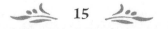

smooth in my hand. I brought the knife up to the high, square window that offered the only light in our sleeping loft. The sheath pulled off with a tug, revealing a blade that was flint rather than iron, and a full two handbreadths long. I had never seen one like it. A copper inlay decorated the hilt, with a design showing two claws with three toes each, the inner toe of each claw gently touching.

A lump blocked my throat. My father had held this knife.

"Lev…" My uncle sounded far away, but there was a strange tone in his voice that got my attention. "The prophets are the chief servants of the Holy One. They mean only good; I believe that." He looked as if he was about to say more, but then turned to go so quickly that I had no chance to respond.

I watched him climb down the ladder. I sheathed the knife, added it to the pile on the mat, rolled it up and tied it together.

I descended the ladder to find Aunt Leah standing before the hearth. "Sit down and eat before you go," she said. There was a plate on the table with cheese and my special bread. Ever since I could remember, she always set aside the first piece of bread baked each day for me.

"Thank you, Aunt Leah," I said, then quickly washed my hands and sat down without meeting her gaze.

She sat opposite me, watching me eat, her eyes tinged with red.

I ate quickly, mostly as an excuse to keep my attention on my food. The bread disappeared, but other than rubbing her eyes with the back of her hands, my aunt didn't budge. There was no use putting it off; she wasn't going to let me leave without talking. Without looking up, I said, "You don't want me to go, do you, Aunt Leah?"

Tears ran down her cheeks and she forced a half-smile. "Yes, I do."

My eyes rose up to meet hers. "You do?"

"I do." She wiped the tears with her palm. "Menachem said you were too young, but I told him you were ready."

So my uncle hadn't wanted me going—that explained his reluctance. "If you want me to go, then why are you crying?"

She smiled, as two more tears spilled over her cheeks. "Hasn't your uncle taught you that more than the lamb wants to drink, the ewe wants to give milk?"

I just stared back. Why was she suddenly talking about the flock?

Aunt Leah laughed, releasing more tears. "You don't understand now, but when you're blessed with children you will. You're my sister's son, but you know you're the same to me as one of my own, don't you Lev?"

A wet stinging filled my eyes—I hoped my aunt didn't notice. "Yes, Aunt Leah."

"And no matter what happens, you'll always have a home here."

I nodded—no words would come.

There was a soft knock.

My aunt rose and opened the door. Uriel stood a little way off, his back to us, leaving us the space to say goodbye. Aunt Leah held me in a tight embrace. I took a final glance at my home over her shoulder as I hugged her back, my eyes open and dry. Though I was destined to return, I would always remember this as the moment that I left home for good.

Shimon son of Azai said: Do not despise any person, and do not dismiss any thing, for there is no one who does not have his hour, and no thing that does not have its place.

Pirkei Avot 4:3

2

The Three Keys

Uriel stood at the edge of Uncle Menachem's land. "Why have you come, Lev?"

"My uncle told me I was hired to play."

"So you are here because you were sent?"

I hadn't asked for this old man to come tear me from my family—what did he want from me?

"Know, if it is only by your uncle's wish that you come, then it is my wish that you remain here."

Eliav would surely laugh at me if I went back. Aunt Leah would be disappointed. Would Dahlia be happy, or think I'd failed?

"Do not be afraid of embarrassment for turning back. Your uncle will be relieved. There is much you can do here to help your family."

"Are you offering me the choice?" All my life others had made decisions for me. I didn't choose to live with my uncle, nor to become a shepherd. I may have complained to Dahlia about not having a choice, but I never really expected to have one.

"The Prophet's Way is a path of choice; its servants are not for hire. So, tell me now—do you choose to come with me, or are you being sent?"

Was it true? Could I choose to let the prophet leave without me? No, that was just another silly dream. My uncle had spoken, and I would not upset my aunt. Yet, I knew that we would not move until I told the prophet what he wanted to hear, so I looked straight into his eyes and lied. "I choose to come with you."

Uriel held my gaze, as if he knew my words to be empty. "So be it," he said at last. "Put your belongings on Balaam." He indicated an old, one-eared donkey by his side.

When I finished tying down my things, Uriel started down the path, his donkey following without being drawn.

As we passed by the fig tree where we had met the day before, I felt the prophet's eyes upon me. "You have a question?"

How did he know? "Yesterday, when the couple came to you, you used prophecy to find something?"

"They lost a valuable ring."

"You find rings?"

Uriel chuckled, slowing his pace and turning toward me. "You thought prophecy was only for more important things?"

"Well…yes."

"I assure you," Uriel said, his eyes no longer laughing, "that ring was extremely important to them."

I hadn't meant to say that what he did was unimportant—I was just surprised. I ought to keep silent. But there was another question I wanted to ask, one that had been on my mind since I woke that morning. My uncle always taught me that the bashful can't learn. "And then you received prophecy about me?"

"About you?"

"Yes, about hiring me?"

Uriel's shoulders relaxed. "No, Lev, I did not receive a prophecy about hiring you."

"Then why?"

Uriel watched me out of the corner of his eyes. "Why what?"

The tips of my ears grew hot. Was he playing with me? "Why me? There must be better musicians. I'm just…" My voice trailed off. What was I?

"You want to know what, other than prophecy, would drive me to hire a shepherd boy to play for the prophets?"

I nodded.

"That is a wise question, and thus deserves a response." Uriel stopped and faced me. "My heart told me."

His heart? "You didn't want to…check?"

"I have learned never to use prophecy to question my heart."

"But prophecy—"

"An open heart knows more than you realize. At times its intuition is more valuable than prophecy. There is no faster way to dull its voice than to doubt it."

Even if he was right, what did it matter? How many times had I watched the distant hills, dreaming of a mother who would never return? How many times had I questioned my uncle about land that would never be mine? I learned long ago the dangers of an open heart. Why rely on his heart when he had a better tool? "Isn't prophecy more powerful than intuition? Your heart couldn't have found that lost ring, could it?"

"True, it could not. Yet, my heart is mine to know, while prophecy is not at my command. Yesterday I was unable to receive prophecy until I heard your kinnor."

"My kinnor?"

"Your music is pure and beautiful. It cleared away many barriers."

We reached the King's Road and took it toward the south. None of the stories my uncle told me about the prophets ever involved beauty.

"You are confused," Uriel said, again responding to my thoughts. "Your uncle told me you learn the stories of our Fathers. Tell me, after Yosef's brothers sold him into slavery, how did they deceive their father Yaakov?"

"They dipped Yosef's coat in the blood of a goat. Yaakov thought Yosef was killed by a wild beast."

"Good, I see you know the story. Now, do you understand it? Yaakov was a prophet and a rich man. Shouldn't he have known his sons were lying to him? Couldn't the Holy One tell him where Yosef was held in Egypt? Why didn't he go down and redeem him from slavery?"

I stopped walking. I had known this story most of my life—at least I thought I had. "I don't know."

Uriel continued on in silence. I fell behind him on the road. How could I know why Yaakov didn't ask the Holy One? What did that have to do with my music?

My uncle told me that Yaakov mourned his son every day he was gone as if he had died that very morning. That was why the story stuck in my mind. Yaakov's grieving for his son felt like my own grieving for my parents. Could that be it? I ran ahead, slowing only when I drew even with the elderly prophet. "Was it his grief?"

"Are you asking me a question or giving me an answer?"

I tried again. "Yaakov couldn't receive prophecy because he was mourning the loss of Yosef."

Uriel smiled, the first show of warmth I felt from him that day. "Indeed. Sadness closes the heart. Prophecy can only be received in a state of joy."

Sweat ran down my neck as the summer sun burned directly overhead. At the side of the road, a man cut the last of his wheat, hacking at the bases of the stalks with a curved iron blade. A young woman collected the cut wheat, laying it flat to dry. As soon as she caught sight of us, the woman dropped her stalks to the ground and smoothed her dress over her pregnant belly. She stepped over to the road, then bowed her head low before us. "Master Uriel, won't you turn aside and eat a meal from your maidservant?"

He nodded to her request, and the two of us stepped into the shade of a carob tree to wait. The woman whispered something in her husband's ear. He dropped his sheaves to the ground and ran off through the fields.

She returned and led us into her small, mud-brick house. She seated us at a low table, poured a small bowl of wine into a pitcher, filled the rest with water, and placed it before us with two clay cups.

"Thank you, Milcah," Uriel said, pouring for the two of us. She brought out a pot of freshly salted cheese, then quickly patted dough into two cakes and placed them directly on the coals in the hearth.

Soon after the bread was done, the husband returned with a second woman. She looked like Milcah, but with a slimmer body and pinched face. She stepped into the house and walked directly to the prophet.

"Peace unto you, Master Uriel," she said. "I have come for another blessing."

"Another, Rumah? Has the first brought what you sought?"

"Of course not!"

"Why then do you ask for another?"

"Any fool can look at the two of us and see why. My sister and I received the same blessing from you nine months ago. Now here she is with her belly between her teeth, and I am just as I was, only older. Why? Why her and not me? She'd been married for two years when we came to you, I for almost ten. People say you can work miracles. Why didn't your blessing work for me?"

"It is not truly my blessing, but that of the Holy One."

"I told my pain to you. It was you who promised me a child. Of course the Holy One is the source of life, but you are a prophet."

"I never promised you a child." Uriel rose from his stool, his thick, gray hair brushing the low roof. "There are three keys that the Holy One does not give to any servant, even the prophets: the Key of Life, the Key of Resurrection of the Dead, and the Key of Rain. Without them, there can be no birth, no resurrection, no rain. Even our father, Yaakov, could do little for our mother, Rachel, when she cried before him, demanding a child. And despite what you may have heard, my power is small compared to Yaakov's."

Rumah wept into her empty hands. "So you can do nothing? I am lost?"

"No blessing is in vain," he replied, his voice softer now, "but the blessing alone may not be enough."

"But the Holy One heard my sister's cry."

"There are many things that can block the channels of blessing. Perhaps you have not come into this world for the children you wish to bear. And perhaps you yourself are closed to the blessing which is ready to be born into your life." Uriel turned to the pregnant sister. "Milcah, when I left here last, did you do anything to prepare for the baby?"

"Well, it's silly," she said as she reached for a loosely woven fabric of heavy wool. "The next day I started weaving this blanket. At first my husband laughed at me, but then he started building that cradle."

Uriel smiled as he looked upon the cradle next to their reed sleeping mats.

The older sister glared at the blanket. "You're not suggesting that if I wove a blanket I would have conceived too, are you?"

"Of course not. The blanket itself was insignificant, as was the cradle, but her beliefs were not." Rumah's mouth was a thin line, and her eyes darted back and forth between the blanket and Uriel. "Milcah acted with certainty that the blessing would come true. This created a space in her heart for the blessing to rest, allowing it to bear fruit." Rumah's hands unclenched as her eyes settled on his face. "Do you remember what you thought when you left me last?"

"I do." She bent her head with a short laugh. "I even remember talking to my husband when I got home. He asked me, 'Do you think it will work?' I told him, 'Who can tell? Milcah thinks it will. What harm could there be in going along?'" Her eyes rose back to Uriel's, filled with a new light. "So if I believe, it will work?"

"I cannot promise you that. As I said, the key of birth is beyond my grasp."

"And if it fails? If there is no child?"

"Then you can choose to embrace your life as it is, seeing your challenges as opportunities for growth, and approaching each day with joy. Or you can remain bitter that your life does not match your dreams. Just know that bitterness will never bring you what you desire."

Rabbi Eliezer said: Warm yourself by the fire of the Sages, but beware of their glowing coals lest you get burnt—for their bite is the bite of a fox, their sting is the sting of a scorpion, their hiss is the hiss of a serpent, and all their words are like fiery coals.

Pirkei Avot 2:15

3

Honoring the Calf

"When you find Yosef son of Avner," Uriel said the following morning, "tell him we shall meet tomorrow at the junction."

I looked toward the ancient walls of Beit El, my morning meal untouched before me. "How will I find him?"

"Quite easily, I imagine. There is no other like him in the city."

"But where does he live?"

"He once lived in the weavers' quarter, but I do not know if he has remained there. I have not entered Beit El in over sixty years."

Sixty years? The men in Levonah who reached sixty years ground their food to mash before eating it, yet Uriel still had a full set of teeth. Just how old was he?

The prophet pointed at my untouched bread. "Eat. There is no knowing how long you'll be gone."

I took a bite, forcing myself to chew—I didn't want to fail in my task because of hunger. Uriel sat down at the edge of a cliff overlooking the junction.

"Are you going to sit here alone all day?"

"Probably, though sometimes visitors come to me even here."

I swallowed another bite. "Why haven't you entered Beit El in sixty years?"

The prophet turned his eyes to a cloud of dust rising above the road in the distance. "That looks like a royal messenger riding toward Beit El. If you hurry you can catch him. There might be news."

I shoved the last chunk of bread into my mouth, slung my water skin over my shoulder, and ran toward the path. My legs ached from the long march the day before, but I pushed myself into a run down the steep path. This was a mistake. I slipped on a loose rock and fell to the ground. I slid down the trail until my left knee banged into a boulder.

I was a musician, not a messenger. Why did I have to go running off while Uriel just sat all day? I got up, rubbing my leg, and limped carefully down the path.

I tried running again once I reached the road, but it was no use. The rider rode past me before I was halfway to the city gates, leaving me coughing in a cloud of dust. Soon after, three ram's horn blasts came from the city, signaling a public announcement.

A public announcement directly from a royal messenger was something we heard in Levonah only three or four times a year. I pushed myself to hear it, running through the gate, to where a crowd already stood in the city square. I came to a stop at the edge of the crowd. I had made it in time.

The messenger brought a silver-tipped ram's horn to his lips and blew a single blast. "By authority of the great King Ahav!" A hush fell across the square. "It gives His Majesty great pleasure to announce his engagement!"

The crowd roared its approval. Still gasping for breath, I added a feeble cheer. Aunt Leah always said, "It is not good for a man to be alone." To her, even a king was lacking without a wife.

"King Ahav will marry Princess Izevel of Tzidon on the ninth day of the fifth month in the royal capital of Shomron. Let all of Israel come and rejoice!"

This time, there was no cheer from the crowd. The messenger sneered at their stunned looks. He kicked his horse, swung it around, and was not yet clear of the crowd when he pushed it into a gallop.

I wasn't sure why news of the King's engagement would bother the people, but the anger written on their faces made me too nervous to approach any of them. Yet, with the messenger gone, now was the time to find out about Yosef, son of Avner, before the crowd dispersed. I bit my lower lip. I never liked asking for help, especially from strangers.

"Are you Lev?"

I turned to meet the smiling eyes of a squat young man with a bushy black beard and bent nose. "Yes, I am."

"Excellent. I am Raphael, son of Eshek. Master Yosef sent me to find you. Come, he is waiting."

Is this how it would be among the prophets? Would they answer my questions before I could even ask? Raphael turned to go, and I followed, still limping from my bruised knee.

"How long have you been with Master Uriel?" Raphael asked.

At least Raphael didn't know everything about me. "Two days."

"Ahhhhh," he chuckled. "My first week with my master, half the time I had no idea what was happening."

I laughed louder than I intended. "That's how I feel right now."

Raphael looked at my swelling knee, with the trail of dried blood leading down to my shin. "Is this fresh?"

I nodded.

"We'll put something on that when we arrive. For now, let me help you." Raphael thrust his stout arm under mine and drew me toward a narrow street.

Raphael smelled clean, like a fresh rosemary bush. Could he tell that I had not properly bathed since the last new moon? His tunic was linen, not the rough wool of a servant's. Who was he, exactly? "Are you Yosef's assistant?" I asked.

"No, his disciple."

"You're training to become a prophet?" None of the stories of the prophets ever involved training.

"Yes." Raphael beamed, revealing a set of large, crooked teeth. I couldn't help but smile back; his eyes gleamed like those of my young cousins whenever Aunt Leah treated them to roasted nuts.

"How long have you been with Yosef?"

"Five years."

"Five years?" I spent only six months going out with my uncle before I was ready to take the flock by myself.

"Oh, yes. Prophecy comes only after many years of training—if at all."

"And have you ever received prophecy?"

"Not yet."

We stopped in front of a flat-roofed house made from chiseled stone. The door swung outward, and an old man stepped into the street, his dark eyes fixed, unblinking, on my own. His gray hair and beard were darker and better groomed than Uriel's.

"Welcome, Lev, son of Yochanan, I am Yosef, son of Avner. I am aware of Uriel's instructions to you; nonetheless, speak your message and fulfill your master's command."

Uriel was hardly my master, yet I kept my mouth shut—I could already see that Yosef was not someone to argue with. "The time has come for the gathering. Master Uriel has informed the others. He will await you at the junction in the morning."

"Very good. We will be there. Raphael, I see that Lev's knee needs care. In my quarters you will find clean fabric and ointment in the remedy box."

As Raphael entered the house, I tried to catch a glimpse of what was happening inside, but couldn't see anything. Yosef said, "You would like to observe my disciples? They are engaged in training now, so I do not wish to disturb them." His eyes flickered over me from head to toe. "Yet, there is one way you can help. Then you could enter and enhance, rather than disturb, their experience."

Curious though I was to see what was going on inside, Yosef's piercing eyes made me glad that I had a ready excuse. "My kinnor is with Master Uriel."

"No matter, you will not need it."

Raphael returned with a cloth and a bowl of water, and bent to the ground to carefully clean the wound. He then brought out from within his robe a small clay jar filled with some evil-smelling substance. I clenched my teeth when the herbs touched my knee, but the sting lasted only a moment. I asked Yosef, "What else would I do?"

"You will see a stool in the middle of the room." Yosef nodded to Raphael, who entered the house, closing the door behind him. "All you must do is walk in and sit down."

"That's it?"

"That is all."

How could sitting on a stool help the disciples in their training? Were they going to do something to me while I sat defenseless?

Inside, eight disciples sat on reed mats, legs folded, eyes closed. In the middle of the room sat the only piece of furniture, an empty stool. I limped quietly to the stool, and sat down. No one reacted to my entrance. Other than one disciple scratching his nose, the only sound came from disciples' breathing. Yosef leaned against the doorframe and watched.

I rubbed the back of my neck, suddenly hot and itchy. Uriel and Yosef both knew things about me without being told. Is that what the disciples were doing now, reading my thoughts? Would I even know it if they were?

I had agreed to help, but my thoughts were my own. My forehead creased as I tried to empty my mind. It didn't work. Memories came pouring in on me, the very ones I least wanted to share: almost losing the flock in a thunderstorm; the feel of Mother's hair on my cheek. Sweat beaded on my forehead, but my failed efforts only proved I couldn't clear my mind by force. When playing my kinnor I could sit without thoughts, but at this moment it was far away. But did I need my kinnor to create music? I closed my eyes and concentrated on one of my favorite melodies. Immediately, my shoulders relaxed.

Yosef finally broke the silence. "What can you tell me about our guest?"

The disciples turned toward their teacher, eyes still closed. One replied, "He is a boy, Master."

"Why do you say so?"

"His footsteps. It took him eight steps to get from the door to the chair. It takes me five or six. Also, his steps were soft, lighter than a man's."

"But slightly uneven," the disciple next to him added, "as if he's walking with a limp." I touched my left knee, still aching from the fall that morning.

Yosef was not yet satisfied. "What else?"

"He's a musician, Master."

"Interesting. Why do you say so, Nadav?"

"He's tapping his feet."

I peered down at my feet. I hadn't realized they were tapping out the melody in my head.

"Do only musicians tap their feet?"

"No, I even do it myself sometimes." The disciple cocked his head to the side. "But there's something different about the way he taps; the rhythm is more...complex...than when I do it."

"I see." Yosef's voice gave nothing away, but he was smiling. "What else?"

The prophet's eyes swept back and forth across the disciples, but no one responded. Finally, the one who had scratched his nose earlier said, "He's uncomfortable with us speaking about him."

"What tells you this, Elad?"

"When Nadav described him tapping his feet, he stopped, and he's breathing faster than he was before." Instantly my cheeks grew hot.

"Very perceptive."

This was my first experience with using the ears to see, and I was amazed at how much the disciples were able to learn just by listening. Yet, within a year, the skills of these disciples would seem basic to me. When one enters a place that light cannot enter, his ears become his eyes. I would learn to hear the difference between a wall and a doorway, and to distinguish the footstep of friend from enemy.

"The time has come to take mercy on our guest. Open your eyes and greet Lev, a musician that Master Uriel hired to play for us during the gathering." Yosef smiled at Nadav, the one who had guessed I was a musician. From the look of gratitude on Nadav's face, I gathered that a smile from Yosef was a rare reward.

"I must ask you to excuse us now, Lev. We will meet again tomorrow at the junction."

The sun had not yet reached its midpoint in the sky when I left Yosef's house. I walked back, thinking over everything I had seen. In all the stories my uncle had taught me, the Holy One simply chose the prophet—there was never any mention of training. Yet, Raphael had said that all the prophets, every single one of them, had trained. Avraham and Moshe had been alone, cut off from any other prophets—where could they have trained?

I turned the stories of my favorite prophets over in my mind. Each Sukkot, Uncle Menachem had told us the story of the seven shepherds of Israel: Avraham, Yitzchak, Yaakov, Moshe, Aaron, Yosef and David. It couldn't just be coincidence that they were all shepherds like me, could it? Could they have trained for prophecy while in the wilderness with their flocks?

As my mind wandered, my feet led me back to the gate of Beit El. I stopped just inside the heavy wooden doors, realizing that Uriel would not look for me much before sundown. I had time for myself, a rarity in Levonah. I turned my head up and sniffed—the scent of roasting meat hung in the air. I immediately knew where I wanted to go; I just needed to get there.

Hurrying back to the main square, I stood watching until I spotted what I was looking for—a farmer drawing a lamb. I crossed the square to follow, and the aroma of meat thickened. I was on the right trail.

I followed my guide through the winding alleys of Beit El until the street broadened into a marketplace. Open storefronts lined the sides and freestanding stalls ran down the middle. A familiar animal odor filled the air, and sheep bleated from a storefront on my right.

"How much for a sheep?" I asked the shopkeeper, though I knew I didn't have enough copper to buy one.

The shopkeeper eyed my dirty tunic. "The lambs start at three shekel silver, the rams go up to eight."

"Eight shekel silver? We get only half of that for a ram that size."

"A shepherd on your first trip to Beit El, eh? The sheep you sell are for eating; it doesn't matter if they have a bad eye or walk with a limp. Mine have no flaws. If you get any big ones in your flock like that bring them to me. I'll give you a lot more than you'll get from the slaughterers."

A cooing sound rose from dozens of holes between the white stone blocks of the wall. "How much for a dove?"

"I can give you a good one for half a shekel." He pulled a small iron weight from a pocket of his smock and put it on one end of a scale. On the second pan, I dropped a few copper pieces, my earnings from the wedding earlier in the summer. Just as my fourth copper piece landed on the pan, it sank, bobbing up and down until it came level with the iron. It was most of what I owned, but I couldn't miss this chance. Dahlia's nose would crinkle with envy when I told her I'd gone to Beit El a year early.

The dove struggled when the shopkeeper pulled it from its hole, then relaxed in his grip. "Hold it like this, with both hands over its wings," he said, passing me the bird. "You don't want it to fly away." I gripped it the way I was shown. The small body squirmed in my hands.

"Hold it firm," he said. "If you let it struggle, it might get hurt. A pity to waste your copper on an unfit offering."

I tightened my grip and the bird relaxed. "What do I do now?"

"Take it to the altar. Follow the crowd uphill toward the smoke." Unable to contain my excitement, I snorted out a laugh. The shopkeeper's eyes narrowed, and his beefy hand clapped onto my shoulder. "Wait, I forgot to ask. You're of age, are you not?"

I shook my head. "Not for another year."

He wrapped his big hands around mine, taking control of the passive dove and shaking his head with a half-smile. "I should've asked first. You can't make an offering until you're of age. I'll not have you sin on my account." He returned the bird carefully to its hole, then placed my coppers back in my empty hand.

"Is there nothing I can do?"

"Go and bow before the Holy One. Anyone can do that."

I stepped out of the shop and continued up the center of the marketplace. Eliav would laughing at me if he ever heard about the dove—I'd have to tell Dahlia when we were alone. As I reached the end of the market, I smelled incense and heard music unlike any I had ever heard.

Slipping through the crowd, I sought the source of the music. Across the plaza, I found what I was looking for: seven musicians standing on a wooden platform, brilliant red robes falling to their feet. The cry of a frightened sheep tore my attention from the melody. With the instincts of a shepherd, I sought out the distressed animal. There was another sharp bleat, cut short by a grunt, and I spotted the lamb. Its blood flowed out into a stone bowl. The creature's body sagged, lifeless, as a barefoot priest in white robes lifted it on his shoulders and carried it up a ramp to the altar. A second priest lifted the bowl of blood and splashed it across the base of the altar.

A banner hung on the side of the altar, showing the royal ox of the House of King Omri. The banner blew in the wind, revealing a crack in the stone hidden beneath.

As I stood there, observing the crack, Uriel's words from the morning before came back to me: the Prophet's Way is a path of choice. I hadn't really chosen to follow Uriel; I only told him what he wanted to hear. But it was my choice to come to the altar and bow down before the Holy One.

I ascended to a platform of massive stone blocks towering over the plaza. A second platform stood above the first. Four pillars supported a roof of woven reeds shading the sacred object: the Golden Calf. The Calf wasn't as big as I'd imagined. Its eyes would barely reach my knees, but the gold reflected the sun as brightly as a mirror.

I always expected my first trip to Beit El would be with my uncle, during the annual pilgrimage. He would have taught me what to do, but now I was on my own. A man next to me lowered his knees onto the chiseled stone. I copied him, wincing as my bruised knee hit the ground.

I felt the Calf's eyes watching over me, over all the faithful of Israel, as it had for generations. How many prayers had it heard?

This was my chance to speak directly to the Holy One. When I was younger, I would always pray for my mother to come back. I wasn't sure how long that went on, probably for years. One day, Uncle Menachem took me aside and explained that wasn't the way prayer worked. "We don't pray for the impossible," he explained, "and we don't pray to change what already is. But we can pray for things that haven't happened yet, like strong rains, a good harvest, or that the flock should be safe."

So for years I did just that; I prayed that the flock would be safe from lions and wolves, and in the two years I led the flock, I lost only three lambs. But now, standing before the Holy One, with the flock so far away, the same old prayers felt wrong. This was my chance to pray for what I really wanted. Not the return of my parents or the inheritance of my land—it was still forbidden to pray for the impossible.

But maybe Dahlia was right; maybe I could choose to be something other than a lowly shepherd. If the altar of the Holy One, the holiest place in the Kingdom, could have a crack, then could I, with all of my flaws, also attain holiness?

Raphael said that his master had put him on the path five years ago—the path to prophecy. When I asked Uriel yesterday why he had taken me for the gathering, he said it was for my music. But there was something he was holding back—I was sure of it. Could this be it? Had he brought me to the gathering so that I could catch a glimpse of a different future? Had he put me on the path to prophecy without my even knowing it?

This was finally something worth praying for, a path of devotion to something greater than just my sheep or my stomach. If it was my fate to become a shepherd in the wilderness, then I wanted to be like the seven shepherds of Israel: a shepherd-prophet.

The man next to me stretched out on the flagstones. I copied his position, placing my palms flat before me. Lowering my forehead to the cold stone, my hands trembled at my first real act of devotion.

Yehoshua son of Perachyah said: Choose a master for yourself, acquire a friend,
and judge every person favorably.

Pirkei Avot 1:6

4

The Knife

"Darkness is rising upon the land," Uriel said when I told him of the King's engagement. For the rest of the night he just sat, deep in thought. I didn't even get to tell him about bowing before the Holy One.

We met Yosef and his disciples soon after dawn. The two masters embraced, then led us off eastward on the road toward Jericho. The path descended from the fertile mountain plateau, where I had spent my entire life, into the dry wilderness. I could already see the Jordan River valley below when we turned north off the Jericho road onto a narrow trail that followed the ridge-line. A hot wind blew dust, and I tasted grit between my teeth. Only the toughest creatures called this steep, dry area home. We passed two migrant shepherds guiding their flock of coarse-haired goats toward a patch of brown grasses.

Shepherding here was hard work, with limited grass and springs distant from one another. I had known for years it was my fate to one day build a flock out here, yet this was my first time ever seeing it. Hard as it would be to live out here, there was a peacefulness to the wilderness. If I truly wished to train for prophecy, it was the perfect place.

The Knife

Late that afternoon Raphael swept his hands toward a valley nestled between two hills, and said, "Welcome to Emek HaAsefa, Lev."

Black openings dotted the cliff face opposite. "Are those caves?"

"Yes. They will be our homes during the gathering." Raphael stepped off the road onto a trail down to the valley. "And those are just the ones you can see."

White-robed servants laid out a table with hot bread, chickpea mash, and beet tops lightly cooked to a bright green. An Israelite indentured servant spooned out food for the disciples, while another baked bread over a clay dome. It was my first time seeing a man baking bread, and my first time having food prepared by an indentured servant. In Levonah, there were only non-Israelite slaves whose servitude was for life.

The servant took one glance at me, and his eyes narrowed. "Are you Lev?" I nodded. "Master Uriel had us set this aside for you." He retrieved a piece of bread from behind the cooking area, dotted with small amounts of the chickpea and beet tops. After a full day's march, I had hoped for more food than this. The servant must have caught my expression for he added, "You can take more. I don't care." He put down his spoon, with the handle facing toward me, then went to help with the cooking, leaving me to serve myself. I added only a small amount, remembering my uncle's resentment at how much his workers had eaten during last year's olive harvest.

Food in hand, I gazed around until I found Raphael sitting with two other disciples. Seeing me approach, he said with a warm smile, "Looking for the musicians? They're sitting over there." I caught myself before sitting down—did the musicians not eat with the disciples?

I followed Raphael's gesture and saw three people sitting together in a corner of the field, all dressed in heavy woolen tunics like my own. The whole time we walked together, I hadn't thought how much my clothes, so hot and itchy in the summer heat, must have made me stand out from the disciples in their linen garments.

The youngest musician looked about my age, thickset, sitting hunched over his food. Another, a few years older, leaned back on one of his elbows and ran a hand through his wavy hair as he watched me approach. The third musician appeared close to my uncle's age. He sat erect, his narrow beard almost reaching his waist. "Are you Lev?" he asked. I nodded and sat down next to him. "Excellent, then we're all gathered. I'm Daniel, son of Eliezer, the master musician here. This is Yonaton, son of Baruch," he pointed to the younger boy, "and Zimri, son of—"

"Just Zim," the wavy-haired one interjected, his mouth half full.

Yonaton offered a hesitant smile. I sat down next to him and bit into my bread, glad for the distraction of food that excused us from conversation.

As the first stars appeared in the sky, the chatter among the disciples died down. All turned their attention toward the serving table where Uriel, Yosef, and a third white-haired man stood between three torches in a circle of flickering light.

"When you are dismissed, you will go directly to sleep," Yosef said. "You will be woken in the second watch of the night to begin your training. Remember your dreams; even ordinary dreams are one-sixtieth prophecy. Each night you will discuss your dreams with a master to decipher their—"

"This isn't for us," Daniel whispered. "Come, we can speak in the musicians' cave."

I stood and reluctantly followed Daniel. I knew that prophecy could come through dreams—Yaakov's vision of the ladder came in a dream—but I had never known that my own dreams might contain prophecy. Could studying prophecy help me understand my old nightmare? Probably not. Yosef said that to decipher your dreams, you needed to remember them, and I could never remember the slightest detail. Besides, if I ever could remember what the dream contained, I was pretty sure I wouldn't need a master to help me interpret it—it felt more like a dark memory than a prophecy.

The moon was only a sliver in the sky, making the trail appear little more than a gray smudge on dark ground. Daniel led us, walking with the comfort of one who knew his way.

"Will they also wake us in the middle of the night?" Zim asked.

"No, they don't need us until an hour or two after sunrise."

"Good, because the second watch is when I normally go to sleep."

"Why do you go to sleep so late?" Yonaton asked.

"It's when I play my best music—there's a special energy to the night."

"I wouldn't know," Yonaton replied. "In my house, we go to sleep as soon as we can after sunset and wake before dawn. My father says sleep is the body's reward. I couldn't get up if I stayed awake playing."

"That's why I never rise before the third hour of the day if I can help it."

My jaw dropped. "Are you royalty?"

Zim laughed, "Why would you say that?"

"Whenever I'm slow out of bed, my uncle tells me that only princes sleep until the third hour of the day."

"No, I have no noble blood. My father's a farmer, and so was his. But farming's not for me. I left home for good a year ago."

Our path ended at the highest cave, with a circle of boulders out front under the stars.

"Then how do you eat?" Yonaton asked.

"My music." Zim retrieved a drum from inside the cave and sat down on one of the boulders, gently tapping his drum with his fingertips. "I've found enough work between weddings and festivals."

"What kind of festivals?" Yonaton asked.

"All kinds. The best is coming up at the full moon in Shiloh—I never miss it."

I swung my kinnor off my shoulder and straddled one of the boulders. "But you'll still be here then, won't you?"

"When Master Yosef hired me I told him I'd come only if I could still play Shiloh."

"How about you, Daniel, is that what you do too?" Yonaton asked.

"Me?" Daniel chuckled as he sat down next to Zim, clutching his nevel, a standup harp twice the size of my kinnor. "No, I have a wife and three daughters; I can't be running around to festivals all the time. It's only while my wheat is drying that I can devote myself to music."

"Isn't it hard being away from your family?" Yonaton asked.

"Sure it's hard, but my nevel is easier to work than my land, and copper doesn't spoil." Daniel began to pick out notes and tighten strings.

Zim cocked his head toward Yonaton. "First time away from home?"

Yonaton nodded. "I've never even slept away before."

"How far did you come?" I asked.

"Not far. We live just on the other side of that hill."

"So why not go home at night?"

"My father told me I can't expect the prophets to send someone round to the farm every time they need me. Still, it's nice to know I can run home if I want to." Yonaton pulled a halil, a wooden fife two handbreadths long, from his belt. "How about you, Lev? Do you play festivals or do you also work your father's land?"

I plucked the strings of my kinnor, feeling their eyes but not looking up. "My father's dead. My mother too. I shepherd my uncle's flock."

My words killed the conversation. I knew this moment, having experienced it so many times in the past—the awkward quiet, the eyes turning away. Zim filled the silence with his drumming. Daniel joined in, picking up Zim's beat. My eyes were dry—I learned long ago that tears would neither bring back my parents nor water the flock—but I was surprised to see Yonaton's eyes watering. I smiled and raised my kinnor, indicating that there was no more to say. Yonaton wiped his eyes across his sleeve and smiled back, raising his halil to his lips.

The stars were already bright in the sky when I saw twinkling lights ascend the trail toward the caves. "What are those lights?"

"Lamps," Daniel said. "The disciples are going to sleep."

"And they carry their own lamps?" At my uncle's house, lamps were reserved for holy times—olive oil was too precious to burn during the week.

"I'm glad I'm not one of them," Zim said, watching the lights go out as the disciples reached their caves.

My hand dropped from the strings of my kinnor and I stared across at Zim. "Is it really so hard to go to sleep early?"

Zim laughed and leaned into his drum.

There could be only one explanation for his lack of interest. "You've never seen prophecy, have you?"

Zim reacted to the challenge in my voice, meeting my eyes without breaking his rhythm. "No. Have you?"

"Yes." That one word was enough to silence Zim and draw the stares of Daniel and Yonaton, but I wasn't done. "When you see it you'll understand—"

"Don't envy the prophets, Lev," Daniel said.

"What's not to envy?"

Daniel sighed. "Theirs is a path that will lead you nowhere."

"Why nowhere?" Yonaton asked. "Look at the masters—"

"Yes, Yonaton, look at the masters. Take Master Uriel. Where do you think he'll be come harvest time when our backs are bent with labor? Out in the fields with us?" Zim gave a snort, and Daniel turned to me. "Can you imagine him chasing your sheep over the hillsides?"

Daniel leaned over his nevel to press his point. "I've been playing here for twelve years. The first day, there's always a musician or two who dreams of becoming a prophet; but they learn soon enough that's all they are—dreams. And you'll learn too."

I recalled my last conversation with Dahlia, how she said that there was no telling where my future would lead. "But even dreams can come true—can't they?"

"Not this one. It's as King Solomon said: 'Wisdom is good with an inheritance.'"

I winced at the word inheritance. "What does that mean?"

"It means that it doesn't matter how wise or holy you are, Lev, you'll never become a prophet. Look at the disciples—servants preparing their food, lighting lamps just to walk back to their caves—some of them even rode in on their own horses. They don't dress like you. They don't smell like you." Zim laughed. Yonaton sniffed his tunic. "Most of the disciples study for years before receiving prophecy, if they receive it at all. Who do you think watches their farms or their flocks while they're searching for the Holy One?"

I just shrugged.

"You have to be rich to become a prophet; there's never been one that wasn't. As far as I can tell, it's part of their Way."

I opened my mouth to respond, but shut it again. What could I say? Uncle Menachem always told me that the smart man learns from his mistakes, but I never seemed to. When would I stop falling into the trap of clinging to dreams that could never come true? I was like the fool in Eliav's favorite story, the one who sat by a pool of still water, seeing the moon reflected in its surface. Such a beautiful stone, he thought; if he could only get it for himself he'd be a rich man. But when he grabbed for it, his hands plunged into the cold water and the moon disappeared. He cursed himself for his stupidity, but when the water calmed, the moon reappeared, and he thought that perhaps this time he'd be lucky.

Daniel watched me closely. "Don't look like that. You have a more dependable path open to you."

"What's that?"

"The prophets use your music to lift themselves beyond this world. You may not reach prophecy, but it can uplift you as well. You just need to learn to play properly—start with this." Daniel put down his nevel and came around behind me. He pulled my left hand further down the front of my kinnor, then twisted the angle of my right hand. "Grip it like this, hold it tighter in your left hand, but loosen up on your right. Now listen." Daniel plucked the highest string and the kinnor let out a crisp, clear note.

"It feels awkward."

"You're used to doing it wrong. Give it time—you'll bring out the full voice of your kinnor. It's a fine, fine instrument."

Yonaton pulled his halil away from his lips. "They don't smell like us?"

Daniel laughed, "Sniff one tomorrow. They're obsessed with purity. Most bathe at least once a day." He returned to his nevel and picked up the melody again. "The way I see it, they have little tying them to this world. That's why they rise above it so easily."

"It's not so easy," Zim said, drumming now with his fingertips so as not to drown out his voice. "They need us."

"Just the disciples—the masters don't need musicians."

"But Master Uriel did," I said, sitting straighter now that I knew something

that Daniel didn't. "The day we met, he came to listen to my music when I was with my sheep. That's how I was hired."

Daniel shrugged. "I've never seen a master use a musician before."

Zim waved off our words with the back of his hand. "Enough of this. We may not be prophets, but we know what we need." He stepped up his playing, and the rest of us followed his lead, bringing the conversation to an end.

A servant shook each of us roughly by the shoulder the next morning. "Master Uriel requires you," he said, then stepped out of the cave before I'd even sat up.

I squinted in the sunlight. I'd never slept so far into the morning—nor had I ever stayed up so late. By the time Daniel finally made us go to sleep, the eastern sky had already brightened to a dark gray. All through the night, I kept telling myself I'd regret not getting to bed, but the music was unlike any I had ever played. Guided by Daniel's nevel and driven by Zim's rhythms, I discovered sounds in my kinnor that I never knew existed.

Several buckets of water awaited us outside the cave, and we quickly washed our hands and faces. The cold water chased the sleep from my eyes. The daylight offered me a chance to get my first good look at our cave. None of the walls were smooth like the cave walls near Levonah, but rather grooved, as if hewn out with iron tools. Who would bother carving out caves in the wilderness?

As the others started down the trail, my eyes fell on my father's knife next to my sleeping mat. It didn't seem right leaving it behind. I took out one of my spare strings and used it to secure the sheath around my waist, under my tunic. Then I ran down toward the valley floor to catch up with the others.

Twelve disciples sat in the shade of a large carob tree. Daniel had us stand under a smaller pomegranate tree nearby. Uriel acknowledged us with a nod, then addressed the disciples.

"Picture your soul like a pool of water. When it is perfectly still, it reflects what is above. The slightest ripple on the surface, however, distorts the image. Music helps us quiet the mind and calm the pool." I grinned at this description, thinking again of the fool who tried to grab the moon. "Daniel, just a simple melody. This is the first trial for many."

Daniel plucked a slow tune, and the rest of us joined in once we caught the rhythm. I took advantage of the easy pace to practice the techniques Daniel had taught me the night before. The melody barely held my attention. Was it the simplicity of the music, our lack of sleep, or was Zim right that there was just something special about the night?

The Knife

Uriel walked among the disciples, correcting their posture and whispering advice. One disciple appeared older than the rest, with milky scars mapping his face. He sat upright with legs crossed, eyes closed, swaying gently with the melody. He listened to Uriel's whispering, nodded once, then returned to his swaying.

My heavy eyelids kept fighting to close. All the things I normally did to keep myself awake—pacing, talking, even playing faster or harder—would have disturbed the disciples. It was a relief when the session finally ended and we were given a break before the midday meal.

"Do you mind holding my halil?" Yonaton asked me. "I want to run home; I'm sure that my mother is worried."

"I don't mind," I said, suspecting that Yonaton was running home less for his mother's need than his own.

"I'll be back in time for the meal."

I watched him go until he passed over the hill, out of sight. I thought about my family back in Levonah. Eliav would be out with the sheep, Dahlia would already be baking the midday bread. Did they miss me?

I lay down on my back, enjoying the sun on my face, thinking about what I would tell Dahlia at the end of the gathering. The look of awe in her eyes was the last thing I saw as I drifted off to sleep.

I awoke to Yonaton standing over me, a melon in his hands. "We're going to miss the meal."

"What? Oh, right." I stood up, stretched my arms above my head, and followed Yonaton down to the eating area, hazy from sleep.

Bread, cheese and bright green leeks were laid out on the serving table. Again, one of the servants handed me a prepared dish, but only me, offering no explanation why he did not do the same for Yonaton. My portion was a bit bigger than the night before, but lacked cheese. Did Uriel really feel that I deserved so little, especially when Yonaton was allowed to take as much as he wanted? Well, if he objected to my taking more, he'd have to tell me himself. I took more leeks and laid a big spoonful of cheese over the top. Food in hand, we sat down next to Zim, who was already finishing his meal.

"So that was prophecy?" Yonaton asked.

I shook my head, fighting back a smile. "No, no one there received prophecy. It looks more like this—" I put down my bread, leaned over, and trembled the way Uriel had done. Two passing disciples flashed me cold stares.

"Whoa," Yonaton's eyes went wide. "So what do we do when it happens?"

"We keep playing, right?" Zim said through a mouthful of bread. "If they need us for prophecy, we have to keep going."

"I don't think it matters. When Uriel had prophecy, it didn't seem as if he'd notice anything, really."

"So he was completely vulnerable?" Zim asked. "Anyone could just come over and slit his throat?"

"I guess so."

"But he's a prophet," Yonaton said. "He can see things no one else can. He would know if he's in danger."

"You think?" Zim asked. "From what I've heard, prophets see only really important things."

"But if someone wanted to hurt him, that would be really important to him—don't you think, Lev?"

"It would be," I said, trying to sound confident, but wondering if Zim was actually right. If Uriel was vulnerable, it seemed best not to share that information. "Besides, prophets see things all the time that aren't so important, they just don't tell stories about them. I saw Uriel find a lost ring."

Zim stood up to leave, his remaining bread still piled high with more leeks than Yonaton and I had taken together. "You're not finishing your meal?" Yonaton asked.

"These are almost raw," Zim said, pointing to the leeks. "They've got all these servants, why don't they cook their food?" He walked off toward our cave, shaking his head.

The two of us were the last to finish eating. When we were done, Yonaton held up his melon. "You want to split this with me?"

"Sure."

Yonaton took the fruit over to a large rock and lifted it over his head.

"Wait, no need to smash it, I've got a knife." I reached under my tunic and pulled out my father's knife, then hesitated as Yonaton stretched out his hand. I hadn't shown it to anyone, nor even used it myself. But I'd already offered—I couldn't refuse now. I turned the blade around and held out the hilt, hoping he hadn't noticed the hesitation. He cut off two pieces, then thrust the knife back into the melon.

Yonaton bit into his slice, but his eyes were on the handle sticking out from the fruit. "Where did you get that knife? I've never seen one like it."

I turned away, wishing I hadn't brought it out. "This is a great melon. Did you grow it?"

"It's from my own plot." Yonaton said with a grin. "I saw it was ripe when I went home."

"Where did you get that?" We both jumped at the deep voice behind us. We turned to see the older disciple from that morning's session, the one with the milky scars across his face, pointing at the melon. The three of us were now alone in the clearing.

"From my family's farm on the other side of the hill. Cut yourself off a slice if you like."

"Not the melon, boy. The knife." He plucked it out of the fruit and held it up before his eyes.

My mouth went dry as I held out my hand to take it back. "It was my father's. Now it's mine. Give it here."

The man ignored my outstretched hand. "Your father's, you say?" His eyes moved from the knife to me. "And what's your name?"

"Lev."

"Lev, son of?"

There was something about him I didn't trust. "Lev, son of Menachem," I lied. "And yours?"

His let out a harsh laugh. "Shimon son of Naftali. Very wise to use your uncle's name, Lev, son of Yochanan." He took a step toward me, holding my knife in his left hand, and pulling a dagger from his belt with his right. I was defenseless.

Yonaton reacted immediately, jumping to his feet, snatching a rock from the ground, and cocking his arm back, ready to throw at the first sign of attack.

I stood paralyzed, hand still extended, gaping at this stranger who knew my father's name.

Shimon ignored both our reactions, his eyes returning to my knife as he turned his small dagger around and offered me the hilt. "Take this."

I reached out and took the weapon—though if we were going to fight I'd rather have my knife back. But Shimon simply wiped my knife clean on his tunic and laid it down next to the melon. He bent down, bringing his eyes even with mine. "Never let anyone see this knife. The danger it brings is very real. Besides, this is not a tool for cutting fruit. It has only one purpose, and should be used for nothing else. If you want to cut melon, use that one," he pointed to the dagger in my hand. "You can keep it. I've got another."

Without another word, Shimon turned and headed down the hill, in the opposite direction from where the disciples were gathering. As he retreated, I examined the bronze weapon in my hand. Its value was equal to two sheep at least, probably three. Even if the disciples were rich, as Daniel said, surely they didn't just give away such valuable gifts for nothing? My eyes moved to my father's knife, sitting on a rock, still moist from the melon. It didn't look dangerous. What was he afraid of? But I had a more pressing question. "Wait!" I shouted at Shimon's back. "How did you know my name?"

Shimon replied over his shoulder. "I brought you to your uncle."

Rabbi Elazar HaKapar said: Envy, desire, and the pursuit of honor remove a person from the world.

Pirkei Avot 4:28

ה

The Song of the World

"What just happened here?" Yonaton's arm dropped to his side, but he still held the rock he'd picked up to defend me.

I avoided Yonaton's eyes. "My parents were killed when I was two."

"Killed? By who?"

"I don't know. It was during the civil war." I didn't look up—I didn't want to see the pity in his eyes. "All I know is that a stranger left me at my uncle's house...afterwards. I guess now I know who that was." I changed the subject. "Are we playing again today?"

"No, the masters gave us the rest of the day to prepare for Shabbat. I know a spring not far from here where we can bathe."

It was the best answer I could have hoped for. I was in no mood for more of the slow music we played that morning, which left my mind too free to wander. I tucked Shimon's blade into my belt, picked up my father's knife, and followed Yonaton toward the edge of the valley.

"I've never seen a knife like that—what's it for?"

"I've never seen one like it either. My uncle gave it to me the day I left, but

42

he didn't tell me anything about it. Just that it belonged to my father."

"Can I hold it?"

I again hesitated. It was my father's—my only inheritance. Yonaton threw the rock in his hand, hitting a distant boulder. He had good aim and a strong arm; I couldn't have hit that boulder even if I could have thrown that far. Yet Yonaton hadn't picked up that rock to throw it at some boulder, he'd picked it up to defend me from Shimon. I turned the knife around and held it out, handle first.

Yonaton took it and ran a finger over the dark gray edge. "I never knew stone could be so sharp. It looks ancient." He turned his attention to the insignia on the hilt. "Are these claws?"

"I think so, but I don't know what they mean."

"It looks like a small sword." He swung the broad blade in short, chopping arcs.

I thought back to Shimon's warning, "But who would get so upset about using a sword to cut a melon?"

Yonaton shrugged and handed back the knife.

Our trail ended at a crumbling, white cliff. Clear water bubbled out of a crack at its base and flowed into a pool cut into the rock.

Yonaton stripped quickly, wincing as he slipped into the cold water. I undressed and sat at the edge of the pool. My mind was still on Shimon. If he had brought me to my uncle, would he know how my parents died?

"Come in!" A splash of water hit me in the face. Yonaton smacked the surface again and I put my hands up in a useless attempt to block the spray. I kicked at the water, splashing him back. Yonaton fought back with the full force of both arms, drenching me. I pushed off the edge of the pool, dove under the water, and pulled my new friend's legs out from under him.

We were still laughing when we returned to our cave late in the afternoon. Zim stood at the entrance, holding a polished bronze mirror in one hand, shaping his long hair into a wave with the other.

"Have you ever seen a boy with his own mirror before?" Yonaton whispered in my ear.

I shook my head. "My aunt has one, but she doesn't look in it this long."

"If I was your aunt, I wouldn't either," Zim said, entering the cave. "You should be more careful if you're going to talk about me. I may drum loudly, but my hearing is excellent." My ears grew hot and Yonaton turned away, but

Zim wore the same carefree expression as always. "Laugh if you like, but if you ever want to feed yourself with your music, you should think about getting one yourself."

"A mirror won't help our playing," Yonaton said.

"True, but it will get you more work. All eyes are on the musicians—you get hired for more festivals if you look right." Though answering Yonaton, Zim held out his mirror to me.

I took the sheet of flat, shiny metal. It had been a long time since I'd seen my reflection. My brown hair was curled from the water, but I was mostly struck by my eyes. They were light today, the color of bee honey, and seemed older than I felt.

From the valley rose the blast of a ram's horn, the signal of the coming Shabbat. The three of us headed down to the clearing where we joined Daniel. The food was better than the night before; the vegetables were still barely cooked, but the smell of roasted lamb also filled the clearing. My mouth watered. Aunt Leah prepared meat only for festivals.

Again, a servant handed me a piece of bread and portion of beet greens that had been set aside for me behind the cooking area, where they had already turned cold. I received no meat, and the amount, though larger for Shabbat, didn't come close to meeting my appetite. Daniel, Zim, and Yonaton all eyed my food curiously; none of them had food set aside. I took the bread and piled meat onto it, making sure the servant saw I wouldn't quietly accept so little. Zim piled as much lamb on his bread as it would hold, not wasting any space on the vegetables. Daniel pointed out a spot for us closer to the disciples than we had sat the night before.

The meat was pink and tender, and the vegetables were so well flavored that I almost didn't mind that they were undercooked. Though I had taken a large portion, I soon went back for more of everything.

I was just finishing my second helping when conversation among the disciples died. Tzadok, the elderly third master, stood by the fire in the center of the eating area. Zim still ate, but Yonaton and I stood, knowing that when the masters spoke it was time for us to go. Daniel put a hand on each of our shoulders. "On Shabbat we stay."

Tzadok closed his eyes and began to sing. Daniel and a number of the disciples joined him immediately. The rest of us came in little by little as we picked up the melody. I closed my eyes, and let my body sway with the music.

Our voices echoed in the open air of the valley. For the first time since coming to the gathering, I felt united with the disciples. When Tzadok reached the end, he lifted his voice higher, holding the final note until his breath ran

The Song of the World

out. His silence brought the song to a close, and quiet settled over the clearing.

I opened my eyes to see Uriel standing alone, his face lit by the red light of the dwindling fire.

"There was once a man who lived in a kingdom in the middle of the desert." The prophet spoke softly, but in the stillness of the night, his voice carried across the open ground. "Every day, this man walked past the King's palace in the morning as he went out to his field, and again in the evening when he walked home. Each time he wondered, 'Why is it that the King has so much while I have so little?' His envy of the King grew and grew, until he was unable to pass the palace without anger.

"The man formed a plan: he would dig a tunnel under the palace, come up inside the treasury, and take just a tiny amount for himself. He worked for years and years on his tunnel. As his effort grew, so did his desire, until he no longer felt the need to leave the King anything at all. Finally, the tunnel was complete, and he broke through the floor of the palace in the middle of the night. He expected to see piles of gold and gems, but found himself in an empty hallway, just outside the treasury. If he kept on digging, there was a chance that he could still get the treasure and escape before dawn. But now that he had broken through the floor, fear struck his heart—he could be discovered at any time, and discovery would cost him his head. So, he returned to his tunnel and fled the palace with nothing.

"It happened that a second thief, who knew nothing of the first, had formed an identical plan to rob the King, and tunneled into the palace on the very same night. Unlike the first, he emerged inside the treasury itself. He saw mountains of gold and streams of jewels, and filled his bags and pockets with treasure. As he was about to leave, he spotted a large ruby in the corner of the treasury, so beautiful that he could not imagine leaving it behind. Lacking any room for it in his bags or pockets, he placed the gem in his mouth.

"The thief lowered his bags into the tunnel and was about to jump in, when he stopped. He spat the gem back into his hand and restored it gently to its place. Then, he emptied his bags and pockets, returned the treasure, then climbed into his tunnel—leaving the palace with nothing.

"The next morning, the two tunnels were discovered. The head of the guards came running to the King. 'My King,' he said, 'two thieves tunneled into the palace last night.'

"The King was shocked. No one had ever broken into his palace before. 'How much did they take?' he asked.

"The guard said, They didn't take anything. One thief missed the treasury and left with nothing. The second thief entered the treasury, but we've counted the treasure and nothing is missing.

"The King said, 'I want to meet these two men. Let it be known that they will not be punished if they come forward.'

"Such was the power of the King that both thieves presented themselves at the palace by day's end. The guards brought the first thief before the King. The King said to him, 'Explain how it was that you broke into my palace and left with nothing?'

"The thief stood shaking before the King and said, 'I planned to tunnel into the royal treasury, but when I came out I found that I had not dug far enough. I feared capture, so I went back into my tunnel and fled.'

"The King said, 'Very well. Had you remained, you might have caused me great loss, but you turned away from the evil. As promised, you will not be punished. I reward your honesty today with your life. You may go.'

"Guards then brought in the second thief. The King turned to him and asked, 'Explain how it was that you broke into my treasury and left with nothing.'

"The second thief dropped his head. 'I did intend to rob you, sire. When I emerged inside your treasury, I filled all my bags, my pockets, and even my mouth with your treasure. Then, when I was about to climb into the tunnel and escape, an image of your face came to my mind. You have been a just and generous king to your people. I should be proud to serve such a king. How could I rob you? So, I returned all the treasure to its rightful place and left the way I came.'

"A tear came to the King's eye. 'Guard,' he called, 'I want you to take this man into the treasury and let him take anything he wants.'"

Uriel paused, staring into the glowing coals. "There are two ways to turn from evil in this world. If we correct ourselves from fear of punishment then, like the first thief, we are forgiven. But there is a higher way—to correct ourselves out of great love for our King. Then our very sins bring us merit, for the Holy One knows how far we had gone along the path of evil, and how great an effort it took to reverse our course."

The prophet's voice grew loud in the silence. "Some of you are here because you desire the prophets' power. You want to cry out, to correct the errors of the people, and when your cries are not heard, you will be tempted to force the people to change. You must remember that the Holy One seeks true service of the heart. You may sway the people by threatening them, but only through fear.

"Israel is a holy nation. The task of the prophets is to guide them to the highest level of service, so that their holiness can elevate all of creation. To do this, we must awaken in them the desire to improve themselves out of love. I wish you all a peaceful Shabbat."

"Blessed is the One who divides between the sacred and the ordinary," Uriel chanted the following evening at the close of Shabbat, "between light and darkness, between Israel and the nations, between the seventh day and the six days of creating—"

"And between the prophets and the musicians," Zim said just loud enough for the three of us to hear. "Can we play now?"

"Yes," Daniel answered, his voice strained. "Let's go back to the cave."

When he and Zim played music together, they worked off each other beautifully. But instruments were forbidden in Emek HaAsefa on Shabbat. Throughout the Shabbat day, while I enjoyed the quiet, walking through the valley with Yonaton and playing Stones, Zim just lay in the cave, his eyes on his drum.

At midday on Shabbat, Daniel had sat with eyes closed, listening. "I love coming to this valley," he said. "It's so peaceful. Without our music, you can really hear the song of the world."

"The world has a song?" I asked.

"Each thing in the world has its own melody. Together their notes rise to form the song of the world."

Zim had replied, "Call it the noise of the world if you must—what you're hearing is too much silence. You're right that there's beautiful music in the world, and you'll hear it as soon as I can get my drum."

Now that Shabbat was finally over, Zim sped up the dark trail. I wondered if the tension between Daniel and Zim over Shabbat would keep them from playing together, but once we all had our instruments, Zim waved toward Daniel with a gesture that said, "You lead." Daniel struck up the melody that Tzadok had led us in the night before. He began the song slowly, increasing his pace with each pass through the melody. We played on into the night, not speaking, letting the music reunite us in a way that words could not.

It was rare in Levonah that I found the time to play my kinnor without having to keep one eye on my sheep. All I had were those few precious moments after the evening meal each night when I could let myself dive fully into my music. That night in Emek HaAsefa, we must have passed through that same melody a hundred times or more, but it never grew old. I felt the notes flow through me, vibrating up through my chest. For the first time, I sensed what the prophets were seeking in our music.

It was not until well after the moon set, after the ram's horn sounded to wake the disciples, that Daniel finally broke off the melody. My eyes went to Zim, whose energy only increased as the night went on, expecting a protest. Yet, I read no disappointment on his face. Only after I lay down did I realize that he had not rejoined us in the cave.

Sometime later, a hand shook me awake. "Don't make a sound," Zim whispered in my ear. "Get dressed and follow me."

When I stepped out of the cave and saw how far the stars had rotated in the sky, I knew it was late into the second watch of the night. "Why did you wake me?"

"I want to show you what I found. Come." He turned without further explanation, and I was too clouded by sleep to protest. Zim all but ran down the path, and I hurried to keep up, careful not to stumble into the darkness below. It was only when I paused to catch my breath that I heard it: a low, bass hum. "Zim, what's that sound?"

"You've finally heard it? I was beginning to wonder whether you three were deaf or I was crazy. I've heard it every night since we've arrived, but tonight I finally found the source. Come."

We reached the valley floor, and continued onto a faint trail that ended at the mouth of a cave. The sound grew deeper, its rhythm vibrating along the stone walls of the cave. The cavern floor sloped steadily down into darkness. Seeing nothing, I kept one hand on the cave wall as I followed after Zim.

There would come a time when I would grow used to the underground world, but at this moment I still feared the darkness. Had I been alone, I certainly would have fled back to the comfort of the starlight. But I continued on after Zim, not wanting to be mocked for turning around.

The music grew more complex as we went. Finally, a light gleamed in the distance, and the tunnel widened out to meet it. Torches high on the wall lit the floor of the cavern. Flickering light danced over three circles of men swaying in rhythm, chanting a song that felt ancient.

I edged toward the swaying men, eager to join them in their song. Before I made two steps, Zim grabbed my arm and pulled me back into the shadows, shaking his head, reminding me that we were intruders. I nodded that I understood and Zim released me.

Tzadok led the melody, his hands on his knees, his body loose as he rocked forward and back. Down here in the cave, I felt the power in music as I had never experienced it before.

The song built steadily, until their voices rose to a peak, then ceased all at once.

The disciples' clothing rustled as they stood. Once they left the circle of light, we would no longer be hidden. Zim's voice trembled in my ear, "We have to get out of here."

We moved as quickly as possible without making a sound. No one stopped us, though I could not be sure we had escaped unnoticed.

I did not risk my first words until we again stood again stood beneath the stars. "Warming to the prophets now, are you?"

"I had no idea they had music like this," Zim replied, shaking his head. "Imagine having such power and keeping it hidden underground!"

"What else should they do with it?"

"What else? You heard Uriel on Shabbat. He said that the prophets must uplift the people. So, what do they do? They travel the land teaching the Law. If they want to inspire, they should bring their music out into the daylight!"

"It looks as if they don't agree with you."

"Of course they don't, and the more fools they are. They don't know how to use what they have—but we can."

"We work for them."

"Just for the gathering. In two months we'll be free."

"Free? Once the gathering ends I have to go home."

Zim led the way up the narrow trail crossing the cliff face. "You mean to your uncle's? And how long will that last? I heard you talking to Yonaton yesterday."

I scratched the back of my neck. "I thought you were asleep."

"I told you, you have to be careful what you say around me. You have three years left at most in your uncle's house. Then what will you do? Wander alone through the wilderness?"

The words stung. "What choice do I have?"

"Fool, you have your kinnor! If we spent our nights in this cave, learning the ancient songs of the prophets, just think what it would do for our music. We could go anywhere—even to Shomron to play for the King."

"The King?" Zim was clearly repeating some fantasy of his.

"Yes, the King! Why not? Come with me."

Suddenly, I understood why Zim handed me his mirror the other day, even while speaking to Yonaton. It was the same reason that he woke me alone to hear the prophets' chant. I was the one with no future. I could go anywhere and hardly be missed. And two wandering musicians would be better than one; we could keep each other company, perhaps even find more work. As we reached our cave, I was glad for an excuse to break off the conversation. "I don't know, Zim."

Zim appeared ready to say more, but Daniel rolled over in his sleep, and he held back.

I dropped exhausted onto my sleeping mat, eager for sleep. But neither of us got what we wanted. Zim never did make it back to the chanting cave, nor did I get a good night's rest.

I woke next in the pre-dawn light, hearing birdsong rising from the valley below. Their calls sounded like a melody, strangely similar to the song in the chanting cave. I felt a hand on my back and rolled over to find Daniel standing over me. He put a finger to his lips and beckoned me to follow. I slipped my tunic over my head, wondering for the second time that night why I was leaving my warm nest behind.

Daniel hurried along one of the trails, and turned to wave me on without a word. What could be so pressing at this hour?

At first I thought that Daniel was bringing me back to the chanting cave, but then he left the path and slowed his pace, stepping through the tall yellow grass, heavy with dew. A few paces on he stopped, dropped to his knees, and crawled on the ground, his eyes fixed on a single point. Gradually my tired eyes gained focus. There, on a stalk of wild barley, sat a grasshopper. I turned to Daniel and mouthed, "What are we doing here?"

Daniel put a hand to his ear and pointed to the grasshopper. I closed my eyes to listen. The birdsong overwhelmed the high-pitched chirps of the tiny grasshopper. With focus, I blocked out the sound of the birds, and heard the calls of the grasshopper. I felt a gentle touch on my back and brought my eyes up to Daniel's. "Why are we here so early?"

"The birdsong is loudest before sunrise."

"But doesn't that make it harder to hear the grasshopper?"

"You think I woke you to listen to a grasshopper? To hear the song of the world you need to hear everything—the grasshopper and the birds."

I closed my eyes and leaned back in, listening without filtering out the birdsong. But I couldn't hold the two sounds at once—the song of the birds overpowered the chirps of the grasshopper. I gave up and got back to my feet. "Why did you bring me here?"

"I told you, to hear the song of the world."

"Why didn't you wake the others?"

"Not everyone can hear it. Look at Zim, he has no interest in listening to birdsong or the sound of the wind blowing through the trees."

"And why not Yonaton?"

Daniel placed a hand on my shoulder. "Yonaton will be a farmer. His time is better spent learning to sow than learning to listen."

"You think I'm different because I can play music while watching my sheep?"

Daniel shook his head. "Yonaton's an only son, just like I was. He has no choice but to inherit his father's farm and care for his parents when they grow old. You have a choice."

I snorted. "The choice to be a landless orphan?"

"The choice to pursue your music."

I suddenly understood why Daniel woke me a second time. He'd overheard the end of my conversation with Zim earlier. "So you also think I should leave my sheep to play festivals and weddings with Zim?"

Again, Daniel shook his head. "That's a desolate life. Besides, to play festivals and weddings you don't need to hear the song of the world."

"Then what?"

"I saw your face the other night when we were speaking about the prophets. It's not only in the summer that they need musicians. One who can hear the song of the world could play for them all year round."

"I couldn't hear the cricket and the birds together. I'm not even sure what I'm listening for." I once again thought how similar the birdsong was to the melody from the chanting cave. Was that the secret? Were the melodies of the prophets somehow connected to the song of the world?

"It takes practice, but you can learn. I already hear the song of the sheep in your music—it's subtle, but it's there."

"Sheep sing?" I understood why Daniel termed the bird-calls a song, but the bleating of my sheep—that was music?

Daniel started back across the meadow toward the path. "I heard a story many years ago from my master, who played before the prophets for forty years, and who first taught me to hear the song of the world. When King David finished writing the Psalms, he said to the Holy One, 'Is there any creature in this world that sings more songs and praises than I?' A frog came and said, 'Do not become proud, David. I sing more songs and praises than you do.'"

"The frog could talk?"

"It's a story. But after hearing the frog, David set out to discover the songs and praises of other creatures. How he understood them I don't know, but he wrote their meanings down in a scroll." Daniel studied my face. "You find this hard to accept?"

"I've never heard any praises from my sheep."

"Neither have I. But we can hear the rhythms of the animals, and we can help the disciples hear them too. Listening to the world is one of their tools; it helps them find their place in the Way."

"I thought we play to bring them joy?"

"True, but joy is only one thing that we can do for them." Daniel yawned, stretching his arms up over his head, clearly intending to go back to sleep.

"So are the songs we play part of the song of the world?"

Daniel paused at the cave mouth. "I don't know if we sing in the song of the world. You'd have to ask one of the masters that."

I lay down and spread my tunic over me. It seemed that everyone had an opinion on my future. I hadn't always liked what my uncle taught me, but I always believed it: that without land I had one choice—to become a shepherd. Since arriving at the gathering, new paths had opened before me, but were they any better?

Zim wanted me as a companion; we'd wander from place to place to place, looking for enough work to feed ourselves. A desolate life, Daniel called it. Daniel thought I should learn to hear the song of the world and play before the prophets. Perhaps that was a little better: I wouldn't have to move so much and it would be easier to build a family. But even if I could hear the song, wouldn't I be just like the grasshopper, whose chirps were drowned out before the powerful birdsong? Was that my destiny—to become the servant of prophecy, playing a part no one would notice?

As a shepherd, at least I could be my own master, have my own flock, and my successes would be my own. One last thought floated through my mind as I drifted back to sleep: my uncle had chosen wisely.

Rabbi Akiva said: All that will be is already known, yet one still has the power to choose.

Pirkei Avot 3:19

The Rogue Vision

It began as a jerking in Raphael's hand, like the twitch of a heavy sleeper. I exhaled to relax my chest muscles, a technique Daniel had shown me the night before. Raphael's back arched, his forehead extending upward as if drawn by an invisible cord.

The invisible cord snapped, and Raphael slumped forward, motionless. A tremor crept up his arms, meeting at the base of his neck. His head snapped up, and convulsions surged through his body.

Yonaton stopped playing and stood mouth agape. He caught my eye with an expression that said, "Now I see what you mean." He quickly returned his halil to his lips, blushing at having stopped playing. But the music no longer mattered. Raphael couldn't hear it. The other disciples broke out of their meditations, watching the first prophecy since the gathering began.

Raphael's arms gave a final jolt, then went limp. He pushed himself into a sitting position, his eyes wide. Only when his gaze fell on Uriel did he regain his focus. "I saw the King's servant," he said.

"Ovadia?"

"Yes."

"What was he doing?"

Raphael's forehead creased and his eyes narrowed, as if examining a picture only he could see. "He is coming." Raphael closed his eyes and rocked gently, as if trying to launch back into the vision. "And there was a voice."

"A voice? What did it say?"

"'Heed his request.'"

Uriel's forehead tightened. "Who should heed his request?"

"You should, Master."

"Me?" Uriel pulled the collar of his tunic away from his throat. "Was there anything more?"

"That's all I heard."

In the silence that followed, I heard hoofbeats thudding faintly in the distance. The tremor grew to a rumble. Four chestnut horses, with one rider apiece, appeared on the trail at the head of the valley, then descended toward the clearing. Yosef and Tzadok emerged from their caves to join Uriel.

Three soldiers stopped at a distance. The fourth rider approached the masters, his eyes pausing briefly upon the musicians. He had thick red hair, and was dressed like no servant I had ever seen. He wore an embroidered blue tunic adorned with silver, a leather belt studded with copper, and a short sword at his hip. A beam of sunlight glinted off a seal hanging from his neck. I knew from watching Yoel son of Beerah in Levonah that the King's men wore seals around their necks—but I had never seen one that reflected the sun.

He embraced each of the masters, holding Uriel longer than the other two. "Is there a place we can speak?"

"Let us go to my cave," Uriel said. "You are hungry after your journey, Ovadia?"

"I'll eat when you eat; I never have much appetite after a hard ride." There was a nasal accent to his speech—was the servant of the King not from Israel?

Uriel's eyes fell on me. "Lev, please bring us wine."

I laid down my kinnor and ran to the cooking area where fires burned in three large, earthen hearths. I approached a servant, sweating over the midday meal. "I need a wine skin."

The cook's lip rose in a sneer. "If the musicians desire wine, they'll just have to wait." He turned back to his cook fire abruptly.

The indentured servants were debt slaves, usually thieves sold by the court into servitude for up to six years to pay back double what they had stolen. Why would the prophets surround themselves with such people? "It's not for us; it's for the masters and an emissary from the King."

"Ah, you should have said so." The sneer disappeared and the servant retrieved a skin and four clay cups.

I ran to Uriel's cave and found the prophets and their guest seated around a low table. "So, Ovadia," Uriel said, "to what do we owe your visit?"

"Let us wait until we're alone," Yosef said, nodding in my direction.

"No, no, it is fine that he hear," Ovadia said lightly. "It concerns him as well. You see, I've come for the musicians." I was filling the cups and nearly spilled wine on the table.

"Why would you want the musicians?" Yosef asked.

"For the wedding, of course. The King heard that the prophets assemble excellent musicians for their gathering, and he wants the very best in the land for his wedding."

"Interesting," Uriel said, leaning forward to take one of the cups. "Thank you for the wine, Lev." The wrinkled skin between his eyes creased in thought. "It's a little dark in here. Would you mind lighting the lamps as well?"

Sunlight shone into the mouth of the cave, making it quite easy to see. Yet, wanting to overhear more, I quickly ran to fetch fire from the cooking area.

"I won't consent to send them," Yosef said as I reentered the cave. I stepped quietly toward a lamp in the back of the cave and took my time lighting it so that I could listen as long as possible.

Ovadia's eyes widened as his hand clenched. "How can you refuse your king? He has the right to anything in the land that he desires."

"He may be the King, but the prophets do not give their full allegiance to any king of flesh and blood. I've heard about Ahav's bride, and I can only imagine what this wedding will be like. Must we contribute to such a travesty? And we also have a duty to the musicians in our service. They come here to play before disciples striving for holiness." Yosef turned now to Uriel. "How can we expose them to such practices?"

Uriel broke eye contact with Yosef and focused on Ovadia. "There are two things I don't understand. I'm surprised to hear that the King is even aware of our gathering, and all the more that we hire talented musicians to play for us. And even if he is aware and wants our musicians, why not send a simple messenger to retrieve them? Why send the steward of the palace on such a journey?"

"Two excellent questions. The King knows about the gathering and the caliber of your musicians because I told him. He sent me here because I advised him to handle the prophets tactfully before the wedding, something we could not depend on an ordinary messenger to do. I convinced him of this so that King Ahav would suggest that I go personally."

"Why would you do such a thing?"

"Because there are serious matters that I need to discuss with you, and I needed a reason to come."

Yosef said, "Ovadia, you have come to us many times in the past. Why should you suddenly need an excuse?"

The King's steward raised his cup to his mouth, but returned it to the table without tasting it. "Everything's changed since the King's engagement. He knows that many oppose the marriage and fears that his servants will turn against him as well."

"And this is why the wedding has been so rushed...?" Yosef asked.

Ovadia nodded. "He wants it over before opposition can be raised. He is constantly on the watch now for who is loyal and who is not. For me to meet with you there needed to be a reason; otherwise, it would arouse the King's suspicions. He assumes that you are opposed to the match."

"That still doesn't justify taking our musicians to play before such a ceremony," Yosef responded. "Uriel, you must agree with me?"

Uriel held Yosef's gaze for a long moment, then dropped his eyes to his cup. "I'm inclined to let them go. King Ahav has the right to anything in the land. Now is not the time to make an enemy of him."

Yosef scowled, but didn't respond. He turned to Tzadok. "We have given our opinions; it is up to you to decide."

There was a pause as Tzadok shut his eyes to consider the issue. Opening them, he glanced at each of the masters, and then, without a word, nodded in Uriel's direction.

"Very well," Yosef said. "I won't oppose both of you. The musicians may go. Now tell us, Ovadia, what is so important that you had to invent such an excuse?"

Uriel cut across Ovadia before he could speak. "Thank you, Lev, that is enough light for now. Please make sure that the soldiers are fed and their horses are looked after."

Yosef surveyed me with his dark, unblinking eyes. Had he forgotten I was there, or was he simply annoyed that Uriel had allowed me to stay and listen? I kept my expression blank as I walked toward the mouth of the cave. Once outside, I broke into a run. I had to find Yonaton. I had a lot to tell him—and we had to pack.

"What do you think they're talking about?" Yonaton asked me for the third time as we gathered our things.

"I wish I knew, but I don't think that we're going to find out. Master Uriel seemed to want me to hear the first part, but not the rest."

"My father always said my time would be better spent working the land than playing my halil. I wonder if this will change his mind?"

"What are you packing for?" Zim asked as he and Daniel walked into the cave. "Does this have anything to do with the King's servant and the mysterious request Raphael was talking about? Lev, did you overhear anything when you brought them their wine?"

"Yes," Yonaton said, his voice cracking with excitement. "Ovadia came to get us to play at the wedding."

"We're going to play for the King?" Zim snatched up his drum with one hand and pounded it with the other. "I knew it! I knew my moment would come!"

Daniel sat down, his forehead furrowed in thought. "If that's all he came for, we should be leaving already."

"Well—" Yonaton began, but I cut him off.

"Yosef didn't want us to go. They were still discussing it when I left." Yonaton shot me a glance that the other two missed. I had overheard a private conversation—it wasn't my place to tell Zim and Daniel everything that I'd heard. Somehow telling Yonaton felt different.

Zim turned to Daniel. "You don't sound so excited."

"I've played for the King before. There will be many musicians there. We may not even see the King."

"I've never been to Shomron," Zim said, tapping the edge of his drum with his fingertips. "The King keeps a small group of musicians to play in the palace," he added with a wink in my direction. "You never know what could happen…"

Ovadia spoke with the masters until the late afternoon. When they emerged from the cave, Uriel sent word that we would leave in the morning.

"I'm going to tell my parents," Yonaton told me. "Do you want to come? They want to meet you, anyway."

I nodded and laid my kinnor on my sleeping mat. We stepped out of the cave and saw one of the servants climbing the path toward us. "Master Uriel wishes to speak with you, Lev."

"Me?"

"Yes, he awaits you in his cave."

I waved goodbye to Yonaton and followed the white robed servant down the trail. As we turned on one of the switchbacks on the path, I noticed a puncture in his right ear. Only one thing could have mangled him in that way.

"You're staring at my ear?"

"Does that mean—?"

"That when my first service was complete, I chose not to go free. Yes, I am a slave until the Yovel…if it ever comes. Forever, probably."

"But you could have been free."

"Free to do what? Go back to being a thief? We all serve, Lev. Before I served my desires. Now I serve a worthy master."

I found Uriel sitting in the same spot as earlier that day. "You heard quite a bit today."

"I was surprised you let me hear as much as I did."

"As was I."

"Why did you let me stay?"

"It began with Raphael—such an unusual way to receive a prophecy."

"It didn't seem very different from when I saw you."

"True, it is not at all unusual for a prophet to receive a message for others. But if the Holy One wished to send me a message, why not send it to me directly? This is the first time I've ever received a prophecy through another prophet."

"Why do you think you received the prophecy this way?"

"I believe that the prophecy was not directed to me alone."

"Then why didn't you tell Master Yosef about the prophecy? Wouldn't that have been easier than arguing?"

"Yes, it would. And since Raphael spoke publicly, I could have shared his words if I desired. But the fact that the message was not addressed to Yosef gave me pause. I was told to heed Ovadia's request, but he was not. He was right to rely on his own understanding."

"But you said the message wasn't intended only for you. If not for Master Yosef, then who else?"

"I believe that it was for you."

"Me?"

"I noticed Ovadia looking intently at the musicians when he arrived. He clearly had an interest in the four of you."

Even if that were the case, the prophecy could just as easily have been for one of the others. "There's more, isn't there?"

"Yes," Uriel replied, but said no more.

I felt blood rising to my cheeks and reached under my tunic for my father's knife. The weapon hit the table with a dull thud. "It has something to do with this, doesn't it?"

Uriel picked up the sheathed knife with a faraway look in his eye. At that moment, I was certain that he had seen the knife before.

"What are you hiding from me?" I asked, my voice rising.

Uriel sighed. "I understand how difficult this must be, but it is not yet safe to tell you all that I know."

"If it's my safety, shouldn't I be able to decide—"

"No! When I took you with me, I promised your uncle I would look after you. I question his judgment in giving you this knife. You heard what Ovadia said—we are entering dangerous times!

"Much as I would like to protect you, Raphael's prophecy shows that there is a greater will than my own involved. I must...I will allow events to take their course.

"Do the others know your father's name?"

"Only Yonaton and Shimon, the one with the scars."

"Good. From now on, call yourself Lev son of Menachem. Tell Yonaton so he won't be surprised, but instruct him not to tell the others. I'm not concerned about Shimon."

Uriel rose. "Be careful in Shomron. Darkness is rising in the Kingdom—I have felt it building for some time. Trust your heart. If something feels wrong to you, it probably is. Keep your eyes open. I won't be in Shomron to see for myself, so I'm counting on you to be my eyes and tell me everything when you return." Uriel walked me to the mouth of the cave, placing his hands on my shoulders. "Perhaps it is best if you leave the knife here with me?"

I shook my head—it was my only inheritance.

"Very well, take it with you, but show it to no one."

Shamaya said: Love work, be loath to assume leadership, and do not become intimate with the government.

Pirkei Avot 1:10

Taming the Bear

"While you're in Shomron, the two of you will stay with me," Ovadia told Yonaton and me as we rode through the gates of Shomron the next afternoon.

My arms were tight around Ovadia's waist and my backside ached after a long day of riding. "What about Daniel and Zim?" I asked.

"They will be in the musicians' quarters."

"We don't mind being with the musicians too," Yonaton said.

Ovadia shook his head. "Master Uriel made me promise to look after the two of you while you are here. He would not agree to send you without my giving my word."

Ovadia's house was the largest and most beautiful I had ever seen. A servant carried our meager belongings up the ladder to a room reserved just for us. Ovadia and his wife Batya saw to it that we wanted for nothing, yet they hardly spoke in our presence, even to each other. As I soaked up the last of my stew with my bread, Batya said, "You two look exhausted; you ought to get to sleep."

Though the sun had not yet set, Yonaton nudged my shoulder as if to say, "Don't argue." It was clear that the family wanted its privacy. We said goodnight and climbed the ladder to our room where two fresh straw beds awaited. I had never slept on straw before—in my house, only my aunt and uncle enjoyed such luxury. I leaned out of the window and stared at the palace on the hilltop until darkness fell and the palace disappeared from view. Only a week ago, I mainly played my kinnor before my sheep. Now I was in Shomron, about to play before the King. Perhaps Dahlia was right: our lives could change in an instant.

The next morning, we went first to the musicians' quarters, a single room that could comfortably sleep six, but which had more than twice that number crammed inside. Daniel sat right up when Yonaton jostled his shoulder, but when I shook Zim he just opened his eyes, moaned, and rolled back over.

"Have a late night?" Yonaton asked.

"More like an early morning." Daniel said.

"Well, help us wake the others; we've got to get down to rehearsal." I shook Zim's shoulder again. "Come on, Zim, you've always managed to get up to play for the prophets. This time it's for the King."

"Yes," Daniel said, pulling on his clothes, "but the prophets water down their wine."

Daniel eventually got all sixteen visiting musicians up, dressed, and out through the city gates. Most could barely keep their eyes open as we headed toward an open field where the six court musicians awaited.

"I'm sure you're all good musicians; otherwise, you wouldn't have made it here," said Dov, the chief musician in the King's court. "We have only two days to learn to play together, so we're going to have to be diligent. The court musicians have been working on the music for the wedding ever since the engagement, so we'll lead. When you feel that you've caught on, join in."

Dov picked up his tall nevel and began the first melody. The other court musicians joined him immediately, the rest of us bit by bit. As soon as all of us were playing, Dov put down his nevel and walked among us. "You need to slow down," he said to Zim. "Focus on staying in time with the rest of us." Zim scowled at the criticism, but did slow his beat.

"I think you've got it," Dov said to Yonaton. "Play louder. I want to hear you more." Dov then stopped in front of me, closing his eyes to filter out the other musicians. He opened them, nodded, and walked onto the next player without saying a word.

Once he had finished his rounds, Dov brought the song to a close. He immediately started a new melody, and began the process began.

Yonaton and I walked back toward Ovadia's after rehearsal, passing merchants who lined the main road of Shomron as it climbed the hill toward the palace. I stopped in front of a cart loaded with milky rocks. Licking my finger, I touched it to the rock, and brought it back to my mouth. "Salt!"

"From the Salt Sea itself," the merchant said. "Don't go eating it, and mind your hands now that you've touched it—you could blind yourself if you rub your eyes with this on your fingers. But I promise you, friend, sheep love it. So do shepherds—keeps the flock healthy like nothing else."

I put my hand on the rock again, feeling the sharp points of the crystals pressing into my palm. No shepherd in Levonah had a rock like this. Yonaton tugged on my arm. "Come on, we can't afford this stuff."

"Now, you don't know that," the salt merchant held up both hands to stop us. "A little one costs just this much copper…" He held up a small iron weight and dropped it on one side of a scale.

Yonaton pulled on my arm again, but I couldn't take my eyes away from those rocks. Would it really keep the flock healthy? With the extra copper from the wedding it might be only two years now until my flock grew too large to keep at my uncle's house.

I suddenly pictured Dov smiling at me that morning, the one musician he didn't criticize even once during the rehearsal. True, I mainly stood out because I wasn't suffering the effects of wine like the others, but Dov didn't know that. Without even meaning to, I had impressed the most influential musician in the Kingdom. Would Dov offer me a place in the King's court if I continued to prove myself?

Daniel told me that the King paid visiting musicians well—surely he did no worse for members of his own court. It might take me twenty years as a shepherd to save enough to buy a piece of rocky hillside, but all the court musicians that morning were dressed in linen tunics, not the woolen ones that farmers and shepherds wore. Perhaps as a court musician I could buy land in ten, maybe even five, years. And Dahlia was right; if the Yovel was not coming, then any land I managed to purchase would be mine forever.

The salt merchant hadn't taken his eyes off me this entire time. No doubt, he thought I was dreaming of returning to my flock with one of his rocks, but I was no longer interested. Here, finally, was a dream worth leaving my flock over, a path that even a landless orphan could take toward a normal life.

A woman shrieked in the distance, her voice immediately drowned out by the rough cheers of a crowd of men. As the cheers faded, her cries rose again, only to be drowned out a second time by a deep roar.

The salt merchant laughed.

"What's that noise?"

"Go see," he said with a grin.

Yonaton and I ran off in the direction of the noise. I fell behind because of my kinnor slung over my shoulder and called ahead to Yonaton, who could see her first. "Is she all right?"

"The woman's fine," Yonaton replied, flinching as the crowd roared again. "It's her husband that's got the problem."

"What's wrong with him?"

"He might be torn apart by a bear."

"A bear's chasing her husband?"

"No. Her husband's chasing the bear."

I caught up to Yonaton and saw a powerfully built man edging closer to a shaggy, brown bear, both of them inside an enormous iron cage. Over a hundred people stood around the cage, cheering him on while his wife pulled at the bars, screaming at him. He ignored her, his eyes focused on the bear that was crouched on four legs, its head reaching as high as the man's chest. As the animal threw open its jaws and roared, glints of sunlight sparkled off its neck.

"Yonaton, is that bear wearing…?"

"Jewels," he said.

The man in the cage stepped forward, and the bear reared up on its hind legs, swatting at him with its massive, brown paw. He jumped back, but not far enough. A sharp claw caught the end of his nose. The smell of blood only provoked the beast. It launched forward, slashing its paws. The man ducked under its arm and lunged for the back of the bear's neck. His fingers closed around the golden chain of a ruby necklace. The beast whirled around, the back of a paw slamming into the man's head. He crashed into the iron bars of the cage and slid down the bars, collapsing at the bear's feet.

Two soldiers with spears leapt into the cage. The bear growled, but retreated before the sharp iron points. A third soldier dragged the challenger out and left him in the dirt outside the cage. The man unclenched his fist and examined his palm. It was empty. The red stone still hung from the bear's neck.

Someone from the crowd helped the man to his feet. As he staggered forward, his wife hit him in the chest with both fists, less powerfully than the bear, but no less fiercely. A scrawny man with bulging eyes climbed to the top of the cage and called out, "A handsbreadth away from a lifetime of riches! Who will be the next to try?"

Two men stepped forward from different parts of the crowd. "One at a time," the announcer said. "You. You climb in. You can go next. Unless…Ovadia, have you come to try? I'll let you go first!"

The crowd turned to watch Ovadia approach the cage. He stared long and hard at the bear, now back on four legs, circling its enclosure. The crowd was quiet, silenced by the prospect of seeing the King's steward in a death struggle for treasure. "Not today, Aviad," Ovadia replied, his calm gaze meeting the shaky eyes of the announcer.

But his refusal only excited Aviad. "Come, come…surely one who enters the throne room of the King isn't afraid to step into a bear's den?" The crowd laughed at the bold taunt but Ovadia just shook his head. Aviad raised his voice higher, "Can any man have too many riches?"

"A fool may be blinded by the jewels, Aviad, but a wise man sees the claws."

Ovadia eyes fell upon the two of us. "Ah, boys, I was hoping to find you here. Can you come with me?" We nodded and followed him away from the crowd. Once out of earshot, Ovadia pulled out a sealed scroll. "Please take this to Uzziah, son of Hanan. He is the foreman in charge of readying the gates. Wait for his response, then come report to me at the palace. I'll instruct the guards to let you in."

I was looking forward to a meal after a long morning of practice but I could not bring myself to refuse. We found workmen washing the city gates under the supervision of a man standing over them, inspecting their work. Yonaton approached him. "Are you Uzziah, son of Hanan?"

He nodded, taking the scroll. "So, what does Ovadia want now?" He broke the seal, read the scroll, then turned to one of his workmen. "Shama, take your horn and position yourself on that hill. When Tzidon's caravan comes into view, sound three long blasts." Turning back to Yonaton, he said, "You may tell Ovadia that everything has been arranged."

The first part of our task done, we headed back up the hill toward the palace at the top—but something about our errand didn't feel right to me. "Does it seem strange to you that Ovadia would use us as his messengers?"

"He's far too busy to go himself," Yonaton replied.

"Of course he is, but he must have other servants."

"Look around, everyone's busy. He probably needs all the help he can get."

"Maybe." But something still didn't feel right.

We found Ovadia standing under the arched entryway to the palace, inspecting an oak throne. Beside him, a man pointed to a carved cedar tree on the back of the throne. "Had there been more time—"

"Nonsense," Ovadia said, cutting him off. "No visiting king could expect more. King Ahav will be pleased." He turned at our approach. "Ah, boys, everything's been arranged? Excellent. I'm sure you're hungry. You can return to the house and Batya will make sure you're fixed something to eat. I may join you there soon, once I find servants to carry this into the throne room."

The throne looked heavy, but not too heavy for us to carry. The next time I saw Seguv, he would surely tell me about his appearance in the King's court. I would love to tell him that I'd been there as well.

Yonaton read my face and nodded—he wanted to do it too. "We can carry it," I said.

Ovadia smiled. "You probably can. But the King is sitting on his throne and will be watching. You do not want to drop this throne in front of King Ahav."

"We won't drop it," I said, trying to sound more confident than I felt.

Ovadia ran his eyes slowly over my face, then down to my chest and hands. He gave the same inspection to Yonaton, who was shorter and more solidly built. I expected Ovadia to refuse, but he nodded. "Very well. Two stout hearts are worth many strong arms. The throne belongs next to the King, on his left side. It is unacceptable to set it down in the throne room or to show any strain. If you feel it slipping, say 'Where would you like it, sir?' and I will come to your aid."

We picked up the throne, immediately discovering that it was heavier than it looked. The effort I saw on Yonaton's face mirrored my own. Ovadia hesitated but then took a step backward and directed us forward. At his nod, servants opened two tall wooden doors, and Ovadia backed into the throne room. We entered, and with great effort wiped the strain from our faces.

We were only halfway into the long, narrow room when I saw the tension creeping back into Yonaton's face and felt the muscles of my own jaw tighten. Both of us leaned forward, using the back of the throne to hide our faces from the King, but this only made it harder to carry. The King's throne sat on a raised platform, and to put this one next to him we'd have to lift it waist high and pass right before the King.

"Where shall we put it, sir?" Yonaton asked with clear strain in his voice.

Ovadia grabbed the back of the throne and lifted it with surprising power. "Right over here," he said. The three of us carried it onto the platform with ease, and Yonaton and I were able to relax our expressions before passing the King.

"Nicely done, Ovadia," the King said. "It is truly as beautiful as you claimed." A loud cheer came from outside, and everyone but the King turned toward the sound of the commotion. "Has someone just taken a jewel from the bear?"

"I believe so, my King."

"A rather brutal form of entertainment."

"Apparently quite popular in Tzidon. Princess Izevel thought it would amuse our guests."

"They do sound as if they're enjoying themselves. Still, we don't need any more cripples in Shomron—I'm feeding quite enough already."

Three long blasts echoed from outside the city. The King sat up straighter. "Could King Ethbaal have arrived already?" He sank back into his throne. "Ovadia, go and meet him outside the walls and escort him to me."

"Very good, my King. What of his wife and daughter?"

"Show them to their rooms." Ovadia bowed and turned to take his leave, motioning to the two of us to follow. "Wait a moment," the King said, noticing the kinnor slung across my back. "These boys. Are they the musicians that you fetched from the prophets?"

I heard the question in the King's voice. Now that he saw that we were just boys, would he guess that Ovadia's journey had nothing to do with musicians?

If Ovadia was nervous, his face didn't show it. "Yes, my King. These are two of the four I brought."

"You said they are quite talented, correct?"

"Superb, my King."

That was a risky thing for Ovadia to say. What if the King asked us to play and found us wanting? But the King had other ideas. "Bring them with you. It will make a nice impression for them to play upon his arrival."

"An excellent idea, my King." Ovadia bowed again and exited the throne room, with the two of us trailing closely behind.

Once out of the palace, we broke into a run, covering the distance down to the city gates in a quarter of the time it had taken us to climb up to the palace. My stomach growled—I hadn't eaten since before the rehearsal.

Outside the gates, Ovadia directed us to a hill overlooking the western road. "The two of you will play from here. When they come into view, I will descend to greet them at the bottom of the hill."

"Who are we waiting for?" Yonaton asked.

"King Ethbaal of Tzidon and his daughter Izevel, who is to marry King Ahav in two days' time."

"Where's Tzidon?"

"It's to the north of Israel, on the sea. The people of Tzidon are great sailors. King Ethbaal has made his capital city into the greatest port in the world."

"Is that why the King wants to marry his daughter?" I asked.

"Yes. An alliance with Tzidon will expand our ability to trade. The King expects this to bring great prosperity to the land."

"Do you think it will?"

"The King's reasoning is sound."

Ovadia had not really answered my question, but before I could ask another, three battle chariots came into view, each carrying a spearman and a bowman. They scanned the sides of the road, weapons gripped at the ready.

"I thought this was a wedding," Yonaton said. "They look as if they're going to war."

Next came a golden chariot carrying three passengers seated side by side. In the middle sat an older man, draped in purple robes, with a high forehead and neatly groomed beard. At his right sat a woman with steel-gray hair, the sun flashing off her many jewels. On his left sat a woman in a gray dress, her face and hair covered by a white veil. A line of chariots stretched down the road behind them. At the end of the caravan rode at least a hundred soldiers on horseback, each with a cedar tree emblem on his chest.

Ovadia signaled to us with a wave. Yonaton looked to me to start, and I began the first melody that came to mind, one we had learned just that morning. It was too cheerful for a march, but Yonaton joined in without objection, and I doubted King Ethbaal could even hear us over the noise of the horses. Ovadia spoke with the King, then climbed in beside the driver, beckoning us to follow.

We passed through the city gates and right up the main road of the city. At the top, Ovadia escorted the royal family into the palace. The maidservant followed Izevel, carrying nothing but an intricately embroidered sack.

I wasn't sure what we should do, but as no one had told us to stop the music, we followed. At the inner gates, Ovadia turned to King Ethbaal and asked, "Would the King like to be shown to his room to refresh himself before meeting with King Ahav?"

"No, I'll see Ahav immediately."

"Very well, my master awaits you. Please follow me. I will return immediately to accompany the Queen and the Princess to their chambers."

Once her father had gone, the Princess pointed around at the plaza and said something to her mother in a foreign tongue.

"You will be Queen of Israel soon," her mother replied in broken Hebrew. "If you wish to enter hearts of people, you must speak their tongue."

"As you say, Mother," the Princess replied, in a Hebrew far more fluid than her mother's. Izevel swept her hand across the plaza again. "It's little more than a fortress."

"Remember, palace is Queen's domain. You cannot expect an unmarried King to keep it properly."

"I'm so glad you were able to make the journey, Mother. I will miss your wisdom once you are gone. You are right. The dignity of the palace is my responsibility now." The Princess turned to her attendant. "Put it there."

The maidservant reached into her sack and put something on top of a pedestal near the entrance. Then she stepped back, revealing a bronze statue of a man, a war helmet on his head, with a jagged lightning sword grasped in his upraised hand.

"Yes," the Princess almost sighed. "That's better already."

I inhaled sharply and bit my lip. An idol—in the palace of the King of Israel?

My sleep was broken that night, but not by the old nightmare.

The caged bear, larger and fiercer than before, roared. The sun sparkled off the jewels hanging around its neck, but the ruby pendant was gone—in its place hung the Princess's bronze statue.

The bear grabbed an iron bar above his head and pulled down until it snapped under his weight. It broke another bar in the side of the cage, then another, and another. Once the cage lay in ruins at its feet, the beast stepped free.

No longer confined, the animal grew at a terrifying pace. It climbed uphill, expanding with each step until it grew taller than the palace itself. The monster grabbed the sides of the palace, tearing it from its foundations. It placed the palace on its head, now fitting it as tightly as a crown. In one giant step, the bear stepped over the walls of Shomron, heading north.

I woke up, my heart pounding. I stepped to the window, relieved to see the palace still perched on the hill, bathed in moonlight. Still trembling, I reached for my kinnor. Nothing calmed me like music.

I slipped down the ladder and stepped out into the cool night air. I didn't want to play near the house lest I disturb others' sleep. It took only a moment to decide where to go.

The bear slept, its shaggy back rising and falling with each breath. Its jewelry was gone, somehow removed for the night. I crouched nearby and plucked a melody my aunt used to sing to me when I woke from a nightmare. The music woke the bear. I stopped playing, but it was too late. The beast rose to its full height and growled, thrusting its paws between the bars at me.

I backed up to a safe distance, closed my eyes and listened to its voice. Daniel said he heard the song of the sheep in my music. I heard the bear's rhythm, slower and more powerful than that of the sheep. I plucked again at my kinnor, searching for the right sound.

A simple melody emerged from the deeper notes of my instrument. It just felt...right. I opened my eyes to see the bear standing silently, no longer lunging for me through the bars. I stepped forward, closer, but it still did not move. I began to hum, adding my voice to the notes of the kinnor. The beast tilted its head and released a groaning sigh. I took another step forward—the bear was now within my reach. Still humming, I removed my hand from the strings and extended it between the bars. The bear didn't move. I laid my hand on the back of its mammoth paw, probing the thick fur.

The animal turned its head—I pulled my hand back, fearing a strike that never came. I returned my hand to the strings, quietly strumming the bear's song. The animal closed its eyes with a low grunt. It crouched and lay down, resting its head on the back of its paws. I reached in again through the bars, scratching the bear behind its neck, the same place where the man grabbed for the ruby necklace earlier that day. I continued to stroke the spot until the bear sank again into a deep sleep.

Rabban Gamliel said: Beware of rulers: They act friendly when it is to their advantage; faithless during times of need.

Pirkei Avot 2:3

8

The Alliance

The High Priest stood alone under the wedding canopy. His eyes had a commanding look, set beneath thick, black eyebrows and a broad forehead. Dov struck the first three notes alone and the rest of us joined in on the fourth. An expectant silence fell over the crowd as all turned their attention up the aisle.

King Ahav walked alone, with no father or mother to march by his side. Next appeared a towering man in violet robes, holding the handle of a sword at his side. His eyes swept across the aisle, examining the crowd with each step. I knew there were many in Israel opposed to the marriage. Did Princess Izevel need protection at her own wedding? He stepped under the canopy and positioned himself next to the High Priest, who took a half step away from the bodyguard.

The royal family of Tzidon now appeared. Princess Izevel stood veiled in the middle, her smooth black hair flowing over her shoulders, dark against the white of her dress. King Ethbaal's proud face tipped upwards, honoring neither crowd nor king with his attention.

At the end of the aisle, King Ethbaal dropped his gaze to his daughter, lifted her veil and kissed her gently on the forehead. A soft pink flushed in Izevel's light cheeks. She appeared only a few years older than me—she couldn't have been more than sixteen. A familiar scent of wildflowers surrounded the Princess, and I suddenly knew what had become of the afarsimon oil Seguv brought to Shomron.

The High Priest stepped forward. "May all who have assembled here be blessed. We are the children of Avraham, whose tent opened to all sides to welcome guests. We placed our canopy under the sky, recalling the Holy One's blessing to Avraham that his children would be as abundant as the stars of the heavens…"

I was barely listening, my attention more on the music than on the words of the High Priest. I glanced at Dov, who in the final days of rehearsal continued to be impressed by my playing. I had not yet asked him about returning to play in the King's court—I would have to do that after the wedding.

Princess Izevel motioned to the High Priest. He broke off his speech and leaned in, allowing the Princess to whisper in his ear. The priest turned to King Ahav, who nodded. The High Priest winced, then restored the calm to his face. "This marriage is more than a union of two people; it is the joining together of two nations. The High Priest of Tzidon will bless the union as well."

The man in the violet robes, who I had mistaken for the Princess's bodyguard, stepped forward, his hand still resting on the hilt of his sword. "I am Yambalya. I serve Baal, the mighty storm god, patron god of Tzidon." His voice was deeper than any I had ever heard.

"Long ago, when the heavens were young, the children of El fought for mastery. In his struggle against Ya'am, lord of the seas, Baal turned to Koshar, the craftsman, for weapons that would make him invincible. With these tools in hand, Baal threw down the lord of the seas and climbed supreme into the heavens.

"As Baal's faithful, we follow his ways. Baal was mighty on his own. But he did not achieve victory until he formed an alliance. So too, Tzidon and Israel apart are mighty nations. But their union will be incomparable. With the blessing of Baal, the fertile soil of Israel and the merchants of Tzidon will bring the nations of the world to our feet."

Yambalya stepped back to the side of the platform. The High Priest of Israel stood pale and silent. He did not resume his speech, but rather nodded to King Ahav, who took a ring from a waiting servant and slid it smoothly onto Princess Izevel's outstretched finger. The High Priest announced, "I give you King Ahav and Queen Izevel." The King and his new Queen clasped hands, stepped out from under the canopy, and headed toward the palace.

Three court musicians escorted the King and Queen while the rest of us followed the guests out through the city gates and into the fields around the city. The feast area was divided into three sections: one for the soldiers, one for the nobility, and one for the commoners.

The aroma of sizzling fat reached my nose, making my stomach rumble. Zim grabbed my arm, "Did you see the size of those cows they're roasting?"

"That's for the nobility," Yonaton said. "Come on, the food on our side looks fine. I'm starving."

"We could get in there if we wanted to," Zim said.

"How?"

"With these." Zim indicated our instruments and the dark red sashes that we had been given for the wedding.

"Look at us; we hardly dress like nobility," I said.

"As long as we look as if we're supposed to be there, the guards will let us pass through."

"I don't know," Yonaton said. "That one on the left looks pretty mean."

"Stop worrying. Just start playing and follow me—and remember to look straight ahead."

Could Zim be right? If we acted as if we belonged, would the guards let us pass? I glanced at Yonaton, who arched his eyebrows as he raised his halil to his lips. I lifted my kinnor, feeling the thrill of the challenge. When we reached the guards, Zim stepped up his beat and closed his eyes. Despite his rough tunic and wild hair, Zim passed through, drawing the two of us after him.

"Wait." The guard on the left stepped in front of Yonaton—he had looked.

Zim called back to us, "Come on, they're waiting for us." Zim's voice carried so much confidence that the guard looked sheepish and stepped out of the way. Once out of earshot, Zim struck a final drum roll, ending in a belly laugh. "Remember: if you believe it, it's true."

Zim walked straight to a serving table, wrapped a chunk of roast lamb in bread, and bit into it like a wolf, letting the juices flow down his chin.

Then I saw, standing at the edge of the serving table, Seguv. I so wanted to go up and say hi to my friend. But Seguv's family were nobility, he actually belonged here, and he knew I did not. What would he think of me if he knew I took food that didn't belong to me?

"I want to go back and eat in our area," I said. Zim laughed, but Yonaton's shoulders relaxed in relief.

"If you two want to go back, I'll come with you. Let me take a little more meat first."

Back in the commoners' section, Yonaton and I waited in line to get our food.

There was no fish and the meats weren't spiced, but it still smelled wonderful. Food in hand, we rejoined Zim, who handed us each a clay goblet. "I got us wine," he said, his own goblet already half empty.

I remembered our first morning in Shomron, when I could barely wake Zim for all the wine he'd drunk the night before. The only reason I distinguished myself at the rehearsal was because I hadn't stayed up drinking with the musicians. Now Zim was handing me a goblet with far more wine than I'd ever drunk. This was my last opportunity to impress Dov—I couldn't take any chances now. "I'll pass."

"Don't worry. I got it from this side; you don't have to feel bad about drinking it."

"It's not that. I don't want it to hurt my playing."

"A little wine isn't going to hurt your playing—it might even improve it." Zim downed a quarter of his goblet in one gulp, then wiped his mouth with the back of a greasy hand. "You're not with the prophets now. You're at a feast—probably the biggest you'll ever enjoy. Everyone is drinking and having a good time. Stop thinking so much." He held out the goblet again.

Slowly, I reached out and grasped it. It was much stronger than I was used to—not watered down at all. All around me people were drinking and laughing. I closed my eyes, took a large swallow, and felt my nervousness melt away.

I was swallowing the dregs of my second goblet when three sharp trumpet blasts sounded from the palace: the signal we were waiting for. We walked back into the city in time to see the palace gates thrown open and King Ahav and Queen Izevel come forth to loud cheering.

Ahav and Izevel joined her parents on a raised stage at the edge of a large clearing. The musicians played just to the side of the stage, next to the section reserved for the sick and crippled, who, according to the King's custom, were given seats at the very front of the commoners' area. Ovadia stood next to the stage, commanding a constant stream of servants. He had been working non-stop since returning to Shomron. Yonaton and I had helped him as much as we could when we weren't in rehearsals, delivering messages and lending our hands to the endless details which he attended to personally. I hadn't even seen him at the ceremony—he must have been too busy preparing the celebration to attend.

A single man stepped into the open space before the stage, so thin that his white robes swayed as if empty. Approaching the platform, he bowed deeply to King Ahav. "Your Majesty, my performers and I were brought by the dyers'

guild of Tzidon in honor of the royal wedding. With the King's permission..."
King Ahav nodded in assent, "We will begin."

Dov struck the first note, and the musicians jumped into the music that we had prepared for the performance. It was a wild piece in parts, with a foreign rhythm, and despite all our practice, I feared I wouldn't keep up with the driving pace. But the wine loosened my fingertips, my dizziness was gone, and I felt a wonderful sense of freedom in its place.

Avidah withdrew to the side of the circle, as one of his performers ran in carrying a torch. With a loud "Hiyah!" he threw his torch high in the air where it broke apart into six, smaller flames. The crowd cheered, stomping and clapping their hands. The juggler caught three torches in his right hand, two in his left, and the final one in his mouth, then stepped to the side of the clearing.

A second performer stepped toward the stage and withdrew a sword with a jeweled handle from a scabbard around his waist. Falling to his knees, he held the sword straight above him, tipped his head back so far that the tendons on his neck stood out like ropes, and opened his mouth wide. How could a man kill himself just to entertain the King and Queen?

As the point of the sword entered his mouth, I turned away, not wanting to watch. Women screamed. I plucked furiously at my kinnor, grateful that the complex rhythm demanded so much concentration. Silence fell over the crowd and I glanced up, expecting to see the man writhing on the ground. The performer was still on his knees, gazing up, with half the length of the sword sticking out of his mouth. Yet the blade kept descending.

The sword sank until nothing except the jeweled handle remained visible. Then he grasped the hilt and drew the sword from his mouth. He held it high in the torchlight, showing that it was clean, without a trace of blood.

The juggler handed him a flaming torch. Again, he threw back his head and lowered it into his mouth. He removed the extinguished torch and handed it back, receiving another one in return. When the final torch was extinguished, both men bowed toward the stage.

The musicians didn't pause for a moment. Zim was right; despite my initial dizziness, the wine hadn't hurt my playing at all. I felt an unfamiliar looseness, playing faster and with more passion. Dov kept turning to watch me. Every time his eyes fell upon me, I felt a jolt of energy, picturing myself playing in the King's Court.

But the transformation in me was nothing compared to what came over Zim. Sweat poured down his head and neck, and his hands were a blur. I wasn't the only one who noticed. Yambalya worked his way over to the musicians, drawn by Zim's ferocious rhythm, and danced to the beat of his drums.

More and more performers came forward to carry out their feats, one after the next. A contortionist was followed by a man who wrestled a bear, then a snake charmer. When they finished, Dov signaled for the musicians to pause. I stretched my fingers and rubbed my palms, never having pushed my hands so hard before.

From beyond the edge the crowd, a chanting rose in the guttural tongue of Tzidon. It grew louder and the crowd parted to allow Yambalya to enter the clearing. Ten men dressed in identical violet robes, all wearing swords at their sides, followed behind. Four of them carried a large wooden chest suspended from poles on their shoulders. Yambalya directed them to lower the chest to the ground before the stage.

We hadn't rehearsed any music for this. We all watched Dov for a signal, but for the first time that evening he had no plan. With a quick strike of his nevel, he started us back into the piece we had performed for the juggler, but we didn't get far. Yambalya waved his arms at us and the song died on our strings. He put his arm around Zim's shoulder. "Just you. You come play."

Yambalya faced the stage and raised his arms. "We must now give thanks to Baal for arranging this union, binding it with blood." His voice boomed across the clearing. "We must humble ourselves before Baal. Ask that he bless this union. And bring prosperity to this land." A murmur rippled through the crowd. Yambalya signaled Zim, who began a fast-paced rhythm.

The violet-robed priests lifted the heavy cover of their box. From inside, they removed a carved pedestal. Then, with heads bowed, they placed a golden statue upon it. It was a larger version of the bronze statue that Izevel had placed in the palace, with a jagged sword in its upraised arm and the war helmet rising straight behind its head. Yambalya splashed blood-red wine before the pedestal. Then he knelt, torch in hand, and lit a pile of incense before the statue.

Yambalya touched his forehead to the ground. When he arose, he tightened his belt and slipped his arms out of his sleeves. The top of his robes fell away, revealing scars across his back and chest.

"We are the servants of Baal!" cried Yambalya. He drew the weapon from his scabbard, and I gasped as he held it high above his head. It wasn't a sword at all, but a broad, flat knife.

"We have no master but Baal!" He drew the blade of the knife across his chest, then slapped the flat of the blade against his chest, speckling the golden statue with blood.

I stared at Yambalya's knife. Had it been stone rather than iron, it would have been nearly identical to my father's. Shimon told me my knife had only one purpose and should never be used for anything else. Could this have been the purpose? Was this the reason that Uriel didn't want me to know what it was for?

Zim's drumming surged in intensity. The crowd stood silent now, too stunned to do anything but stare.

Yambalya faced the royal couples. "The offering of blood has been made. We must now bow down. We must humble ourselves before Baal. Then Baal, master of the storm, will hear our pleas. He will bring rain upon this land. And it will flow with his blessing."

Queen Izevel fell quickly to her knees, pressing her face to the ground. She was followed by both her parents. King Ahav remained seated, his eyes on the crowd. Ovadia stood next to the stage, glaring at Yambalya.

"People of Tzidon," Yambalya called out in his booming voice, "Humble yourselves before Baal." There was a rustling of clothes as the foreign guests dropped to the earth.

Yambalya faced King Ahav. "Great King! You wish prosperity for your land. Humble yourself! Bow down before Baal, most powerful of gods! Only he can fulfill your desire."

Queen Izevel raised her face from the ground. Green eyes wide, Izevel reached toward Ahav, beckoning. He rose at the request of his young bride, moving like a man half asleep. His eyes still on hers, he knelt to the ground, bowing until his forehead touched the wood of the stage.

"People of Israel. Your King and Queen want rain and prosperity for you. Show Baal that you desire it for yourselves and you will be answered." One by one, noblemen lowered themselves to the ground to bow before the Baal. Dov hesitated, but once most of the nobles prostrated themselves, he too knelt and pressed his forehead to the ground. Once he bowed, the rest of the court musicians bowed as well.

If Yambalya was unafraid to shed his own blood, what would he do to those who resisted? It would be so easy to join them, to drop to the ground and be spared their wrath. Yonaton's hands trembled on his halil. Daniel stood resolute, clutching his nevel. Seeing his defiance strengthened me. If he could resist, so could I. Yonaton moved in closer, and we remained standing together. I gazed toward the stage to see what Ovadia would do, but he was gone.

Most of the nobility were now on the ground, but the majority of the commoners still stood. I glanced at the section next to ours, that special section reserved for the crippled who depended upon the kindness of King Ahav for their very bread. Not one of them bowed. One man, bent with age, who had sat throughout the entire performance, pushed hard upon his walking stick with a trembling hand and drew himself to his feet. He stared at Yambalya, a challenge in his eye.

The Alliance

The High Priest of the Baal surveyed the crowd. He nodded approvingly at the Israelite nobility but shook his head as he scanned the rest of the people, almost none of whom met his eyes. He gazed upon the crippled, his eyes locking upon those of the bent old man. I watched Yambalya's knife, waiting for him to strike. But Yambalya only shook with laughter. He sheathed his knife, lowered himself to his knees, and touched his head to the ground before the golden statue.

When Yambalya stood, everyone on the ground rose with him. He raised his arms again, shaking the dirt and blood from his chest, and danced to Zim's frantic beat. The other priests joined in, drawing others into the clearing to dance.

On the stage, Izevel twirled her long, thin wrists in time to the music. Order broke down as people on all sides entered the clearing to dance. Dov signaled that we musicians were on our own. Some picked up their instruments and tried to keep up with Zim, while others jumped into the circle to join the dancing.

I picked up my kinnor and started to play, but Yonaton tucked his halil into his belt and said, "Come on, let's dance." My eyes scanned the clearing—the box holding the Baal was gone. What could be the harm in dancing now? I slung my instrument onto my back and followed Yonaton into the thick of the crowd.

Whoever leads the people on the right path will not come to sin. But one who leads the people astray will not even get a chance to repent.

Pirkei Avot 5:21

9

The Dispersal

The tight grip on my shoulder woke me, but it was cold rain on my face that forced my eyes open. I lay on my back, squinting dumbly at the clouds hanging just above the mountaintops.

My head throbbed—I wanted nothing more than to slide back into sleep, rain or no rain. Yonaton grabbed my hand and pulled me up. The world tilted as my body came to a sitting position. A bitter taste rose in my throat, bringing with it memories of dancing around the huge bonfire late into the night. I could not remember lying down.

The rain fell heavier, rousing sleepers all around us. Grunts gave way to groans and curses as farmers staggered to their feet. It wasn't just the wet awakening that upset them: it was the season. Still mid-summer, the early rains were not due for another two months. All across the Kingdom, the abundant wheat harvest—blessed by the same late rains that had destroyed so much of the barley crop—was cut and drying in the fields. If a downpour soaked the grain, it could rot in storage, destroying the year's harvest.

The farmers stared wildly at the clouds above them. They moved in a pack

toward the sound of drumming, which still echoed from the clearing. "Come on," Yonaton said, pulling me to my feet. I followed, stumbling behind him over the uneven ground.

I had never seen rains this early before, but I had heard other shepherds call them the shepherd's gift. Even a brief downpour now would bring up grasses all around Levonah, creating perfect grazing to nourish the flock.

In the clearing, Yambalya and his disciples still danced to Zim's beat. They called out in celebration of Baal's speedy answer to their prayers. Yambalya's belly shook with laughter at the panic on the farmers' faces. He stretched his head back so that raindrops fell into his mouth. "Baal is merciful," he called out. "He will not destroy your crops. Not yet. This is but a sign. A sign..." he lowered his gaze to the crowd, "...and a test.

"You will bring in your harvest before Baal unleashes the power of the storm wind. He who fails to heed Baal's power and leaves his grain in the field will surely see his harvest rot." Yambalya gave a final triumphant shout, and the rain came to an end.

The royal family would continue to celebrate for a full seven days, but most of the crowd had already planned to leave today. Now with Yambalya's threat, they ran to gather their belongings and begin their journeys home.

Yonaton and I walked silently toward Ovadia's house. We were also leaving that day. The court musicians would suffice to play for the week of celebrations, and we were still needed at the gathering.

"You look awful," Batya said as we entered. "You boys get ready to go, and I'll fix you something."

When we descended the ladder with our sacks, one of the maidservants poured out two steaming cups of steeped herbs. "Drink that," Batya said. I took a sip and gagged. "I know it tastes awful, but it will help. You boys should also have something to eat. You have a long journey ahead."

We had barely begun our meal when Daniel arrived. "Finish up," he said. "The donkeys are ready. If we start soon, we might make it back before nightfall."

"We haven't been paid," Yonaton said.

Daniel held up a leather pouch. "Dov came to pay us this morning. I collected for both of you."

Daniel's pouch held more copper than I'd ever owned, almost as much as promised for the entire gathering. I tried to look pleased, but I had looked forward to speaking to Dov myself about playing in the King's Court. Of course, all of the Court musicians had bowed to the Baal. Would I have to bow too if I wished to join them? I hadn't bowed last night, even when afraid of Yambalya's wrath. I made my choice, and once my stubborn heart decided on a path, it was set. I wouldn't bow now either, despite the possible rewards.

I took my last bite and rose to follow Daniel. While we packed the donkeys, Zim came over to the house, clutching his drum under one arm. His eyes were glassy, but his smile was wild with joy.

"Hey, Zim," Yonaton called. "Where are your things?"

"They're still in the musicians' quarters."

"You better run and get them. We're leaving."

"I'm not coming with you. I came to say goodbye."

"You're staying for the week of celebrations?" I asked.

"Longer. Yambalya invited me to join him."

"You're not coming back to play for the prophets at all?"

"Playing for Yambalya through the night, I poured all of my body and soul into my drum. That's what devotion should look like."

"We'll miss you," Yonaton said.

"I'll miss you too. But I have a feeling it won't be for long. You've both got talent, and you're only going to get better. From what I've seen, good musicians rarely stay in one place for too long. Unless they decide to marry like Daniel here," he added, giving Daniel a slap on the shoulder.

"So you'll be moving up to Tzur?" I asked.

Zim shook his head with a grin.

"Isn't Tzur the capital of Tzidon?"

"It is, but Yambalya isn't going back. Queen Izevel asked him to stay. She promised to build him a temple right here in Shomron."

Zim threw one arm around me and the other around Yonaton, drawing us both roughly to his body. When he released us, he picked up his drum and stood playing while we rode away.

Once past the city gates, Daniel tied our donkey to his with a lead rope. "This way you can sleep and let the donkey do the walking."

The animal's slow plodding made me think back to our swift ride to the wedding. On horseback, the journey took less than a day, even with lightly burdened donkeys following along behind. Now I couldn't see how Daniel hoped to get us back to the gathering before nightfall. Before long Yonaton's head slumped forward against my back. I fought to keep my eyes open, but sleep overtook me as well.

I awoke to a shaking against my back, and turned to see Yonaton crying. "What's wrong?"

"Nothing," Yonaton replied, sitting up and wiping his eyes on his sleeve.

"You can tell me." I twisted on the donkey's back so that I could catch Yonaton's eyes over my shoulder. "What is it?"

Yonaton hesitated, but only for a moment. "It's my father. I know what he's like. He won't gather in his grain early. He'd say it's betrayal to fear the Baal. What if our harvest is ruined? We don't have enough stored to get us through winter."

"You think Yambalya can make the rains come early?"

Yonaton gazed up at the dark patches of clouds moving across the summer sky. "What if he can?" he said softly.

I didn't know what to say—I was a shepherd, not a farmer. I was no more concerned about the early rains spoiling the wheat than I had been a few months earlier when the late rains ruined so much barley. The late rains made grazing easier this summer than in summers past. The early rains would do the same: replenish grasses, keep the flock healthier, and make my life easier.

But Yonaton's pain struck me in an unfamiliar way. A few months ago, it was the farmers who suffered when the barley spoiled. This morning, it was the farmers who would suffer if the rain soaked the wheat. It was easy to bear the pain of farmers I didn't know—especially when they had land and I had none—but it was much harder to gaze into the teary eyes of a friend. Not finding any words, I reached back and squeezed Yonaton's hand.

By early afternoon, the clouds burned off, leaving the sky a bright blue. "You know, I think the wheat will be fine," Yonaton said, his mood brightening with the sky. "The prophets look out for Israel. They wouldn't let Yambalya destroy the harvest of whoever doesn't fear the Baal."

We left the mountains south of Shomron behind and rode through the massive brown hills that I knew so well. We ate the midday meal under a carob tree just past Levonah. "We're making good time," Daniel said. "With a little luck we'll arrive before dark."

"But when I came with Master Uriel it took us two days from here," I said. "We were walking, but we weren't moving much slower than we are now."

"You went through Beit El. Our path will be more direct."

Yonaton swallowed the bread in his mouth. "Then why did Ovadia take us on the Beit El road?"

"Our way is too rough for horses. But the donkeys can make it if we lead them."

After the meal, we continued south on the King's Road for a short stretch, then Daniel turned the donkeys onto a narrow path that climbed up a hillside before Shiloh. Once over the ridge-line, the path dropped into a gully, and we dismounted to lead the donkeys down the descent. Daniel was right; this way was far shorter than the road through Beit El. I recalled how my legs ached from walking those first days with Uriel. He couldn't have led us that way just to alert Master Yosef; a simple messenger could have done that.

When I asked Daniel, he laughed. "How many people have we passed on this path?"

"None."

"There's your answer."

"What do you mean?"

"What do you think Master Uriel does when he's not at the gathering?"

I had never given any thought to the prophet's life before. "Return home to his family?"

Daniel shook his head. "He travels the land. People go to him for prophecy, for advice, for blessings, for judgment of their disputes. It's not his way to seek the shortest path."

The sun was just setting as we descended into Emek HaAsefa. My eye found the musicians' cave. I was surprised at the feeling of warmth in my chest—like coming home.

Daniel approached a servant cleaning up after the evening meal. "Is there anything left? We just returned from Shomron."

"Yes, Master Uriel had us put aside dishes for each of you." The servant gestured to a table with three large portions of bread and lentils. Had the prophet received a vision that Zim wouldn't be returning with us, or was this another instinct of his heart?

The servant approached me and spoke quietly, so that I alone could hear. "The portion on the right is for you." It was curious to me that they kept setting aside food for me, yet at least this time my portion was no smaller than the other two, and even had a helping of cheese. Was Uriel warming to me?

After the evening meal, we walked to our cave in the twilight. "I'll be back later," Yonaton said. "I promised my mother I'd tell her when we got back."

"You're going in the dark?"

"The moon's still up; that'll give me enough light."

I finished laying out my bedroll and retrieved my kinnor. "Then Daniel and I will just have to start playing without you."

Daniel laughed. "You can play on your own." He lay down on his sheepskin mat. "I need to go right to sleep if I'm going to make it back to my farm tomorrow."

I turned to Daniel. "You're leaving too?"

"I've got to get home and bring in my harvest before it rots in the field. You heard Yambalya, this morning's rain was only a warning. If we fail to heed it, we may not be so blessed in the future. I'm leaving at dawn. Yonaton, if I were you, I'd tell your family to bring in theirs as well."

Yonaton's eyes went wide, and without another word, he ran out of the cave toward home.

Zim's reaction to Yambalya was one thing—but Daniel? "After all these years playing for the prophets, you're going to heed the Baal?"

Daniel shook his head. "All these years with the prophets have shown me that all kinds of things are possible."

"But you refused to bow at the wedding."

"True, but I also felt the rain on my face this morning." Daniel folded his arms behind his head. "If Yambalya is wrong and I bring in my crops early, what have I lost? But if he's right, and I leave them in the fields…" Daniel sighed, put down his head, and closed his eyes.

I sat down on one of the boulders in front of the cave. Zim wasn't coming back and Daniel was leaving. Would Yonaton be next? Would I have to play on my own for the rest of the gathering? There was no point in staying awake on my own. I was just turning into the cave when I heard someone stepping up the path.

"Ah Lev, I was hoping to find you," Uriel whispered, resting his hand on my shoulder. "I want to hear about the wedding. Let us go to my cave so that we don't disturb the others."

I followed Uriel in silence. Four lamps burned inside his cave. I sat opposite Uriel, whose blue eyes fell upon mine, expectant. I wasn't sure what he wanted me to say, so I started at the beginning.

"When we got to Shomron, Ovadia told Yonaton and me that we'd be staying with him, not with Daniel and Zim in the musicians' quarters." I paused, hoping he would direct me, but he didn't speak, just nodded for me to continue.

As words spilled out, I found myself saying more than I intended, talking about things of no importance. Why would the prophet care about us delivering Ovadia's messages, or the commoners fighting the bear? I kept watching the prophet for some sign of what he was after, but he just met my eyes with a steady gaze.

When I finally ran out of words, two of the lamps had burned out.

"So Queen Izevel and her family all bowed before the Baal?"

"Yes."

"Then King Ahav bowed, and the people bowed as well?"

"Many of them."

"And Ovadia?"

"I looked for him, but he had gone."

"Then, in the morning, there was rain?"

"Yes."

"The people were afraid, and in their fear they turned to the priest of the Baal."

This wasn't a question, but I still answered, "Yes."

Uriel's eyes rose to the ceiling of the cave. "The lamp of darkness is burning brightly once again," he said, more to himself than to me. "May the Holy One protect Israel."

"The lamp of darkness?"

Uriel lowered himself onto a reed mat on the floor with his feet before him, his knees bent to his chest. "I would like you to play for me. We may need to end the gathering early."

"Why?"

"As you said, the rains might be coming. Whoever leaves his crops in the fields risks ruin. Many of our disciples are farmers. We cannot cause them to suffer such losses."

I thought back to what Yonaton said on our journey back to the valley. "But can't the prophets stop the rains?"

"Even if I could, I wouldn't do so."

"Why not?"

"If we stop the rains, it will only bring the people to fear us more than Yambalya. It becomes a battle of one fear over another."

"Isn't that what you want, that the people should fear the Holy One more than the Baal?"

"No! A true turning to the Holy One is the end of fear, not a step down its path."

"So none of the prophets will do anything to stop this?"

The old prophet hesitated. "I don't think so."

I would have said no more, but I heard uncertainty now in Uriel's voice. Did this mean that not all the prophets agreed with him? Was there still a chance to stop the rains?

"When we were riding home from the gathering, Yonaton cried. That's how scared he was that his father would refuse to listen to Yambalya and their harvest would be lost."

"And you feel that Yonaton's tears show what?"

"They show suffering. They show fear."

"And weakness?"

I didn't want to call Yonaton weak, but Uriel was right—that's exactly what I thought. "Yes."

"You have much to learn about strength, Lev. Would you consider the constipated man strong?" Uriel fixed me with a penetrating glance. Could he see that I, who cried so much as a child, had not cried for over five years? "Yonaton's tears are not a weakness—they're his greatest strength. Indeed, if all of Israel could cry out as Yonaton has, we would have nothing to fear from Yambalya. Now, if you could please play for me."

I didn't see how tears would move Yambalya. The more our tears flowed, the deeper he'd laugh. But the time for discussion had passed. I needed to play, which posed a different problem. "I don't have my kinnor."

"I'm sure you will manage."

Lacking anything better, I drummed on the table and chanted along as best I could. It seemed to work. By the time the third lamp burned out, Uriel trembled with the spirit of prophecy.

An image rose in my mind of Yambalya, drawing his knife across his chest. Next I saw farmers' faces as the rain fell the following morning, and I heard Yambalya's deep laughter at their terror. Then I observed Uriel, old and gray, trembling in a heap on the floor. It was easy to guess which of the two the people would follow.

Uriel's trembling stopped and he pushed himself to a sitting position. "The rains are indeed coming," he said, getting to his feet. "I must speak to the other masters about ending the gathering early."

"You really won't do anything to stop the rains?"

"I will not." Uriel placed both hands on my shoulders this time, holding my eyes in his. "There is no greater blessing than peace, Lev. For its sake the Holy One overlooks our failures, even the people bowing to strange gods. But once peace is broken, there is little left but judgment. In a time of judgment, our sins are recalled and accounted for. The devastation may be great indeed. You are too young to remember the wars that ravaged this kingdom not so long ago. Believe me, it is nothing we want to return to."

Uriel took several steps toward the entrance, then turned back to face me. "I know that your words come from your courage as much as from your youth. This courage will serve you well. Indeed, it already has. It was no small thing refusing to humble yourself before the Baal."

I stood straighter. "No, I've bowed only before the Holy One."

The old prophet's brow furrowed. "You bowed to the Holy One?"

"Yes," I nodded. "In Beit El. When you sent me to Master Yosef, I also visited the altar. I wanted to make an offering," I added with a sigh, "But I'm still too young."

Uriel turned to face me fully, his eyes narrowed. "But you bowed?"

"Yes."

Uriel's eyes boiled with anger. My earlier thoughts of him as a weak, old man disappeared. In his suddenly hard eyes, I sensed an untold strength within his aged body.

Finally, he turned away, stepping toward the cave entrance. "You may sleep now."

I woke in the predawn light to see Daniel rolling up his sheepskin sleeping mat. I dressed quietly, so as not to wake Yonaton, and stepped out of the cave. Daniel emerged, his nevel in one hand, a sack slung over his shoulder. "I'll see you next year?" he asked.

I pictured Uriel's expression of the night before. Would the prophet even want me back? "I don't know."

"Return if you can." Daniel hitched his sack higher. "But even if you don't make it back, even if you have only your sheep for an audience, never stop playing your kinnor."

I didn't need anyone to tell me to keep playing my music; it was the one thing that brought me joy that I could carry with me into the wild. But Daniel's tone got my attention. "Why not?"

"Twelve years ago, my master told me the same thing I told you, that I could stay with the prophets, playing for them year-round, just as he did."

"But you didn't want to?"

"I did. I stayed with them for over a year."

"Why did you leave?"

"My father was getting old—he could no longer handle the farm by himself. One day he fell and injured his leg. I had to go back—I had responsibilities. My master was disappointed, but he understood. Before I left he told me what I've just told you, that I must never stop playing."

"Why not?"

"The music surges inside me. Every power a person has must be expressed, otherwise it decays, and decay is a small death. The Holy One forbids us to resign ourselves to death."

"So that's why you return?"

"That's why I return each summer, even though I now have a family of my own and my responsibilities have only grown."

"So even if I can't return—"

"Even if you can't return, you must continue to play. Never let this spark inside you die. But I believe that you will return. You didn't receive a kinnor like that to play it alone in the wilderness."

My hand slipped to my side where my kinnor normally hung, feeling only empty air. "What do you mean?"

"The workmanship is unmistakable. It's prophet-made."

"Prophet-made? But I got it from my uncle."

"That kinnor was made by no local craftsman. I don't know how it reached your hands, but I doubt whoever gave it to you intended for you to play before sheep."

"What do you mean 'whoever?' I told you my uncle gave it to me."

Daniel allowed himself a half smile. "I see. And your uncle is quite the musician, is he?"

My head cocked to the side. "No, I've never seen him play."

"A collector then? Your uncle has many fine craftsman-made objects lying about the house that he has no need for?" I laughed—we both knew I didn't come from nobility.

"Admit it, Lev, even if you did receive that kinnor from your uncle, there's more to the story than you know. If a prophet's treasure winds up in your hands, it's rarely chance. Now, I must start for home before the sun gets any higher—I have much work ahead of me." Daniel raised a hand in farewell, then turned down the trail.

I stepped into the cave and retrieved my kinnor, then sat back down outside, examining it in the growing daylight. I ran my fingertips along the olive wood frame, as if seeing it for the first time. I admired the smoothness of its surface, the precision of the carving, and the flawless joints. Truly, there was nothing in my uncle's house that came close to it.

Yonaton stepped out of the cave, his arms raised in a yawn. "Has Daniel gone?"

"Yes, he's left for home."

"Too bad, I would have liked to say goodbye."

"How are things with your family?"

"Not good. My father refuses to take in the harvest—he got angry that I even suggested it."

"Well, he might change his mind now. Master Uriel saw last night that the rains are going to come early."

"Oh? If a prophet says so, that will be enough for my father."

"They're serving the morning meal now if you want to go."

"Sounds good. We've never made it to the morning meal here before."

The disciples were already sitting in the field eating by the time we joined them. One of the cooks handed me a small piece of bread, a single dried fig, and twelve kernels of toasted grain from where it had been set aside in the cooking area. The portion was the smallest I had ever received. Was this a further sign of Uriel's disappointment?

The three masters stepped to the center of the eating area. "We have received word," Uriel began. "The rains will indeed come early this year. The gathering will come to a close so that disciples can return home and attend to their harvests."

Uriel and Tzadok both appeared calm, but Yosef scowled.

Uriel continued, "I will remain here with any wishing to stay and continue training. To those who are leaving, may you be blessed with an early and abundant harvest. You are now free to go."

A disciple named Tuvia approached me. "Master Uriel asked me to escort you back to your uncle's. I need to ride past Levonah on my way back home."

"But I'm not a farmer. I don't need to go back for the harvest."

"Then speak to Master Uriel—but do it fast, because I need to go. He also asked me to give each of you one of these." He handed each of us a pouch of copper.

Yonaton turned his pouch over in his hand and examined the contents. "This is how much we were supposed to receive for the entire gathering, but we haven't even played for a week."

I poured out my pouch and counted as well. Yonaton was right—the entire summer's wages were there.

Tuvia gazed up at a small cloud in the otherwise clear sky. "I'm just the messenger. Speak to Master Uriel if you want, but you'll need to do it quickly."

Uriel was on the far side of the clearing talking to Yosef, his back to us. He wouldn't have arranged a ride home and paid full wages for the entire summer if he wanted me to stay. "I'll get my things."

Tuvia nodded. "I'll wait for you at the top of the hill."

"Master Uriel might not realize that you're not needed for the harvest," Yonaton said. "Maybe you should speak to him."

"He knows," I replied, avoiding his eyes. "If he's sending me home, he doesn't want…" I swallowed. "He doesn't need me." I didn't understand why bowing to the Holy One would anger Uriel, but I had no desire to talk about it—not even to Yonaton. "We should go pack."

Neither of us spoke as we gathered our few possessions. Saying goodbye to Yonaton felt different than parting from Zim or Daniel. But words were never my strength. I stepped forward and embraced my friend, then walked off to meet Tuvia.

Rabbi Shimon said: Do not be wicked in your own sight.

Pirkei Avot 2:18

10

Eliav's Choice

"Tell us about the man eating the sword again," six-year-old Shimi asked for the third time at dinner that night.

"As I said, he didn't exactly eat it." I dropped my spoonful of lentil stew — everyone else had finished eating, but my bowl was still half full. "He bent his head back like this and held the sword over his head —" I held my spoon over my upturned mouth in demonstration— "then he lowered it down his throat." I lowered the handle until I gagged. "But he kept it going all the way down."

"How long was the sword?" Eliav asked.

"About this long." I held my arms out.

"But it must have gone down to his stomach." Dahlia wrinkled her nose at this. "And it came out without any blood?"

"Not a drop."

"I think you should all let Lev eat," Aunt Leah said. "You can ask him about his adventures tomorrow. He's home now. Come Ruth, Shimi, Naamah. To sleep."

The youngest children followed their mother up the ladder as Dahlia cleared the table. Eliav went outside to check on the flock, and Uncle Menachem stayed at the table while I finished. He had passed the meal in silence, hardly taking his eyes off me as he ate.

Eliav returned and climbed the ladder without a word. I wiped the clay bowl with the last of my bread, handed the bowl to Dahlia, then turned toward the door.

"Eliav's already seen to the sheep," Uncle Menachem said.

"I know, Uncle." But I walked outside anyway and leaned against the edge of the pen, patting the head of the nearest sheep, which stared up, then pulled away.

"You didn't mention the rest of the wedding," my uncle said, coming up behind me.

"I didn't want to scare them. I wasn't sure if you even knew."

"We felt the rain here too, Lev. It didn't take long to learn the reason why. Everyone's in a panic to gather in their crops. What does Master Uriel say?"

"The rains will come, just as Yambalya promised. He ended the gathering early."

"That's why he sent you home?"

"No, Uncle. That's not why he sent me away."

"No? What did he say?"

"He didn't say anything. He closed the gathering and told everyone they could go home to bring in the harvest."

"But if the gathering was closed, it was closed."

"No, Uncle." I wanted to understand the truth, and to do that, I needed to tell my uncle everything. "He stayed behind with any disciples wishing to remain."

"Then it probably wasn't worth paying a musician for just a few disciples."

"No, Uncle. He paid me for the entire summer." One of the sheep crossed the pen to lick my hand. "He sent me away because he's angry."

"Angry?"

"On the way to the gathering, Uriel sent me into Beit El to deliver a message. I had time, so I went and bowed to the Holy One. I told him this last night when I returned from the wedding."

Whatever response I may have expected, it wasn't the burst of laughter I received. "You told a prophet that you bowed to the Golden Calf?"

My face grew hot. "Why not? You taught me that bowing to the calf is bowing to the Holy One. You go every year."

"Yes, yes I do," he said. "I'm not proud of it. But I go. And I bow."

"Why wouldn't you be proud? And if you're not proud, then why do you go?"

"I didn't used to go. Of course, when I came of age, my father took me. But once I married your aunt, your father wouldn't hear of it."

My uncle almost never spoke of my father. "What do you mean?"

"The tale of the calf is a troubled one. Have I ever told you why the Kingdom was split?"

I sensed a story coming and sat down on the wall of the pen, shaking my head.

"When King Solomon died, the tribes called his son Rechavaum to Shechem to crown him King of all Israel. Now King David was a mighty warrior, and the people followed him with all their hearts. His son Solomon was a great builder who set the people to build the Holy One's Temple and his own palace in Jerusalem. Twenty years of sending people north, thousands at a time, to fell trees and cut stones in the mountains of Tzidon. Twenty years of fathers gone from their families, husbands from their wives, sons from their farms.

"So when Rechavaum came to Shechem, the tribes said to him, 'Your father placed a heavy yoke upon us. Lighten our burden and we will serve you as we served him.' Unwilling to answer right away, Rechavaum took three days to consider.

"The elders who had advised Solomon told Rechavaum to bend to their will. But Rechavaum's friends did not agree. They told him that it was dangerous to meet demands with weakness. They advised him to say, 'My father laid a heavy yoke on you, I will add to it. If Solomon beat you with sticks, I will whip you with scorpions.'"

"Why would they say that?"

"I think they were afraid."

"Afraid? Afraid of what?"

"Of what the tribes would do. Of having to hold together the Kingdom without King Solomon. And when men are afraid, they feel safer if they can make others afraid as well—afraid of them."

"So he listened to his friends?"

My uncle nodded. "His friends convinced him that the strong hand is the one that holds the whip. But he didn't count on the strength of the tribe of Ephraim. They killed his tax collector and sent Rechavaum fleeing back to Jerusalem. Only his own tribe of Yehudah and the small tribe of Binyamin stayed loyal to the House of David. The other tribes chose Yeravaum as their king, and he declared the new Kingdom of Israel, independent from the Kingdom of Yehudah."

"But how could they do that?"

"As I said, Ephraim is a powerful tribe, and the northern tribes resented twenty years of forced labor to build a capital in the south."

"But you told me the Holy One granted an eternal kingdom to the House of David."

Uncle Menachem's eyes narrowed. "Well, this is where your friends, the prophets, enter the story."

"They fought against Yeravaum?"

He shook his head. "King Solomon marrying foreign wives angered the Holy One. Achia of Shiloh, Uriel's master, anointed Yeravaum as king even during Solomon's lifetime."

"The prophets declared Yeravaum king even before the people rejected Rechavaum?"

My uncle nodded.

"But what does this have to do with my bowing to the calf?"

"Well, Yeravaum had the support of most of the people, especially after it became known that he was anointed by a prophet. But there was one thing he didn't have: the Holy Temple. All the men of Israel are obligated to go up to the Temple for the three yearly festivals."

"So?"

"So, only a king from the House of David is allowed to sit in the Temple; all others must stand. Yeravaum was afraid that if he allowed the people to go to Jerusalem, they would see Rechavaum sitting in the Temple courts while he stood. Who would look like the greater king then? He feared their loyalty would return to the House of David. So he closed the roads to Jerusalem and forbade the people from making the pilgrimage."

I pictured the faces of the nobles bowing to the Baal at the wedding. "Yeravaum was afraid, so he frightened the people?"

Uncle Menachem nodded. "He put soldiers on the road. After he killed the first few who defied his orders, most stopped trying. But Yeravaum was not opposed to the people serving the Holy One, just to them going to Jerusalem. So he crafted two golden calves, placing one in Beit El in the south of the Kingdom and one in Dan in the north, and declared: 'Here are your gods that brought you up from Egypt.' Then he created a new pilgrimage festival one month after Sukkot."

"Why did he choose the calf?"

"I think it was because our ancestors already worshipped the calf in the desert—it was already in our hearts."

"Uncle, if you know all this, why did you start going again?"

Uncle Menachem dropped his eyes. "It's what everyone does, Lev. It's a time for the people to come together and strengthen our connections to each other and the Holy One. I loved going with my father when I was young. Is it better to go to the Temple? Of course. But the road to Jerusalem is closed. Your father made me ashamed to go, but when he was no longer here, I started again."

I nodded, glad my uncle had answered, but not wanting to push him further.

"So you'll be taking out the flock in the morning?"

Now it was my turn to look away. The question had been on my mind the whole journey back. "No. I'll go, but only to help Eliav. He leads the flock now."

"Lev, you know you are no less to me than my own children, don't you?"

I swallowed but didn't reply.

"It's true that you can't inherit the land. But your aunt and I have spoken. We want each of you to inherit part of the flock. You needn't give way to Eliav. You're the elder and the better shepherd. He should help you."

My lower jaw trembled, but I had decided my path—there would be no more silly dreams. "No, I'll help him. Between the prophets and the wedding, I have enough copper to buy seven ewes and two rams in the spring." Uncle Menachem raised his eyebrows. "I'll go out with Eliav through the winter, then start a flock of my own."

Uncle Menachem pulled on his beard. "This is what you want?"

"Yes," I said, though the word came out weaker than I intended.

"Very well. I'll give you another ram and three ewes from the calves. With that many to start, you should have a strong flock by the time you're ready to marry."

I knew he would want to help, but hadn't expected such a generous gift. "Thank you, Uncle."

Uncle Menachem stepped back toward the house, then turned to face me. "You're sure this is what you want?"

"Yes," I said with confidence I didn't feel. "Eliav should take the flock."

"I meant, are you sure you want to be a shepherd?"

The dream of playing in the King's Court still called to me, but not if it meant bowing to the Baal. "What else would I do?"

Uncle Menachem shrugged. "That morning when you went off with Master Uriel, you didn't see me. I was working in the olive trees and watched you go. I wondered if you'd ever return to this life. You have a lot of your father in you."

Three mentions of my father in one conversation. Was Uncle Menachem suddenly willing to talk? "Uncle, what really happened to my parents?"

"The truth? I don't know most of it. A man came to us in the night with cuts all over his face. Didn't appear as if anyone had treated his wounds at all. He was carrying you. You just kept screaming. You weren't hurt, but it looked as if you'd not been fed all day. He told me that he saw your parents killed. He wouldn't say any more. I tried to convince him to stay, to eat something and let us care for his wounds. But he refused. He just refilled his water skin, took a little food, and left."

I nodded, not trusting my voice. Menachem rested his hand on my shoulder, then stepped back toward the house. I sat alone with my thoughts as darkness fell.

"Where's your kinnor?" Eliav asked me the next morning.

"I'm not bringing it." I held a shepherd's staff, which I hadn't carried in over a year. "You're in charge of the flock now. We'll do it your way."

Eliav didn't respond, just stared at me with a blank expression, as if unsure whether to be happy about this change or not. With a shrug, he turned his back, unlocked the pen, and let out a sharp "Yah!" that brought the sheep pouring out. I hemmed in the flock with my outstretched staff, and Eliav turned them downhill toward the fields on the back side of the town.

"The rain brought up fresh grasses by the road," I called from behind the flock. "No one's grazed there yet."

Eliav didn't turn. "The rain brought up grasses everywhere. This way's closer."

"But you need to go through Zimmah son of Merari's field this way. They might eat from the cut grain."

Eliav stopped and the sheep bunched up behind him, bleating and snorting. "All the shepherds pass through his field and no one grazes there, you know that. But if you'd rather go to the road, we can go to the road."

"It's your flock—I'll follow you."

Eliav spit on the ground, then turned the flock back up toward the road. How long had it taken Eliav to change my grazing spot? Had he done it the very day I left? And why? Was it because the road was farther or because all the other shepherds went behind the town?

We found good pasture on the slope immediately below the town's gates. I missed my kinnor. A staff might keep the sheep in line, but it was a poor tool for occupying heart and mind.

In early afternoon, I noticed a rider turning up from the King's Road, dressed in violet robes. A priest of the Baal in Levonah?

Eliav gaped, and I elbowed him so that he wouldn't stare. I needn't have bothered—two shepherd boys were beneath the priest's notice. He approached the gate and addressed the guard loudly in poor Hebrew. "I want Yoel son of Beerah."

Yoel son of Beerah was the King's minister in Levonah—what could a priest of the Baal want with him? Without thinking, I motioned to Eliav to watch the sheep and slipped up to the town wall. I stopped in the shadow of the gate where I could hear without being easily seen.

The guard at the gate said, "Who seeks the King's officer?"

"A messenger of the Queen." The priest held out a scroll in one hand.

The guard examined the seal on the scroll. "He is here in the gatehouse. I will summon him."

Yoel son of Beerah stepped into the gate, trailed by two soldiers. "I am Yoel son of Beerah. You may deliver your message."

The priest handed over the scroll and Yoel son of Beerah hastily broke the seal and glanced at the contents of the parchment. "Come, we must discuss this."

"Lev!" Eliav hissed from below.

I cringed at the sound and scurried down from my perch.

"What were you doing?"

"That's a priest of the Baal bringing a message to Yoel son of Beerah."

Eliav's eyes widened. "How do you know he's a priest of the Baal?"

"I recognized him from the wedding."

"You have no business with him. What were you doing? If he had seen you…"

Eliav was right—it was a stupid risk to take. Why did I feel such a strong need to know what they were saying?

"What did he want with Yoel son of Beerah?"

"I don't know." I glared at Eliav. "I had to stop listening."

Eliav gazed up at the clouds. "Do you really think they can bring the rains?"

"Master Uriel says that they will come early."

Eliav grinned. "That'll be a blessing."

I leaned away from him. "But what about all the farmers whose crops will be ruined?"

"What about them?" Eliav planted his staff before him and stood. "Let their blood be on their own heads. Yambalya granted them enough time for the harvest; you heard him yourself. It's only those who don't listen whose crops will be ruined. And any rain is good for us, right?"

Again Eliav was right—hadn't I thought like him when I first felt the rains? Yet, now a fury rose within me that I couldn't explain. I stomped off to gather in a stray ram.

The next day was Shabbat. I passed the time feasting with my family and repeating the stories of my travels, mostly at the request of my younger cousins. On the first day of the week, Eliav again directed the flock toward the fields behind the city. This time I didn't bother protesting.

After the evening meal that night, I retrieved my kinnor for the first

time since returning home. It was not to "keep the spark inside me alive," as Daniel had pressed me to do. No, I needed music to smother all those voices rising in my head since my return: my anger at Eliav, my disappointment in Uncle Menachem, my desire to be more than a shepherd in the wilderness. I'd made my choice, and my kinnor was my best tool to quiet my mind. I leaned against an olive tree opposite the house and gently plucked the strings, trying to replicate the sound of the leaves rustling overhead, imagining myself alone in the wilderness.

"There was no music while you were gone." Dahlia stood over me, a bowl in her hands. "I brought you some toasted wheat."

I grabbed a few wheat berries, still warm from roasting, and popped them into my mouth.

Dahlia sat next to me, pulling her dress down over her feet, and resting the bowl in her lap. "Do you want to sing to me?"

"I don't feel like singing."

"Want to tell me about the wedding again?"

"No," I said, louder than I intended.

She pulled away. "Do you want me to go back in?"

"No, you can stay." In the distance, there were three heavy thuds, the sound of wood striking wood.

"Are you happy to be home?"

Had anyone else in the family asked, I would have replied with a quick "Yes," but it was different with Dahlia. "I was when I first got back."

"You don't seem happy now." Again we heard a thudding sound, this time closer. "I don't think my mother expected you to return."

"Is that why she cried so much when I left?"

"Probably."

"One of the musicians I met was like that. He left home over a year ago, moving from place to place, playing for weddings and festivals."

"He didn't get lonely?"

"I don't think so."

"Would you?"

I closed my eyes, picturing myself moving from festival to festival, carrying a mirror like Zim, never spending more than a couple of weeks in any one place. Maybe if Yonaton was with me it wouldn't be so bad. "I'd get lonely."

"I don't think she saw you becoming some wandering musician."

"No, she thought I'd stay with Master Uriel," I said, clamping my hand on the strings of the kinnor. The music died. Whenever I thought of Uriel now, I saw his cold, narrowed eyes after he learned that I'd bowed to the calf.

"Yes," Dahlia replied, and we sat in silence once again.

Two men crossed Uncle Menachem's property and approached the house, taking no notice of Dahlia or me in the growing darkness. The man in front raised his staff and banged it three times against the door.

"Who's there?" my uncle called, worry in his voice. We did not get many visitors at night—certainly not ones who knocked so loudly.

"It is Yoel, son of Beerah," the shorter man answered.

Eliav opened the door and soft light from the hearth shone from the house, revealing the violet color of the other man's robes. Uncle Menachem appeared next to Eliav in the doorway. "Good evening, Yoel, son of Beerah. Please come in."

"There is no need, we want just a word. Queen Izevel invites all of Israel to humble ourselves before the Baal prior to the rains so that we will be blessed with a bountiful year."

The priest put a box on the ground, opening a flap in the side facing the house.

"I see the Baal. And I see his servant's weapon," my uncle said, staring at the long knife at the priest's side. "Are we being forced to bow?"

"Certainly not. Queen Izevel only invites us. Already tonight several men have declined. If they're not concerned for their crops, I cannot help them. We are here for your sake."

The priest fell to his knees in front of the box, stretching out his arms and pressing his face to the ground. Yoel bowed next to him.

Dahlia clutched my arm. Would Uncle Menachem bow to the Baal as he did to the Golden Calf?

Uncle Menachem hesitated. This was not like the Calf. Even if Uncle Menachem believed bowing to the Calf was bowing to the Holy One, he could claim no confusion here. I watched for my uncle's reaction—but Eliav moved first. Turning away from his father, Eliav fell to the ground beside Yoel, stretching himself out in the dirt of the doorway.

Uncle Menachem's eyes fell on his son.

Dahlia's nails dug deep into the skin of my arm. I choked back a cry.

Uncle Menachem's knees buckled, as if he was trying to hold up a weight greater than himself. He dropped to the ground and pressed his forehead to the earth like the other men.

Yoel stood first, brushing dirt from his cloak. Uncle Menachem followed, but Eliav did not lift himself from the dirt until the priest stood and closed the shrine.

"You are a prudent man, Menachem," Yoel said. "May you receive much blessing for it. Peace to you."

"And peace unto you, Yoel, son of Beerah," Uncle Menachem replied.

The priest handed an object to my uncle. "Gift from the Queen," he said, then followed Yoel away into the darkness.

Uncle Menachem stood in the doorway, watching the two men disappear down the path. As he turned back toward the house, his glance paused under the olive tree where Dahlia and I sat. His chin fell to his chest; he stepped inside and closed the door.

"I didn't think my father would bow," Dahlia said.

"He doesn't like to be different."

The moonlight reflected in two lines down her cheeks. "You're different, but you never seem to mind."

"If I'm different, it's not because I mean to be. Don't think it's easy."

"If it's not easy, why did you come back?"

"Where else was I supposed to go? I told you: I don't want to be some wandering musician."

"You said Master Uriel stayed behind with a few disciples. Why don't you return and play for them?"

"Uriel doesn't want me!"

The bowl of wheat berries toppled to the ground as Dahlia ran toward the house. I hadn't meant to shout. But I didn't move even as she closed the door fast behind her. Instead, I plucked aimlessly at the strings of my kinnor.

Rabbi Elazar HaKapar said: Against your will you were created, against your will you were born, against your will you live, against your will you die, and against your will you will come to give an accounting of your deeds.

Pirkei Avot 4:29

11

The Vineyard of Shiloh

A hand gently shook my shoulder, rousing me from sleep. I awoke to total darkness.

"Get dressed," my aunt whispered against my ear. "Pack your things. Wake no one." Her dress swished down the ladder.

Eliav moaned in his sleep as I pulled my tunic over my head. I rolled my sheepskin sleeping mat as quietly as I could so as not to rouse him further. Holding my things under one arm, I slipped down the ladder. The flickering light of the hearth illuminated a clay statue set in a niche in the wall: the gift from the Queen.

Even in the half-light I could see that Aunt Leah's eyes were red.

"Aunt, have you slept?"

"No."

"What's happening?" I rubbed my eyes to force them awake.

"It's time for you to leave this house."

"Leave?"

"Eat. You'll need your strength." Aunt Leah laid a plate of bread and cheese on the table. I sat opposite her and took a small bite, though I had little appetite.

"Do you remember how, before you left with Master Uriel, I told you that you are the same to me as my own children?"

"Yes."

"Well, I heard everything that happened last night. I know that Menachem and Eliav bowed to the Baal. Dahlia told me that you saw it too. I couldn't sleep thinking of you. I wish Menachem and Eliav hadn't bowed, but Menachem is my husband and Eliav my son, and I love them. I'd rather not have a Baal in the house, but there it is. I don't want to bow down to it, but if my husband insists, I will.

"I love you too, Lev." Aunt Leah stuffed bread and hard cheese into a sack. "But you're not my son." Tears now rolled down her cheeks.

"Your parents never would have raised you in a house with that abomination of an idol. My poor sister would never forgive me. For their sake—for yours—you cannot stay."

"Where will I go?"

"You could return to Master Uriel—"

"I'm not going back to him."

"Why not?"

"I'm not going back." My words were final. "There must be another choice."

Aunt Leah laid a piece of parchment on the table before me, brown in color, tattered at its edges. I tilted it to read by the red light of the coals. Elazar son of Amram, Beit Shemesh was all it said. "What is this?"

"This is the name of your uncle, your father's brother. He lives in the Kingdom of Yehudah. You can go to him and still be with your family, away from all of this."

"Go to Yehudah?" It was the first mention I ever heard of family across the border.

"The road is guarded, but there are many paths through the mountains. Take this." She put a small pile of copper on the table. "Go to Mitzpah. Search there for a guide to lead you through the passes out of the Kingdom."

Ignoring the copper, I lifted the parchment, my heart pounding. "Whose writing is this?"

"It's your father's. He wanted you raised with his family in Yehudah. Menachem thought it too dangerous to move you during the war, and then…" Aunt Leah wiped her eyes again on the back of her hand. "But now I see that your father was right. It will be better for you there than here."

"Why?" I could feel years of unanswered questions welling up inside. "Am I from the tribe of Yehudah? Is that why I have no inheritance here?"

"No, you're not from Yehudah. You have no land there either."

"There's something you're not telling me."

Aunt Leah didn't turn away as she normally did when I asked about my parents. "Master Uriel made us swear never to tell. He said that knowledge would put you at risk. But once you get to Yehudah you will be safe. Your family there can explain everything."

My eyes narrowed. So, Uriel was responsible for the secrets—for no one telling me the truth about my family.

A cough disturbed the quiet of the dark house. "That's your uncle waking. Go now. I won't have the strength to send you away with him here."

Aunt Leah added more bread to the sack and laid it on the table with a full skin of water. "Take the copper. It will get you across."

"I don't need it. I was paid more than that just for the wedding."

"Take it anyway. For me."

I collected the dull pieces of metal and added them to my pouch. It held more wealth than I ever dreamed I'd have at this age. It felt heavy against my thigh but brought me no joy.

Aunt Leah opened the door. Uncle Menachem's foot appeared on the top rung of the ladder, and I hurried through the open doorway.

"I love you, Lev," was the last thing I heard as Aunt Leah closed the door behind me.

I fought the desire to turn and look at my house one last time. I was on a path I had not chosen and it seemed best to keep my feet moving.

The slip of parchment was still in my hand. I hadn't looked at it since learning that it was my father's writing—but I hadn't let go of it either. There was a message in the note, but what was it? Aunt Leah said they would explain everything in Yehudah. Explain what?

I had to stop.

I dropped down onto a flat boulder by the roadside. I'd left so many places in the past weeks, but always with a clear destination. But now…now I was all alone.

The impossibility of this journey suddenly hit me. I'd never heard of anyone crossing into Yehudah before. It was a dangerous path, and who would I even ask to help me? Images whirled through my head: jugglers, prophets, musicians. Uriel rejected me. Aunt Leah sent me away. Who was left?

A shudder passed through my body, and for the first time in five years, I began to cry. It started off slowly, as if my eyes had forgotten how. The salty

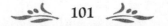

taste hit my lips, bringing back memories of the years when I cried nightly. A wail rose in my throat, and the tears broke free.

I don't know how long I cried, but when I gazed up, the wind blew cool against my cheeks. My uncle's words echoed in my mind, "Israel is wide enough for us all, if we each find our place."

I looked up at the sky and called out, "Where is my place?"

The sun peaked over the mountains, it's rays warming my face. I slipped the parchment, damp with tears, into my pouch, slung my sack over my shoulder, and continued down the hill.

An image of Uriel rose in my mind—not with the anger of our last meeting, but with the compassion and wisdom I had come to know. I could almost hear his advice about trusting my heart.

I reached the junction with the King's Road just ahead of a group of men walking down from the north. They were all older than me, wearing the worn summer clothes of farmers. What were seven farmers doing on the King's Road at dawn? "Peace upon you," I called to the one leading the pack.

"Upon you peace," the man replied.

"Where are you headed?"

"To the festival at Shiloh. And where are you going?"

I opened my mouth to say Mitzpah, but I held myself back. The parchment with my father's writing was the key to answering all my questions. Yet, once I crossed into Yehudah—if I managed to make it alive—I'd probably never return. That piece of parchment had sat in my uncle's house for ten years; another day or two wouldn't make any difference. And hadn't Zim said that Shiloh was not to be missed? Besides, Shiloh was one step closer to Mitzpah. "I'm also going to Shiloh."

"But you're far too young," one of the farmers laughed.

Now the whole group was staring at me—Zim never mentioned anything about age. "I'm a musician," I said, hoping that made a difference.

"Oh, I see. Walk along with us if you like."

"A musician, eh?" a particularly dirty farmer chuckled. "Why don't you play us something?"

I wasn't interested in being their entertainment, but it was good to have company. I drew my kinnor forward and played as we walked.

Dozens of men milled around the hill below Shiloh, all appearing between the ages of twenty and forty. A second group gathered at the east side of the hill, but the two groups didn't mix. Nervous laughter ran through the crowd.

One of my companions pointed to a cluster of trees at the foot of the hill. "The musicians are over there."

I approached the trees, finding five musicians playing as an older man watched on. "Excuse me," I said to the man, who took no notice. "Excuse me," I called a little louder.

The old man turned, first looking over my head, then down until he met my eyes. "Yes?"

I had never asked for work before. "I'm wondering if you…" I began, holding out my kinnor.

"Ah, you'd like to play with us." He smirked. "I'm sorry, I've got all the musicians I need." The other musicians watched me now, a couple of them grinning. "Keep working on your music. Perhaps in a few years you can come join us."

I nodded and walked away. The musicians were good, but no better than me. The leader hadn't even listened to me play. Their song faded as I approached the King's Road, all but the drumming, which grew louder with each step.

I pulled the piece of parchment out of my pouch. It was stupid to think I could just show up and play. At least I hadn't lost much time. If I moved quickly, I might still be able to reach Mitzpah by nightfall. All I could hear now was the drum, pounding louder and louder.

"Lev, you came!"

"Zim!" He stopped drumming and wrapped one arm around me, squeezing my face into his shoulder. "I thought you were staying in Shomron?"

"I told you, I never miss Shiloh. Yambalya said I could come." Zim released me and I rubbed my nose, which itched from scraping against his rough tunic. "You're going the wrong way. The musicians set up over there."

"They didn't want me. The leader didn't even listen to me. He thinks I'm too young."

Zim laughed. "I was barely older than you when I started coming. You're not too young—you just look terrified. Come on." Zim walked past, waving for me to follow, "Emanuel!" he called out.

The old man saw Zim, a genuine smile stretching across his face this time. "Zimri. I was hoping you'd come back. We can use your drum." Emanuel caught sight of me. "I told your friend to come back in a couple of years. We don't need any boys playing."

Zim shook with laughter. "You must have some group this year if you think your musicians are better than the King's."

"The King's?"

"This is Lev, son of Menachem. I played with him at the King's wedding.

I told him to come to Shiloh—I figured you could use the help."

"But he's just a boy."

"You judge too much by appearances." Zim said, running a hand through his wavy hair. "Have you listened to him play?"

"No." Emanuel scratched his beard.

"Lev, let's do that song we played for the juggler. You start and I'll join in. If the rest of you think you can follow along, feel free to try."

All eyes were on me again, but now it felt completely different. I took my time preparing to play, first stretching out the fingers on my left hand, then on my right.

Zim picked the right tune. It was fast, and the melody jumped around a complicated rhythm. If I hadn't spent so much time practicing before the wedding, I would never have been able to lead it. Zim let me start, then filled in the rhythm underneath. After one round, a nevel added its voice, not quite in rhythm.

Before long, all seven musicians were playing—the quality of the music nothing near the caliber of the wedding. I played the notes as crisply as I could in order to guide the others—suddenly aware of how much my abilities had grown since the gathering began. All of Daniel's lessons had taken hold. I had more power and speed than before, but that wasn't all. I was playing more loosely now, as I did at the wedding after two goblets of the King's wine. This time, though, the freedom couldn't have come from drink. In my heart, I knew it came from that morning's flood of tears.

We played through the melody twice, then Zim departed from the rhythm into short rapid beats. I brought the tune to an end, sealing it with a bold final note that continued to reverberate even as I removed my hand from the strings.

Emanuel's attention was locked on me, eyes wide and mouth slack. Zim held back a laugh. "You can stay," Emanuel said. "Let's try that song again. We can add it tonight if the rest of you get it sharper."

A full moon rose in the eastern sky. The crowds on both sides of the hill continued to grow as the day wore on, but they still hadn't mingled. The musicians set up on a hillside overlooking a vineyard that lay between the two groups. An old man approached the near group, and chatter ceased as they surrounded him.

When the old man finished, he left the first group and walked along the edge of the vineyard toward the second, passing directly below the musicians.

I nudged Zim and pointed. "Hey, that's Master Yosef!"

"That's right. He comes here every year. That's how I got hired to play for the prophets this summer—he heard me last year and asked me to come to the gathering."

"I'm surprised to see him at a festival."

"He likes to come and make sure everything happens in 'the right way.'"

"What has to happen in the right way?"

"You don't know what happens here?"

"No, what?"

Zim threw me a mischievous grin. "You'll see soon enough."

The second group now gathered around Yosef. When he finished speaking, he waved a torch back and forth above his head.

"That's our signal." Emanuel said as he raised his hand. "Lev, lead us in that song from the wedding." I struck the first notes and the others joined in, sounding smoother than before, but still struggling.

The signal was not just for us. When the torch waved, both groups moved toward the vineyard, spreading out as they approached. Even from a distance, I could see that the far group were dancing. Yosef sat beside a bonfire on the hillside below us, next to two of his disciples.

As they reached the edge of the trailing vines, I got a better view of the dancers. "Hey, those are girls!"

"That's right." Zim said.

"How can Master Yosef agree to this?"

Zim's laughed. "He says it's one of the holiest days of the year."

The last of the girls danced into the vineyard, and I could no longer make out anyone clearly. Hundreds of shapes moved beneath the vines. We performed our fastest songs, one after the other.

Toward the end of our third song, a couple emerged from the vineyard, walking side-by-side up the hill toward Yosef. They stopped before the prophet, faces lit by the fire, staring into each other's eyes. The man had a severely crooked nose that distorted an otherwise handsome face. She was much younger than he, wearing an elaborately embroidered dress. There was something oddly familiar about her.

I continued to stare until it came to me—I knew her. Her name was Hadassah, the daughter of one of the poorest families in Levonah. She looked so different tonight that I was surprised that I had recognized her at all. She must have spent hours, if not days, cleaning herself and braiding her hair. I had seen her only in dirty, tattered clothes. How could her family afford such an expensive dress?

Yosef addressed them, but his words were lost in the music. The couple glanced at each other and nodded with the expression of children getting away with something forbidden. They bowed their heads, and Yosef placed one hand on the man's head, holding the other just above Hadassah's. When he removed his hands, they gazed at each other again, clasped hands, and withdrew from the fire.

More couples emerged from the vineyard, ascending the hill toward Yosef, and waiting in a line before him. "What is he saying to them?" I asked Zim.

"Go listen."

"I can't do that."

"Why not?"

Something about the expression in Zim's eyes made my fears feel childish. I looked around for Emanuel, but he was nowhere in sight. With six other musicians playing, I wouldn't be missed if I went quickly. I left my kinnor and crept down the hillside until I was close enough to hear Yosef. A new couple stood before him now, both rather short and broadly built.

"It's hard to see in the vineyard," Yosef said, "So I want you to take a good look at each other in the firelight." The couple peered at each other and smiled. "You are certain of your choice?"

The man said "Yes," and the woman nodded.

"Very well. Bow your heads. May the Holy One bless your home to be like the tent of Yitzchak and Rivka, to raise righteous children, and to eat from the bounty of the land." Yosef lowered his hands, indicating the two disciples at his side. "These men are your witnesses that you have been bound today in holiness. You may go." The man stepped away from the fire first, and his bride followed him into the darkness.

I returned to my place next to Zim. "They're getting married?"

"That's right," Zim said.

"But I've been to plenty of weddings, why—"

"Nobody wants to get married this way. But some families can't find good matches for their children. They might have no wealth, no connections. And look around. Some of these people are just plain ugly. But they all come to Shiloh and find each other in the vineyard."

"I recognized that first girl; she's from my town. Her family is really poor, but she was wearing a fancy dress."

"All the girls borrow dresses—it's part of the rules of Shiloh. No one can tell who is rich or poor in the vineyard."

"So how do they find each other?"

"The girls just go under the vines, dancing and calling out to the men. Inside that vineyard is the only place where the people of Israel don't hold back."

A place in Israel where no one holds back—no wonder Zim was drawn to it.

The sun already blazed above the mountains when Zim shook me awake the next morning. My first thought was how strange it was for Zim to be awake before me, and then I realized that I was bathed in sweat.

"You were screaming."

"It's nothing," I said, sitting up, "Just a nightmare." But it wasn't nothing. For the first time, I remembered a detail from my old dream. There was a horse, driven fast. I wanted to close my eyes, to hold onto the vision, to see more.

"You sure you're all right?" The concern on Zim's face appeared so out of place.

If I was going to talk about my nightmares with anyone, it wasn't Zim. I opened the sack of food my aunt had prepared and pulled out bread and cheese, giving up on any hope of slipping back into the dream to learn more. "Come eat," I said. At least it was Zim and not Yonaton who had heard me screaming. Yonaton's concern wouldn't have been pushed aside so easily with a bribe of food.

In the vineyard and the surrounding fields, couples were sitting and walking together. Two groups again formed on opposite sides of the vineyard, each much smaller than the night before. These must be the ones who had failed to find a match. Would they be back next year?

"So you're heading back to the gathering today?" Zim asked between bites.

It hadn't occurred to me that Zim wouldn't know. "No, the gathering was closed after the wedding."

"Why?"

"So that everyone can bring in their harvests before the rains."

"So even the prophets have begun to fear Baal? Yambalya will be pleased."

My first instinct was to defend them, but I held myself back. It did feel as if the prophets were giving way to the Baal.

"So you're going home, then?"

I stopped eating and stared down. "I can't go home."

"Can't go home? Why not?"

"My aunt sent me away."

"Why? What happened?"

"My uncle brought a Baal into the house. My aunt said that my parents would never accept me living in a house with an idol, so she made me leave. She told me to go to my father's family in Yehudah."

"Yehudah? How are you supposed to get across the border?"

THE LAMP OF DARKNESS

"My aunt gave me copper so I can pay someone in Mitzpah to guide me over."

"So that's it? You're going? And you'll just hope that whoever takes your payment can get you there alive?"

"What choice do I have?"

Zim shook his head. "Just because your aunt sent you to Yehudah doesn't mean you have to go. You're almost of age, Lev—it's time to become a man."

I turned away.

"She threw you out—it's no longer her choice. Come back to Shomron with me."

"Shomron?"

"Yes, Shomron. Queen Izevel is building two temples: one for Baal, the other for Ashera. The nobility are competing to offer the biggest feasts each day. There aren't enough musicians for all the ceremonies and banquets. Two nights ago, I even played for Uriel's son."

"Uriel's son?'

"The Chief Priest of Israel." Zim laughed at the look on my face. "Didn't you notice their similarities at the wedding? It might have been Uriel forty years ago!"

I pictured the face of the head priest. If the thick brows were white and the skin across his broad cheekbones wrinkled, it would have been Uriel. How had I not noticed? "But Uriel hates the Golden Calf. How can his son be its priest?"

Zim shrugged. "You can ask him when we get to Shomron."

"I couldn't do that!"

"Why not? I did."

"You did? What did he say?"

"He said he used to walk in his father's ways. But his father was always traveling, tending to the needs of the people. He wasn't there for his own family. Ten years ago, he decided he'd had enough."

"And you're playing for him?"

"I'm playing for everyone. There aren't enough musicians in Shomron. They need you there."

I dropped the bread in my hand, my hunger forgotten. "You heard what my aunt said—my parents wanted me far away from the Baal."

"Your parents are dead, Lev."

My crying the day before must have unblocked my eyes, for fresh drops teared my vision.

"I know it hurts, but it's true. You can't live your life for them. Do you even remember what they look like?"

"You don't understand," I said, my voice flat.

"Maybe I don't." Zim placed a hand on my shoulder. "But you need to hear this. Didn't you learn anything last night?"

I shook off Zim's hand. "What do you mean?"

"I mean, look at those couples down there. Every one of them would have preferred to get married in the usual way, but it didn't work out for them. They could have stayed at home and cried about being alone—but they didn't. They decided not to let a rotten past force them into an empty future."

I gazed at the men and women holding hands under the trees.

"They went into that vineyard with all they had, and they left everything they didn't need behind. Now look at them; most of them aren't alone anymore. How do you think they feel?"

"I don't know… Happy?"

Zim shook his head. "Scared. They're starting a new life with someone they hardly know. But they know one thing: it's better to jump into an unknown future than hold onto a dead past."

I cocked my head. "What are you saying?"

"You were one of the best musicians here last night."

I snorted at the flattery.

"No, really. But if I hadn't come along, you would have walked away and never played a note. Emanuel took one look at you and decided that you were too young. What did you say back to him?"

"Nothing. I left."

"Exactly! Emanuel tells you to leave and you go, even though you're better than his musicians. Your aunt tells you to leave and you go, even though you don't really know why. Did you ever stop to think about what you want?"

Zim stood up. "Learn from the girls of Shiloh. Go into that vineyard and leave the past where it belongs. Come out ready to decide your own future, and let nothing stand in your way."

I picked up a piece of cheese. "I hear what you're saying."

"Clearly you don't, because you're still sitting here." Zim grabbed my arm and drew me to my feet. "Go on, and don't come out until you're ready to claim your life."

Zim pushed me downhill. I continued on my own, then turned back to Zim. "Don't eat all my food while I'm gone."

"Don't worry," Zim said, breaking off another hunk of cheese. "There's plenty to eat in Shomron. Go!"

As I ducked into the vineyard, rows of grapevines stretched out in every direction. The outer world felt far behind.

What Zim said made sense—I was on my own now. I didn't choose to leave, but now every choice was mine. Hadn't I come to Shiloh rather than going right to Mitzpah as my aunt wanted? I could just as easily go to Shomron—or anywhere else for that matter. I followed one path into the vineyard, but there were countless ways out.

What do I really want? And what path will get me there?

A grasshopper landed at my feet. The wind died, and its rhythmic chirps rang out in the still air. I closed my eyes and other sounds emerged: the rustling of leaves, a distant dove's cry. I took a deep breath and descended into their song.

Though I had walked far into the vineyard, it was easy to find my way back out. I just followed the pounding of the drum. My sack of food lay empty on the ground by Zim's side. Zim beat out one last flourish on his drum and got to his feet. "If we want to get back tonight, we'll need to go now," he said.

I nodded, picking up my belongings and following Zim toward the road.

"Put out your hand." Zim dropped three pieces of copper into my palm. "Emanuel paid us while you were gone. It's nothing compared to the wedding, but it's not bad for a night of music. Are you still going to Yehudah?"

"No. You were right. That's what my aunt wanted—not what I want."

"Excellent. Yambalya lent me a donkey for the trip. If we both ride, we should be able to make it back before they close the gates."

I stopped Zim with a hand on his shoulder. "I'm not going to Shomron either."

Zim cocked his head. "No?"

"No. You go on your own."

"Where will you go?"

"On my own path."

"Good. Then for the second time in a week, we part as friends." Zim embraced me with both arms this time. "Until our paths cross again."

Rabban Shimon son of Gamliel said: All my days I was raised among the Sages, and I never found anything better for a person than silence.

Pirkei Avot 1:17

12

The Rains

I filled my lungs, breathing in the dry desert air as the valley opened out below me. It was late afternoon, and my legs still felt strong. I hitched my sack higher and stepped lightly down the trail.

Uriel paced beneath the carob tree, five disciples sitting before him, heads bowed between their knees. The old man's sharp eyes fell on me. Neither of us spoke. I went directly to my old spot under the pomegranate tree, swung my kinnor forward, and held my fingers over the strings, awaiting his signal.

Would Uriel reject me again? Walking from Shiloh to Emek HaAsefa, I realized that fear had been my constant companion since losing my parents. Yet, for the first time I took a strange pleasure in my trembling, having resolved—like the girls of Shiloh—not to let fear stand in my way.

Uriel relented, dropping his chin in the slightest of nods.

I closed my eyes and drew my fingers softly across the strings of the kinnor, not wanting to startle the meditating disciples. At each pass through the melody, I increased the pace.

A firm hand clasped onto my shoulder, and I opened my eyes to find

myself alone with the prophet in the clearing. "You have returned for the rest of the gathering?"

I nodded.

"And after that?"

"If you desire my service, I will go where you go. Master."

One eyebrow lifted at the title. All called him Master Uriel, but only a true servant or disciple called him Master. My stomach churned—would the prophet reject me?

"You have chosen to return. I accept you into my service," Uriel said at last. "Is there anything else you wish to say?"

"Yes, Master. If there are times that you do not need me, I would like to help Yonaton's family bring in their harvest before the rains."

"A generous thought. Come and play for us in the mornings. You may spend the rest of the day helping your friend."

"Thank you, Master."

"Put your things away and come eat. You've had quite a journey."

"Lev!" Yonaton dropped the sheaves in his hands and ran out to meet me. I held onto Yonaton's embrace for a long time, my arms wrapped tightly around his back. After being thrown out by my aunt and Uriel's cool reception, Yonaton's embrace felt like coming home.

"Are you back to play for the disciples?" Yonaton asked.

"Yes, and Master Uriel says that I can help you with the harvest too."

"We could use it. Come meet my father and sisters." All eyes were on me as we approached their donkey cart. "This is my friend, Lev. He came to help us with the harvest."

"You are welcome, Lev. I'm Baruch, son of Naftali. Yonaton told us much about you." Baruch had a strong, stocky build and slow speech, giving me the impression that he didn't talk much. But he met my eyes with a smile that felt sincere.

"These are my little sisters, Yael and Naomi."

I waved to the girls. Naomi blushed and turned away, but Yael, the younger, continued to stare.

"So what can I do?"

"Right now we need to load the grain onto the cart and bring it to the threshing floor. What made you come back?"

I glanced toward his father and sisters, working near me in a tight group.

"I'll tell you later," I said, collecting a bunch of sheaves and tossing them onto the cart. I had never harvested grains before. The sheaves of summer wheat were light, and the bending and stretching felt good. As I warmed up, I quietly sang an old shepherding song. Yonaton picked up the tune and joined in, and even Baruch started to hum along. Seeing that the song wasn't a disturbance, I let my voice soar.

I arrived at the farm the next day to find that Yonaton wasn't in the fields. "Morning, Lev," Baruch called, pointing to the hilltop overlooking the farm. "Yonaton's at the threshing floor. You can join him there."

"I thought we weren't starting threshing until tomorrow?"

"The morning clouds keep getting darker and burning off later in the day. The sooner we start threshing, the more we'll be able to save when—if the rains come." He sighed and returned to gathering the cut wheat.

I climbed up the terraced hillside until I reached the broad threshing floor at the very top.

"Good, you're here," Yonaton called out, raising his voice over the wind. "This is a lot easier with two people. You want to lead the team or ride the sled?"

That was an easy choice. "I'll ride the sled."

Yonaton hopped off the threshing sled and circled around to the front of the oxen, taking the reins. Until I arrived, he had been steering the oxen from behind while weighing down the sled himself.

"I thought farm work was going to be hard," I said, sitting back on the sled. "I think I might just take a nap."

Yonaton laughed while spreading more grain on the ground before the oxen. "Go ahead. Enjoy your time on the sled. We'll be winnowing soon enough."

"In the meantime, I'll lend you my weight." I closed my eyes, enjoying the vibrations as the flint stones on the sled's underside cut into the grain beneath.

"One of Yambalya's priests came by this morning."

"What?" I sat up. "When?"

"Not long before you came. One of the Queen's soldiers was with him too."

"What soldiers?"

"You remember all those soldiers that came down from Tzidon with King Ethbaal for the wedding? I guess he left some of them behind. I recognized the cedar tree symbol on his tunic."

"What happened?"

"The priest was happy that we were bringing in the harvest early. He said we were showing proper fear of the mighty Baal. Then he pulled out a statue and told us we should humble ourselves before Baal so that he would hold off the rains until we finished."

"You didn't, did you?"

"No. My father didn't either. The priest wasn't pleased, but he didn't say anything. The soldier kept fingering his sword, but he never pulled it out, just spat on the ground and followed the priest away. As soon as they left, my father told me to start threshing."

I thought back to my conversation with Baruch—now it made more sense. Yes, the clouds were gathering unusually early, but apparently that wasn't the only thing pushing him to salvage whatever grain he could.

Though the music was better when I played with Daniel, Zim, and Yonaton, my bond with the disciples strengthened now that I was alone. At a nod from my master, I launched into my opening melody and immediately sensed something different. As the melody came back around to its opening note, the disciples collapsed as one, shaking as if a great wind was tossing their bodies like dry leaves in a storm.

My jaw dropped. Uriel said, "For so many souls to rise together is rare, but it does happen. You felt them go?"

I nodded without a word.

Uriel peered deeply into my eyes. "What is the shadow on your heart, Lev?"

"Master, the power of the Baal is spreading throughout the Kingdom. What will the people do? What will happen to those who refuse to bow? What will happen to you and the rest of the prophets?"

Uriel sighed. "I do not know what will be, Lev, not for the people nor for the prophets. The visions I have received lately have all been of the present. I see nothing of the future."

"What will you do?"

"As I have always done."

"Won't they try to stop you? Queen Izevel has her own soldiers. I saw them in Shomron. They're traveling around with the priests, trying to scare people into bowing down to the Baal. Do you think they'll allow you to travel and speak against them?"

"For now, yes. Their power is only growing, even while the prophets are yet free to travel and speak against them. Open conflict would force the people to choose between us, and they are still seen as foreigners. They will not fight openly until they are certain that they hold the hearts of the people. If a struggle is to start before that, it will be because we begin it."

"And you don't think that will happen?"

"Pitting fear against fear will not bring us the goal we seek."

"What do the other prophets say? Does Master Yosef agree?"

"He is less inclined to this way of thinking than I. But I believe he too would prefer to avoid a conflict. For now."

"So then what will happen?"

"I do not know, Lev."

How could a prophet not know?

Uriel placed his hand on my shoulder. "Lev, you must know that there is only one truth. The same hand that fashioned the light also made the darkness."

"Why would the Holy One create darkness?"

"Without darkness there is no choice. Our bodies may grow without darkness, but our souls cannot."

"But if there is just darkness—"

"Then we could not grow either. There must be a balance for our choices to be real. That is why the disciples have progressed so quickly since the wedding. As darkness deepens, hidden light is revealed."

The disciples began to stir. Two of them rose unsteadily to their feet, two remained sitting, and one fell flat on his back, exhausted. "What did you see?" Uriel asked softly.

"The rain will come in three days' time," one of the disciples replied.

"Did you all receive the same vision?"

The others nodded in agreement.

"Very well. Lev, you are excused from playing for us for the next few days so that you can help Yonaton's family complete the harvest."

I grabbed my kinnor and raced toward the farm.

By the third day, the winds whipped across the fields, stripping leaves from trees. Yonaton's father wasn't complaining—we needed wind for winnowing, and better too much than not enough.

The winnowing fork reached above my head. With it, I hoisted the threshed stalks of grain and threw them as high as I could into the air. The wind did the rest. The heavy kernels of grain fell to the ground first. The husks and chaff blew further away, where Yonaton's sisters gathered them to use for animal feed and fuel.

When lightning flashed against the dark sky, Baruch ran over. "Stop winnowing. Gather as much grain as you can. Get it in before it gets wet." Baruch took the fork, tossing the threshed stalks by himself while the rest of us gathered grain and carried it to shelter. Baruch worked the grain pile tirelessly, getting through twice as much by himself as Yonaton and I had together.

When the first drops fell, only a small mound remained of the grain pile, and most of the winnowed grain was gathered. I didn't mind working on in the rain, but as the lightning drew nearer, Baruch ordered us all in the house. We saved most of the harvest, but whatever remained would now be lost. Baruch glared at the dark sky as drops rolled down his cheeks.

Rabbi Yishmael said: Do not judge alone, for only the One may judge alone. Do not say 'accept my view,' for it is for them to decide, not you.

Pirkei Avot 4:10

13

Jericho

The next two months were the quietest of my life. The ceaseless rains dampened my desire to speak. The chatter in my head also diminished. I worried less about the future, finding comfort in the fact that I had chosen a master, letting the burden of deciding both of our paths fall upon him.

Yet, even as I became more peaceful, Uriel's tension built. The time for the planned ending of the gathering came and went, yet the prophet did not leave the valley to resume traveling. As the Sukkot festival drew near, he became obsessed with the rains, watching them for hours at a time at the mouth of his cave.

During breaks in the rain, we managed to build a sukkah, a temporary hut that was to be our home during the weeklong festival of Sukkot. Yet, the rains fell so hard when the holiday began that we were unable to leave the shelter of our caves. Uriel's mood was light, however, as we ate the first meal of the festival in his cave. "There is no sorrow on Sukkot. It is a time of joy," Uriel explained. "If we cannot rejoice in the sukkah, we may not enter. So, we shall delight in our festival despite the rains. And perhaps we will merit to enter the sukkah before the holy days end."

On the fourth day of the festival, a new noise filled the cave. It took me a moment to realize that it wasn't actually a sound at all, but the lack of one: the rains had stopped. The one remaining servant prepared a feast, and for the first time we ate inside our battered Sukkah. Midway through the meal, Uriel's hand paused on the way to his mouth. He stood quickly and strode up the hill toward the road. It was not long until we saw what our master had sensed: a donkey trotting along the hillside.

The prophet reached the road just before the rider passed. The man spoke briefly to Uriel, then continued on his way. There was a shadow on my master's face as he walked back into the valley, but no trace of it remained by the time he entered the sukkah. He stepped inside and, ignoring his meal, led us in a festive song. The rest of us joined in, but though I knew the tune well, I struggled to harmonize. My master sang a bit too fast.

The break in the rain didn't last, and we never returned to our sukkah. The final day of the festival marked the beginning of the rainy season. The ground was already saturated and rain still fell in torrents, but Uriel said that the prophets had prayed for rain at the end of Sukkot ever since Joshua led our people across the Jordan River, regardless of what the skies held. We gathered at the opening of the cave, wrapped in all our clothing and sheepskin sleeping mats, to hear the Uriel's prayers.

"Master of the World! For the sake of Avraham our father, who ran to bring water to the tired and thirsty, do not withhold rain from his children."

A gust of wind stuck Uriel's drenched tunic to his body. "For the sake of Rivka, our mother, who ran to bring water to a stranger and watered even his ten camels, do not withhold rain from her children."

At the end of each statement, we all shouted, "Amen."

"Holy One! For the sake of Moshe, our Teacher, father of the prophets, who stood before you forty days without water, do not withhold rain from his disciples!

"May the rains come as a blessing and not as a curse!"

"Amen!"

"May they come for life and not for death!"

"Amen!"

"May they come for abundance and not for scarcity!"

"Amen!"

"Master of the World! You and only you cause the wind to blow and the rain to fall!"

"Amen!"

Uriel pulled two disciples out into the rain and began to dance. The rest of us joined in, finally relishing the drops on our faces, which for the first time felt like a blessing.

No sooner had the sun set that night, marking the close of the festival, than Uriel drew me aside.

"The first day we met, when I was entering Levonah, you were speaking to a boy leading a donkey. Do you recall?"

"Yes, Master."

"There was an emblem on his saddle bag from the city of Jericho."

"That was my friend, Seguv. His father, Hiel, is rebuilding the city."

"Yes, I know that Hiel of Beit El is rebuilding the city; I wondered if your friend was his son. I'm sorry to tell you that Seguv died six days ago."

Hot tears stung my eyes—they came so easily now. "Is that what the rider told you?"

"Yes, he was on his way to bring the news to the King."

Seguv told me that the King had invested heavily in the rebuilding of the city—of course he would want to know that Hiel had lost another son. But I cared little now about the King or Jericho. My thoughts were on the warm smile, the friendly face that always stopped to greet me whenever he passed through Levonah. I wiped my cheeks with the back of my hand. "Why did you wait to tell me?"

"Sukkot is a time of joy."

Blood rushed to my face. "You should have told me."

"I know it feels that way."

Uriel's words only made me angrier. "Joy isn't always the right feeling. We need to feel other things, too."

"Not on Sukkot. Don't think joy is so simple—I'm not talking about the empty celebrations of fools. Real joy takes work, inside and out—more than any other emotion.

"On Sukkot, we choose to rejoice even when we don't feel joyous. That's why there is no mourning on Sukkot. The mourning period for Seguv will begin now and last for one week. His family will receive anyone wishing to visit."

Uriel paused, but I remained silent. "If you like, you may go."

Now my eyes met his. "You said we would begin traveling immediately after Sukkot."

"The loss of a friend is a deep wound, and it must be mourned if it's to heal." Uriel let out another long sigh. "There is no time to go and return before Shabbat. You may leave early on the first day of the week, and take Balaam to hasten your journey. I will wait for your return to begin traveling."

In better conditions, I could have reached Jericho in one day, but washed-out roads made for a slow ride. On the morning of the second day, I descended into the great valley of the Jordan River, where the ruins of Jericho lay just north of the Salt Sea. Halfway down the mountains, the rains stopped and the sun came out. At the base of the mountains, the road flattened and passed through a grove of tall date palms, where a dozen camels grazed in their shade. There were also rows of newly planted trees whose species I didn't recognize. These must be the balm trees Seguv told me about, the source of the afarsimon oil, the reason for rebuilding the destroyed city despite the costs.

When I reached Hiel's house, I found a middle-aged couple sitting on the floor, barefoot, their clothing torn and their heads dusted with the ashes of mourning. I knew they must be Hiel and his wife, but where was Onan, Seguv's older brother? Could he have died as well?

Four men sat opposite them, but no one spoke. Two of the men looked like brothers, both dressed in dirty work clothes. A third man sat rigidly in his chair, his woolen tunic spotless. The fourth sat in the corner, eyes on the floor. He was clearly a nobleman. His hair and beard were trim and neat. He wore a thick belt made of sheep hide. Despite the heat, he wore a red wrap known as a mantle wrapped around his shoulders.

"Were you a friend of Seguv's?" Hiel asked me.

I returned my attention to the man on the floor. "Yes, sir, I was."

"How did you know him?"

"I live in Levonah. He came up to sell dates."

"You came all the way from Levonah?"

"No, sir, I was in Emek HaAsefa when I heard."

The nobleman with the mantle looked up.

Hiel also sat up straighter at the mention of Emek HaAsefa. "Are you a disciple of the prophets?"

I gave a weak smile, then thought better of it. "No, sir, I am a musician."

"Oh, you are that shepherd boy that...that Seguv spoke of." My smile almost broke through again when I heard that Seguv spoke about me.

Jericho

"Did he...I mean, were you..." Hiel was struggling to find the words.

Without warning, the nobleman rose to his feet, drawing Hiel's attention. "Are you leaving?"

The nobleman motioned with his chin toward the entrance. In the doorway, flanked by two guards, stood King Ahav himself. The other guests and I immediately jumped to our feet. Hiel and his wife attempted to rise from the floor, but Ahav stopped them with a gesture.

"No need to get up, my dear Hiel. The mourner needn't stand before the King. I was broken-hearted when the news reached me." The King pulled a stool toward himself and sat down. "You may wait outside," he said to his two guards.

The King ignored us, his attention fixed on Hiel. "I blame myself, of course."

Hiel's hand rose in protest. "You must not, my King. I knew the risks involved. The dangers of the waters here are well known. I was proud to take on the mission of rebuilding a great city in Israel. Our losses have been tragic, that is true. But we hold you blameless."

King Ahav dropped his eyes saying quietly, "I'm not talking about the waters. I'm speaking of the curse."

Hiel's eyes grew wide. "My Lord, I thought you did not believe in the curse?"

"Well, I didn't. It seemed so ridiculous. Just a story told to children and the ignorant to frighten them away. But now that it has come true, can we continue to deny it?"

"What curse?" I said, then slapped my hand over my mouth. One didn't just speak in front of the King—certainly not to interrupt such a private conversation.

The King turned to me. "You look familiar," he said at last.

I bowed my head. "I am a musician. I played at the King's wedding."

"Ah, yes, I remember." Ahav leaned back with a satisfied smile. "Yes, the curse. When Joshua conquered Jericho over five hundred years ago, he declared, 'Cursed is the man who will rise up and build this city Jericho. With his oldest son he will lay the foundations, with his youngest son he will erect its gates.'"

Hiel and his wife both started to cry. I shrank back against the wall—I shouldn't have asked.

The King turned back to the couple on the floor. "It's so strange that the curse would come true," he said, a tone of pleading in his voice "Who would imagine that the curse of the disciple would come true, when the words of his master have failed?"

"And what does that mean?" The nobleman stepped forward. The hard tone of his voice reminded me of Yambalya.

The King replied, "Come, Eliyahu, you know the story better than I. Moshe pronounced a curse on the people that if they worship idols there will be no rain. Go on, recite it for us."

Eliyahu did not argue with a command from the King. He declared: "Guard yourselves, lest you turn your hearts and serve other gods and bow down to them." Eliyahu's eyes burned with rage. "Then the wrath of the Holy One will blaze against you. The heavens will be restrained, there will be no rain, the ground will not give its abundance, and you will be lost from upon the good land the Holy One gave you."

I had known these verses from the Torah since I was a young boy, but this was the first time that they made me tremble.

The King appeared unmoved. "You see," he said, "it makes no sense that this curse would come upon you, my dear Hiel. Look around you. The people seek the Baal more every day, yet in my entire life I never remember the rain being so plentiful. So why should the curse of Joshua cause your family so much misery, when the curse of his teacher Moshe failed?"

Eliyahu stepped closer to the King. He would have towered over Ahav even if the King had not been sitting. Had the guards been in the room, I'm sure they would have removed Eliyahu to a respectful distance—but they were outside. For the first time, the King shrank as he stared up into Eliyahu's fiery gaze.

I could barely breathe. The air grew heavy, like a gathering storm. Then Eliyahu spoke, his voice barely above a whisper. "As the Holy One, the Lord of Israel, before whom I stand, lives…there will be no dew nor rain during these years except by my word."

Eliyahu strode out of the room. Both guards rushed in. They could not have heard his declaration, but they must have been alarmed by the fury on Eliyahu's face. "Is everything well, my King?"

"Fine," the King said, his voice weak. Clearing his throat loudly, he added in a commanding tone, "You may continue to wait for me outside."

The guards bowed and left, and the King turned back to Hiel and his wife. "Always been unyielding, Eliyahu has. He's quite wise, really, but once he gets an idea into his head there's no reasoning with him."

"Well, he's certainly gone too far this time," Hiel said, no longer crying.

"Nonsense, he's harmless enough. With people like that it is best to just let them be."

An awkward silence descended on the room.

"And how is the King finding married life?" Hiel asked.

"Ah," Ahav smiled, his posture relaxing with the change of subject. "Izevel has been doing wonderful things with the palace. She brought down a beautiful Ashera tree all the way from Tzur to plant at the gates. Are you men leaving?" The two brothers had stepped forward, and the King paused in his description to allow them to take their leave of Hiel and his wife.

I thought this was a good opportunity to slip out as well, so I stepped forward once the brothers turned to leave. I leaned down toward Hiel and his wife and repeated the line that Uriel had made me memorize before I left. "May the Holy One comfort you among the mourners of Israel."

Hiel and his wife lowered their heads. I bowed to the King the way the farmers had and respectfully backed out of the open door.

Mounted on Balaam and on my way, I looked up at the mountain trail and saw a roof of black clouds hiding the mountain tops. The return trip would be harder than the downhill journey had been.

I kicked Balaam into a trot and we were soon back among the date palms. A flash of red caught my eye. Eliyahu's mantle was crumpled at the base of one of the trees. Its owner lay beside it, his head between his knees, gripped by the spirit of prophecy.

Rabban Shimon, son of Gamliel, said: The world rests on three things: on justice, on truth, and on peace.

Pirkei Avot 1:18

14

The Key of Rain

The return journey passed faster than I expected. I made it back without meeting any rain. I reentered Emek HaAsafa to find Uriel waiting for me. "What happened? I want every detail."

He drew me into his cave, seeming far more anxious for my report than when I returned from the wedding.

"When I entered, I didn't know what to say to Seguv's parents, so I just sat."

"You did well. Words rarely penetrate the fresh pain of loss."

I described the house, the visitors, Seguv's parents. Uriel nodded as I spoke, saying nothing. He finally interrupted to question me about Eliyahu's mantle. "Why is that important, Master? Who is he?"

"I might ask you the same question. Continue."

I recounted King Ahav's entrance, how I had been moved by the King's journeying all the way to Jericho to comfort his faithful servant.

"And no doubt to strengthen his resolve. The King has much invested in the rebuilding of Jericho and its balm."

I described Seguv's mother crying as the King conveyed his wonder at

the fulfillment of Joshua's curse, and how King Ahav forced Eliyahu to recite Moshe's words. Uriel's hands trembled on the table as I repeated Eliyahu's oath, "As the Holy One, the Lord of Israel, before whom I stand, lives…there will be no dew nor rain during these years except by my word."

"Once you left Hiel's home, what happened?"

"I mounted Balaam and rode through the gate. Then, as I rode toward the mountains I saw…Eliyahu."

"What exactly did you see?"

"He was lying in a date grove at the side of the road, trembling."

"With the spirit of prophecy?"

I nodded.

"Eliyahu didn't receive prophecy in the house?"

"No, only after he left."

"After you saw Eliyahu in the date grove, what did you do?"

"I continued riding up the mountainside. I knew how long it took me to get there. I was worried that I would not get back before sundown tonight."

Uriel sighed. "You have done well in your tale. It explains much—though one mystery still remains."

"What does it explain, Master?"

"It explains why the heavens are trembling and why the gates of prophecy have swung wide open."

I frowned at Uriel. Prophecy had gates?

"Eliyahu has taken one of the forbidden keys."

"The keys?"

"Yes, the keys. Do you recall the sisters we met on our first day traveling together?"

I nodded, remembering the pain of the older sister who wanted to have a baby.

"I explained then about the three keys that forever remain in the hands of the Holy One: the key of life, the key of resurrection of the dead, and the key of rain. Eliyahu has taken the last one—the key of rain—in many ways the most powerful of the three."

"Taken it?"

"Well, I should say he was given it. None can take a heavenly key by force. While you were in Jericho, I experienced prophecy here in Emek HaAsefa. I saw Eliyahu's soul rise before the Throne of Glory itself. He demanded the key of rain. The angels went into an uproar that a man would demand the key. But the Holy One granted Eliyahu's request."

"What does that mean?"

"It means that as long as he holds the key, Eliyahu will determine if and when we receive rain."

"And the prayers we're offering—?"

"Will not be answered. The Holy One will not bring rain as long as Eliyahu denies it."

"What about Yambalya and the Baal?"

"They are powerless to bring the rain."

I pictured the faces of the farmers standing in the morning rain at the wedding. "But I saw—"

"There is no Baal. Remember, the same hand which created the light made the darkness as well. That hand has now granted the power to bring rain to Eliyahu, and to him alone. Neither myself nor Yambalya can do anything affecting the rain, other than pleading with Eliyahu."

I grinned at the thought of Yambalya cutting himself and calling out to the Baal in vain. "So when Eliyahu swore that there would be no rain other than by his word, he knew that he held the key?"

"That's the question I cannot answer. Did Eliyahu know he would receive the key when he made his oath? Did he already hold it? We may never know."

"But if the key is never given to man, why would he think he could receive it? He wouldn't swear otherwise—he must have known."

"So I believed; that's why I asked you if he received prophecy in Hiel's house." Uriel stroked his beard. "But prophecy is not the only path of power. What the righteous decree, the Holy One carries out."

"The righteous can bind the Holy One?"

Uriel nodded. "You yourself observed a powerful example of this."

"When?"

"I do not believe that the Holy One commanded Joshua to curse the city of Jericho—he was moved on his own to bind the city in ruins forever. But once his lips spoke the curse, the Holy One gave it power."

"That's why Seguv died?"

Uriel nodded. "Hiel's family was destroyed by a curse uttered five hundred years ago."

I swallowed the lump in my throat. "That's what happened with Eliyahu?"

"Perhaps."

I could see the muscles of my master's shoulders tight beneath his tunic. "You don't agree with what he did, do you, Master?"

"It's not for me to agree or disagree, Lev. Eliyahu must be an extremely powerful prophet. To take a key from the Holy One is something that has never happened; something I would have said was impossible. But it is true that his way is not my way."

"His way?"

"Eliyahu is willing to take a path I will not tread. The people fear power. You saw this in their reaction to Yambalya. Eliyahu wants to show them that the Holy One is the only power to fear. By this he hopes to win back the heart of the nation."

"Isn't that what you want as well?"

"Indeed."

"But you don't think it will work?"

"It may work—but will it last?"

"Why wouldn't it?"

"Because fear will not bring the devotion that the Holy One seeks. And will the people truly fear the Holy One, or just Eliyahu? Someday Eliyahu will be gone and the darkness will remain. Then what will the people do, if we have trained them to fear?"

"Return to darkness?"

Uriel nodded. "This is why I left the path of fear. It is a tool most fit to the hands of darkness. The powers of darkness are always greater in number, and often in strength as well."

"Master, why should darkness be more powerful than light?"

"Who would choose night over day? If light and darkness were seen in balance, there would be no real choice between them. The true power of light is hidden, to enable us to choose."

I thought of Eliav bowing before the Baal. "But why hide it? Doesn't the Holy One want us to choose the path of light?"

"Of course, but it must be a real choice. This world exists so that we can perfect ourselves and creation as a whole. We can do this only through the choices we make. If the choice is obvious, then even the right choice will yield no growth.

"In the beginning, there was only the light of the Holy One—a light that shone so brightly that nothing else could exist. In order to create the world, the Holy One withdrew this light, leaving a space of emptiness behind. Only a single ray of light shone into this emptiness. But even this fragment of Divine light filled the emptiness with such radiance that a world of choice could not exist. So, the Holy One made the lamp of darkness as well."

"A lamp of darkness?"

"A lamp that radiates darkness. A lamp that covers the light as night covers the day."

"But why?"

"As I told you, so that we can grow. As we grow we reveal the hidden light."

"But you said the Holy One does not desire too much light."

"That is true. The more light we shine into the world, the deeper the shadow cast by the lamp of darkness. But that is not our concern—our task is to create more light, no matter the cost."

"Why create light if the lamp of darkness will only cover it up?"

"When a child first learns to walk, his father might stand only one or two steps away. But as the child progresses, the father steps farther and farther away, not to punish the child, but to allow him to grow more."

The image of a father teaching a son made me think of my own father. Had he taught me to walk? What else had he taught me before he left the world?

Uriel reached over and touched me gently on the underside of my chin, bringing my moist eyes to meet his. "Your father gave more for you than you can imagine."

The prophet stepped to the back of the cave. "The lamp of darkness is now casting a powerful shadow. Since the gathering began, there has been a great rise in idolatry in the land. Traveling among the people has never been more important." He lowered himself onto a reed mat on the floor. "The remaining disciples left while you were in Jericho. The time has come to resume our travels. Play for me and I will seek our path."

As my kinnor was still in the musicians' cave, I drummed on the table, tapping out a complex rhythm I had learned from Zim at Shiloh. I closed my eyes and chanted softly between the beats.

The sound of chattering teeth alerted me that Uriel had ascended—the prophet could no longer hear my drumming—but I did not stop. I raised my voice even louder, no longer worried about distracting my master.

I heard Uriel rising and broke off my chanting. "Where are we going, Master?"

"Nowhere."

"Nowhere?"

"Nowhere. We are to stay here through Shabbat and begin traveling on the first day of the week."

"Why?"

"I do not know. I thought our work here was finished. All the disciples have gone and very few people live in the surrounding valleys. But perhaps someone is coming to us. Either way, we will know soon enough."

Hillel saw a skull floating in the water. He said to it: Because you drowned others, you were drowned. And ultimately, those who drowned you will be drowned as well.

Pirkei Avot 2:7

15

The Battle

For days we waited, yet except for Yonaton, no one entered the valley. At dawn on the first day I again asked, "Master, where are we going now?"

The prophet sighed. "I do not know." He lowered himself onto the cave floor. "Please play." No sooner had I started playing than my master's body began trembling on the ground, reaching prophecy faster than I had ever seen. I put down my kinnor and began hitching our things to Balaam.

As I tied the last bag to the donkey, Uriel stepped out of the cave, his face ashen.

"Have you received instruction?"

"Yes. We must go now."

I led Balaam up the hill toward the road.

"Not that way," Uriel said, pointing down the hill toward a narrow track that wound north across the valley floor. "This way."

I had only seen someone take that trail once before. Shimon, the one with the scars, disappeared down that same path right after telling me not to use my father's knife. He had not reappeared since.

A voice called out behind me, "Wait! Don't go yet." Yonaton ran down the rocky hillside, his sister Yael trailing behind. "My parents sent food for your journey." Yonaton carried two large loaves and a cake of pressed figs. Yael struggled under a massive, green-skinned melon.

I untied the top of one of the donkey bags and carefully added the food. I quickly embraced Yonaton one last time.

"Go in peace. And take care of Master Uriel."

Uriel still moved down the trail. I squeezed Yonaton's hand one last time. "I'll see you next year," I said, then led Balaam at a trot after my master.

We traveled all that day along the overgrown trail, encountering no one. When the sun dropped below the horizon, Uriel pointed to a cave on the hillside. As we climbed through the trees, I gathered an armful of firewood. The prophet inspected the shelter while I arranged the wood outside its entrance.

"No, Lev," Uriel said, emerging from the darkness within. "Tonight, we light the fire inside."

I gazed up at the cloudless sky—it was a shame to spend the night in a smoke-filled cave when we knew there was no chance of rain. Did Uriel think that Eliyahu had relented already?

Uriel sat outside, gazing out into the darkness as I cooked dinner. When I finished, Uriel accepted a bowl of wheat porridge without a word, laid it beside him, then turned back to his thoughts.

"Master?" I asked quietly.

"Yes?"

"I've been thinking about Eliyahu. Won't his curse also hurt those who don't bow to the Baal? Like Yonaton's family?"

"Indeed," he said, his eyes shining in the reflected firelight. "A curse brings suffering to all. It falls upon the guilty and the innocent alike." Tears welled in his eyes. "Even the one who called down the curse is not spared its destruction." He turned back to the darkness, his bowl of porridge untouched.

I dreamed of the throne room. Two thrones sat side by side, just as I remembered. The King's was empty, but Izevel sat upon the one crafted for her father.

"You summoned me, my Queen?" Yambalya's deep voice echoed through the room.

"Yes. Have I acted too soon?"

"No, my Queen. You were right to act now."

"And the people will not protect them?"

"They are sheep. They will not rise against us without the leadership of their king."

"That they will not have." Her lips curled in a snake-like smile. "Baal has not informed you where he is to be found?"

"No, my Queen. The movements of one man are not a matter of note to mighty Baal."

Izevel leaned forward. "But he stopped the rains."

"Yes, he stopped the rains. Their god is still strong in this land. But when their prophets are gone, the people will learn to fear Baal."

"Their prophets, yes. Most of their prophets are weak. But as long as he remains alive, he gives the people strength. We must find him."

"The servants of Baal seek him even now. They have never failed in the hunt. He has not been seen since casting his curse. We believe that he has fled the land."

Izevel laughed. "There is nowhere for him to flee. I watch the roads, and I have sent word to my father. He rules the sea. We will find him."

"Indeed we will, my Queen. I have read his future in the stars."

Izevel bent her head forward, close to Yambalya's. "What have you seen?"

"Eliyahu will not die the natural death of men—to this I will swear."

Izevel settled back in her throne, her face flushed with pleasure. "Excellent. Let his death be a message to all who would stand against us."

"Yes, my Queen. It will be done."

Uriel shook me awake before the sun. "We have to move quickly. There isn't much time."

The prophet kept up a driving pace all day. Daniel once told me that Uriel did not concern himself with taking the shortest or fastest paths, that his goal was to travel among the people. What had changed?

It was late afternoon when Uriel finally stopped with a raised hand, gazing back up the trail. I spotted a man in the distance running toward us. Uriel increased his pace, but in that brief pause I noticed a sad smile cross my master's face.

The runner drew closer, but Uriel did not slow or turn again. When our pursuer reached the hilltop directly behind us, he paused and bent forward to catch his breath. In that moment, I realized that he was not a man at all, just a boy: Yonaton.

Uriel did not pause until Yonaton caught up with us. Gasping for air, he tried to speak, "They're looking—"

Uriel cut him off with his own skin of water. "First drink. You've had a hard journey—it was brave of you to come."

Yonaton gulped down the skin of water and began again to deliver his message. "Yesterday afternoon they came looking for you. They were part of the Queen's personal guard. I recognized them from the wedding. They heard that I played during the gathering. They came to my house and had me lead them to the valley, where they searched all the caves with swords drawn. They asked me where everyone had gone. I told them that you were the last ones to leave that morning. They asked which direction you went, and I pointed them toward Jericho."

My mouth went dry. I pictured the long column of soldiers that had escorted Izevel to her wedding. How many had remained behind?

"How many were they?" Uriel asked.

"Four."

"You saw them go toward Jericho?"

"Yes. I wanted to come and warn you immediately, but it was already too dark, so I came at first light." I thought of the fire inside the cave—had Uriel known?

"You brought nothing with you?"

"When I finished my food and water, I dropped the skins so that I could run faster."

"Again, that was very brave of you. I doubt you can appreciate how much you risked coming after us. You will need to stay with us now. It is no longer safe to return."

"Why? They don't know I've come."

"They do. You were followed."

Yonaton and I turned as one, but saw nothing.

"You won't see them," Uriel said with a shake of his head. "They will stay out of sight until they are ready."

I gazed up at my master. "Ready for what?"

"Surely you can figure that out for yourself?" Uriel started again up the trail. "Come, we must go on."

Despite the prophet's words, Yonaton was too drained by his run to do more than trudge along. When the sun set, we moved even slower. Uriel gazed up at a rocky outcrop on the hillside above us. "Stay here. I want to examine that cave."

Moments later, Uriel came out of the cave and yelled down to us, "Come up. This looks like a good place to spend the night. Lev, see to the donkey.

Yonaton, gather wood."

When Yonaton came back with a double armful of wood, I said, "Build the fire inside the cave, that way it won't be easily seen."

"No, build it outside tonight," Uriel corrected, then turned away before either of us could question him.

I gazed up at the stars as I cooked the evening meal. Was it really less than three months since Dahlia and I lay on the wall watching them, wondering what the future held? Was I now gazing at them for the last time?

Uriel repacked all of our gear in the back of the cave. When he finished, he said, "Take the food off the fire, it is time to eat."

"It's not done yet, Master."

"We have given it as much time as we can afford."

Yonaton, after the long day's run, ate as much as Uriel and myself combined. Once we had finished, I picked up the pot to scrape it, but Uriel put up his hand. "There is no time for that. In any case, we cannot take it with us. Yonaton, throw the remaining wood on the fire. As long as it is burning high, it will appear as if it is tended. There will be no attack until they think we're asleep. When you're done, we'll leave."

Yonaton dumped the last armload of wood on the fire. Uriel led us to the back of the cave and handed us each a pack. "I've gone through and separated out only the most essential things. We'll need all our strength."

"What about Balaam?" I turned back toward the donkey, tied at the entrance.

"He stays. Leaving him in front is the best sign that we are still in the cave."

I opened my mouth to protest.

"You think this poor payment for hard service?" Uriel raised his eyebrows. "Fear not. Men do not kill a beast of burden without cause. Balaam is wise. He will make his way with a new master. Or perhaps find his way back to his old one."

I looked over the pile of belongings to be left behind. My kinnor rested on top. I trusted Uriel that we would need all our strength, but the kinnor wasn't a drain on my strength—it was a source of it. "I won't…" I insisted, "I can't…" I picked up the instrument, cradling it against my chest. "I'll carry it. The extra weight won't slow me down. I promise."

"I'm sorry, Lev." Uriel pulled the instrument from my hands and tucked it behind a rock. "It is well hidden there. May we merit to retrieve it."

I swallowed the lump in my throat, avoiding Yonaton's eyes. I touched my father's knife beneath my tunic, suddenly grateful that I kept it on me at all times. Would Uriel have made me leave that behind as well? Probably not. Shimon's dagger was tucked in my belt, and Uriel hadn't mentioned that.

Yonaton looked up into the crack at the back of the cave. "You don't expect us to get out this way, do you?"

"There is no other path. They are watching the front."

"But it's too narrow—even Lev won't fit through."

Uriel approached the wall, running his hand up and down it. Behind him, the new logs already burned down. How much longer would our attackers wait? Uriel's eyes rolled back in his head as he spoke. "You split the rock for Samson at Lehi. Only you can open our way and bring us out into life."

The prophet struck the rock with his staff. Nothing happened.

"You opened the mouth of the well for Israel, sustaining us in the wilderness. Open now our way and bring us out into life." Uriel swung again, with the same result.

Balaam brayed in the silence. Was he just restless, or did he sense someone approaching?

Fists now clenched, Uriel leaned in close to the wall and hissed between clenched teeth, "In the name of the Holy One, I say this is the moment for which you were formed!"

A low rumble shook the cave. I grabbed Yonaton for support. When the tremor stopped, the opening at the top of the crack had grown to twice its width.

Uriel led the way. Sharp rocks scraped my arms and cut into my fingertips as I pulled myself up after him.

I emerged into the moonlight on a slender ledge on the far side of the hill. A half-moon illuminated the cliff face as we climbed down. At the bottom of the cliff we hit a rocky hillside. Years shepherding along similar terrain allowed me to slip smoothly down the hillside. At the bottom, I followed Uriel into a muddy streambed. A muffled cry came from above. Yonaton joined us in the streambed in obvious pain.

Uriel pulled Yonaton into a patch of moonlight to examine his leg—which bled from a gash along his shin. Uriel tore off a long strip from his linen cloak, wrapped the cut and pulled hard on the ends. Yonaton winced and bit his lip as the prophet tied off the bandage.

We crossed the narrow streambed and picked up a faint trail. Despite his limp, Yonaton scurried uphill, keeping up with our pace.

Voices drew my attention back toward the opening we'd escaped from. Someone peeked through the crack in the cave. Uriel said, "Come, we must move quickly. They'll circle around the hill. It will be faster for them."

"Where are we going?" Yonaton asked.

Uriel didn't answer.

The moon soon dropped beneath the horizon, forcing us to slow our pace even further. But I didn't mind the darkness: it concealed us as well.

We pushed forward until the light of the new day crept up in the east. Now it was a race.

The glow of a fire appeared ahead of us, brighter than the dawn that quickly rose behind us. That's when I knew we had won. Uriel picked up his pace, hurrying toward the firelight, and we matched him easily, drawn on by the promise of safety. Yet, as we drew nearer to the warm light, it became clear that this blaze would offer us no protection at all.

Had we walked up the trail two days earlier, we would have crossed a clearing to a large house, at least three times the size of Uncle Menachem's. Now, with the roof gone, it seemed even larger. The walls still stood, their stones black with ash. A red glow radiated from the burnt remains, still smoldering from their destruction.

Uriel staggered forward with a low moan. He dropped to his knees at the side of a dark figure on the ground. The firelight reflected off the silver beard of the body. I stepped closer, recognizing familiar wrinkles around the mouth that sang so beautifully it never required words. Tzadok. Other shadows dotted the clearing around the ruin. We had arrived at the scene of a massacre.

A ram's horn blast split the dawn: a soldier with dark, hawk-like eyes had reached the edge of the clearing.

I expected the soldier to kick his horse into a charge, but he just sat, watching us from a distance.

Uriel rose from Tzadok's side. "You two run. It's my blood they want. They'll take yours as well, but if you get far enough away, they won't bother giving chase."

"There are three of us," I said. "We'll fight."

"If he were going to attack on his own, he would have done so already. He's just watching us until the others arrive. Then it will be one old man and two unarmed boys against four soldiers with swords and horses." He spun us away from the soldier and gave us each a hard push in the back. "Go!"

Uriel yelled the command with so much force that I didn't even consider disobeying. We ran across the clearing, past the destroyed house, and into the cover of thick pine trees on the far side. There I stopped for one last glimpse of my master.

Uriel twirled his staff above his head as the soldier circled, well out of striking range. A second rider charged up the trail. Would they wait for all four, or would the two attack? Yonaton grabbed my arm. "He told us to get out of here!"

Yonaton was right; there was nothing more we could do for the prophet.

There was no way he could hope to defeat four armed soldiers with just his staff. I realized that his defense was not intended to protect him at all—it was for the two of us, buying us extra time to escape. We dodged between the trees, crashing through branches and stumbling on the uneven ground of a rough trail, no longer caring about keeping quiet, or even where we were going.

Our haste made us careless: we almost collided with the third soldier, riding hard toward the battle. He reined in his horse and a wide grin split his sharp cheekbones, as his eyes fell upon Yonaton. "Thought you'd have a little fun sending us down to Jericho, didya? Knew you were lying. Knew you'd bring us right to him. Ought to thank you, I should. But the Queen says no survivors—no prophets, no disciples. Anyone who'd run to warn a prophet sounds like a disciple to me." He kicked the horse's belly and charged.

We dove to opposite sides of the trail, and the soldier pursued Yonaton. "Run!" Yonaton screamed as the soldier raised his sword.

I took one step down the trail, then froze. I may have left my master to face four soldiers, but I would not leave my friend to fight one alone. I snatched a sharp stone from the edge of the path and flung it with all my might at the rider's back. The rock missed its target, but came close enough to the soldier's ear to make him flinch. That was enough—Yonaton rolled back onto the trail as the sword plunged into empty ground.

The soldier turned his horse, now facing me. I threw a second rock. He ducked it, then raised his sword for the strike. My legs wouldn't move. Even if I had run for the trees, I wouldn't have reached them in time. But then the soldier lurched forward on his horse as blood stained his tunic below the shoulder.

A man jumped out of the trees.

My mouth dropped. It was Shimon, the scarred disciple.

"Give me the other one!" he screamed at me.

I stared, confused. Shimon reached into my belt and pulled out the dagger that he had given me months before.

The soldier was wounded, but not badly enough. He recovered his balance and kicked his horse forward. Shimon threw the dagger, but the soldier ducked low over his knees to avoid it.

The soldier raised his sword, then screamed out in pain as a rock from Yonaton struck his injured shoulder. He turned back and forth between us. He was still better armed, but now it was three against one, and none of us was his intended victim. Pulling up his horse, he turned and thundered back up the trail.

Shimon reached out his hand. "Give it to me."

This time I knew exactly what he meant. I pulled my father's knife from under my tunic and handed it to the man who'd told me never to use it.

Shimon closed his eyes, pressing the flat of the stone blade to his forehead. When he opened his eyes, his face was transformed. The burning anger was gone, replaced by peaceful clarity. Without a word, he bolted up the hill after his injured enemy. The look in Shimon's eye pushed all thoughts of flight from my mind. I took off after him, waving for Yonaton to follow.

All four soldiers now circled Uriel like wild dogs. They jabbed at him with their swords, hemming him in. He held the end of his staff, swinging it in broad circles, keeping them back. They rode just out of reach, knowing that he could not keep up his defense for long, waiting for the opportunity to strike. They would take the easy kill.

Shimon ran out of the trees unnoticed and leapt onto the closest horse. It reared and kicked as his weight crashed down behind its rider. Shimon drove the knife through the soldier's back, then shoved him off the horse.

The other three turned as one at their friend's cry—a mistake. Uriel brought his staff down with a sickening crunch on the knee of a stocky soldier. The rider let out a howl and turned to fight the prophet, while his companions chased after Shimon.

Yonaton and I waited in the shelter of the trees, gripping rocks. As Shimon raced past, we threw. I missed the hawk-eyed soldier's head by a hairsbreadth, but Yonaton's hit the other just above his left eye.

The rider struggled to keep control of his horse. We saw the blood stain below his shoulder—the same soldier we'd faced earlier. He recovered his balance and took off after Yonaton, who eluded him by ducking in and out of the trees. I chased after them throwing rocks, aiming high to avoid hitting Yonaton. I missed twice, but my third throw connected with the back of his head.

The soldier screamed out and spun his horse around to face me. Yonaton grabbed the horse's tail with both hands and pulled down with all his weight. The horse reared its front legs high in the air.

The soldier fell backward, pulling his horse with him. The rider hit the ground first. The horse followed, landing on its rider and Yonaton.

The animal was the first to rise. Yonaton struggled up as well, having absorbed merely the weight of the horse's hind legs in the fall. The soldier absorbed the hardest blow, with the full weight of the horse landing on him.

I ran past Yonaton, grabbing the soldier's fallen sword before he could get it.

The wounded soldier pushed himself upright and let out a cough, his face twisting in pain. I expected the soldier to beg for his life, but all he said was, "Make it fast."

I drew the weapon back to gather more power, but my arms froze there.

"Do it!" the soldier cried. He knew he was dying. The most merciful thing would be to end it quickly. But I couldn't bring myself to deliver the final blow.

A hand closed over mine. I peered into Yonaton's eyes, afraid of finding pity there, but seeing only understanding. Yonaton took the sword and plunged it into the soldier's chest. "Come on!" he said. "There are more of them." Sword in hand he ran back toward the heart of the battle with me running behind.

We stopped again at the edge of the trees. Even with a sword we were no match for mounted opponents—we would wait for another opportunity to strike.

In the clearing, the hawk-eyed soldier still chased Shimon. Uriel smashed his staff into the nose of the stocky soldier's horse. While he fought to get the horse back under control, Uriel slipped in closer, showering blows upon them both. Once the soldier regained his balance, he brandished his sword to hold off Uriel's assault.

But the stocky soldier's focus was diverted from the rest of the battle for a moment too long. Shimon saw the opening and rode toward the center of the clearing. The hawk-eyed soldier giving chase called out, but too late—all his friend's attention was fixed on fending off Uriel's attack. Shimon jammed my knife into the soldier's neck, and he toppled sideways off the horse.

The hawk-eyed soldier swiped at Uriel as he rode past, but the prophet blocked the blow easily with his staff. He rode on after Shimon, who was now unarmed.

Yonaton called out, "Here!" holding the sword in his hands. Shimon's horse leapt forward. I threw a rock at the soldier to keep him back. Shimon snatched the weapon from Yonaton's hand and spun in time to block a thrust from the hawk-eyed soldier's sword.

Now Shimon had no need to run. He closed in on his adversary. Shimon's sword descended like a bolt, and the soldier raised his blade to block it. The soldier's sword broke off its hilt from the force of the blow. Shimon swung his sword in a wide circle around his head, then struck again. The soldier tumbled from his horse. His body slammed to the ground with a thud, while his head rolled to a rest at Uriel's feet.

Hillel said: Be among the disciples of Aharon, loving peace and pursuing peace.
Pirkei Avot 1:12

16

Yochanan's Secret

"I don't understand." Shimon groaned as he and Uriel laid one of the slain prophets beside the ruined house.

"Tell me everything, from the beginning."

"I've been here since I left you. You were right, it was better for me here among the masters than it was among the disciples. The Queen's soldiers rode up at sunset, eight of them. Three of us went out to greet them with food—we had no idea. Foolish as it was, that probably saved my life. I don't think that anyone in the house managed to—Lev, no!"

I jumped back at the rebuke. Yonaton and I had approached one of the bodies—why shouldn't we try to help? And why did he yell only at me? Yonaton was a bit stronger, but not by much.

Uriel edged over to my side, making his body a barrier between me and the dead. "Yes, why don't the two of you gather wood for the morning meal? We will need all of our strength."

My master's tone was softer than Shimon's, but his command was no less clear. I bit back my response, and the two of us retreated from the line of bodies to the first row of trees, where we gathered sticks in silence so as not to miss a word.

Shimon stood over another of the fallen prophets. "The details of the battle are not important. You see the results before you."

"Did anyone else survive?"

"I don't think so. We'll know for certain once we have gathered everyone." He dropped his eyes. "I hid in a cave last night."

Uriel placed a hand on Shimon's shoulder. "Flight is also courageous when it brings hope for return."

Shimon nodded. "The ram's horn woke me. I wasn't sure if the blast was from friend or foe, so I crept back, keeping to the shelter of the trees. Then I saw one of them go after the boys, so I attacked. I managed to plant my knife in him, and he rode off. Coward. I knew he must be going after you. I couldn't help you barehanded, so I asked Lev for Yochanan's knife."

Shimon pulled my knife from the body of the fallen soldier and brought the weapon to Uriel.

Uriel examined the knife. "Yes, Lev has shown it to me. For the second time this blade has saved your life."

"Indeed. But it is a tool of peace, not war. It should never have been used to kill a man."

"It hardly seems you had a choice."

"No, there was no choice. Not this time, and not when Yochanan used it to save me." Shimon sighed. "You know, just before it happened, I...I saw him."

Neither of them heard the branches fall from my arms.

Uriel fixed his eyes on Shimon. "You saw Yochanan?"

"I touched the flat of the blade to my forehead and closed my eyes. I recalled that day years ago. My fear, his sacrifice. I was filled with the injustice of Yochanan's murder, the horror of yesterday's massacre, and the evil of them trying to kill you now..." Shimon's back straightened. "And that's when it happened."

"What did you feel?"

"Power, like nothing I've ever felt. Yesterday I injured my ankle running away, but when I took off after that soldier, I felt no pain—and I ran faster than I ever have.

"Clarity." Shimon closed his eyes. "When I charged into battle, I didn't have to decide what to do. My body just...knew. I leapt onto the back of that horse as if it were a pony!"

"Did you feel anything else?"

"Courage, no fear at all. And so strong. I snapped that soldier's sword in two—I can't do that."

"How did it end?"

"When the last soldier fell, I felt it just...flow out of me. The fear hasn't returned, but my leg is throbbing, and well..." he glanced at his hands, "I won't be shattering any more swords."

"You have sought prophecy for many years, but it always eluded you. Now you finally taste the fruits of your commitment."

"This was prophecy? It's unlike any prophecy I've ever seen."

"But I've seen far more than you have, Shimon. There is a level, close to prophecy, which comes in a time of crisis. One sees injustice and rushes to act. When your heart, mind, and will move you in this way, you can become a fit vessel for the Presence."

The words made little sense to me, and Shimon didn't seem to understand either. The lines on his forehead only deepened.

"Learn from Samson," Uriel continued. "Drawn after his eyes, he could never receive full prophecy. But when he saw the desperate need of Israel, he seized that donkey's jawbone and slew a thousand men in one day."

"So the Presence brings you strength?"

"Not always. It is a spirit that fills you with the power you need at the moment. Samson, whose way was to fight alone, received the power of an army. King Saul, who ran away from kingship, received this spirit in a different way, giving him the power to lead."

"But why wasn't I given this power yesterday? Why did so many have to die?"

"Do not take what you received lightly—it is a rare gift. Yesterday you were afraid and ran. Today you were determined to fight, determined to succeed—you just didn't know how. That determination made you a fit vessel for the spirit. You didn't receive the strength of Samson or the leadership of Saul. But it did bring you enough speed, strength, and knowledge to overcome these four soldiers. For that, I'm grateful."

It wasn't my place to interrupt, but I cut through the clearing in three strides and faced Uriel and Shimon over the line of the dead. "What's this about my father?" I demanded.

Shimon gasped—he hadn't heard me approach. He leapt over a corpse and grabbed my shoulder, drawing me back. I shook his arm free, but allowed him to lead me away from the bodies.

"Lev, I'm sorry. But you can't know. Not yet."

I glared at Shimon. He knew. If Shimon owed his life to my father, then he owed me an answer.

Uriel's voice was softer. "Lev, when you returned to me, you said that where I went, you would go. But even I did not foresee where it would lead.

"I have served the Holy One faithfully my entire life, but I am an old man.

There are more soldiers seeking me, and even if I were not pursued, the time to lie with my fathers is drawing near. It matters not how my soul will leave my body, in sleep or in battle. But your life is ahead of you. I release you from your oath."

Was my master dismissing me rather than tell me the truth?

"The journey to Yehudah is now too dangerous for you to attempt. Even the smallest passes will be watched. If you wish to return to your aunt, tell her that it is with my blessing and she will welcome you home. Your uncle will help you raise a flock of your own. No one will seek your blood. You will marry and build a family. Grow old.

"Or you may continue with me. We will travel fast, eat little, fight if we must. If you go where I go, it may be to the grave before the week is done."

I stared down at the bodies of the massacred prophets on the ground. If I hadn't been there, Uriel could have lain among them. I raised my eyes up to my master's. "Where you go, I will go."

"So be it. Then it's time to hear the truth about your father. The truth about yourself.

"I have hidden things until now because knowledge can be dangerous. But at this point, you could hardly be in more danger—now ignorance is a liability." The old prophet held out the handle of my knife. "I saw your father's courage in you today. Take the knife."

I asked for the truth, but I hadn't expected to get it. My fingers trembled as I grasped the weapon with both hands.

"Do you recognize the imprint?"

How many times had I wondered about its meaning since leaving home? I shrugged. "Claws of some sort?"

Uriel cocked his head to inspect the insignia. "True, it does look like claws now, doesn't it? Much time has passed since I saw it first. Yes, some definition has been lost. Not three fingers, five. The thumb, two fingers held together, a gap, then two fingers held together. Does that help you?"

"No, Master."

"The kohanim, the priests of the Holy One, hold their hands this way when they bless the people. Your father was a kohen." Uriel drew my eyes up from the knife with a gentle touch on my chin. "Which makes you a kohen as well. You were born a priest of the Holy One."

Memories came pouring in. My special bread—my aunt always gave me the first piece of bread. Hadn't Uriel done the same when I came to the gathering, making sure that a portion was always set aside for me? Uncle Menachem taught me that the kohen receives the first bread and the first fruits—why had

I never made the connection?

"Is that why I can't help with the bodies?"

"Yes, you are forbidden contact with the dead."

"And this is why I have no land?"

"Yes, the kohanim are from the tribe of Levi, who received the service of the Holy One as their inheritance. They have no share in the land."

I raised the knife. "And this?"

"That knife was used by your ancestors to slaughter offerings in the Holy Temple."

"Shimon said it was for peace, not war."

"Indeed it is. When the hearts of the kohanim are pure and the people are devoted to their service, there is peace in the land."

"Why was it dangerous for me to know what I am?"

"Did your uncle teach you about the splitting of the Kingdom?"

"Yes," I said, then added quickly, "but only when I went home after the wedding." I wanted it to be clear that I hadn't understood about the Golden Calf when we were in Beit El. "He said that Yeravaum feared that the people would return to the Temple, so he created the calves and commanded the people to worship the Holy One through them."

"Yes, a new form of our old sin in the desert. The annual pilgrimage to the calves will be in one week, at the full moon, exactly one month after Israel should have gone up to the Temple for Sukkot. And did Menachem tell you that not all the people accepted this substitution?"

I shook my head.

"The tribe of Levi rejected the calf in the wilderness and were not going to bow to it here in the Land. When Yeravaum replaced the Temple, he replaced the kohanim as well. New altars meant new priests, an honor bestowed upon one of the most powerful families in the Kingdom, assuring their loyalty to Yeravaum. Most of the true kohanim in the northern Kingdom of Israel fled south to Yehudah. Only a few stayed, and their very presence provoked Yeravaum and the kings who came after him."

"Why?"

"Because the Holy One anointed Aharon and his sons as our priests for all time. The only way to serve the Holy One at the altar is to be a descendant of Aharon. As long as his descendants lived in the land, they were a challenge to Yeravaum and his false priests."

"So the remaining kohanim were hunted down?"

"No. Most went about their lives quietly. They became craftsmen, shepherds, teachers of the young. Yeravaum saw no reason to disturb the peace by dealing harshly with them."

"So why was my father different?"

"Because your father refused to flee or conceal his identity. He wouldn't let the people forget. He traveled the Kingdom, teaching about the Holy One, and rousing the nation to correct its ways."

"But you also do this. You were never hunted before, were you?"

"No, Yeravaum had no desire to break the connection between the people and the Holy One. Just the opposite: he told the people that worshiping his calves was the surest path to connect to the Holy One. Opposing the prophets would have destroyed this illusion, so we remained free to live and teach in the land."

Suddenly the battle made more sense. "But Izevel wants to destroy the connection between the people and the Holy One. She wants them to worship the Baal."

"Indeed."

"Was I never to know who I am?"

"That was to be a question of how you matured. Had you grown into a man who likes to avoid trouble, like the kohanim who abandoned their roots, I would never have burdened you with this knowledge."

"But how could you know which direction I'd take?"

"When we met under the fig tree, I was a stranger to you, but you were well known to me. I have walked the land for over fifty years—almost always alone. Your father was a rare friend; I would not abandon his son. After he died, I visited your uncle whenever my path brought me close to Levonah. It was I who gave you that kinnor, for music is a channel for the soul. I saw early on that you possessed a rare spirit—a spirit like your father's—but I still needed to know you better. The past can be such a heavy burden. I needed to be sure that you could bear it.

"That's why I hired you to accompany me to the gathering. There I was to make my final decision: to leave you in ignorance and allow you to sink into the people of the Kingdom, or to smuggle you to Yehudah once you came of age. There you could learn the ways of the kohanim, and one day serve in the Holy Temple. Your uncle knew this, of course, but he long ago yielded to my desire for secrecy."

"But, Master, I thought that you hired me for my music?"

"Your music is beautiful, Lev—it is an expression of the spirit of which I speak. But I didn't need a musician badly enough to take you from your uncle's flock. I needed to know you better. And you needed to see your father's world before you could make the choice: whether to remain here a shepherd, or join me on the journey to Yehudah to learn the ways of your tribe."

"And what now, Master?"

"Everything has changed. My days of walking the Kingdom are over. We'd be hunted down within days. The watch on the passes will be doubled as well—the way to Yehudah is sealed."

"Where will we go?"

"I don't know. Despite the delay, I must seek vision. Please play for me."

Uriel lowered himself to the ground. He closed his eyes and dropped his head between his knees, but there was no music. Uriel gazed back up. "I forgot that we left your kinnor behind. I will attempt it on my own."

My master's brother prophets lay on the ground next to him, awaiting burial. I couldn't imagine harder circumstances to enter prophecy. I might not have my kinnor, but I still had my voice.

I searched for a melody that could lift Uriel into the state of joy necessary for prophecy. Nothing came. Where was the joy in this place?

I closed my eyes and pictured King Solomon's Temple. If I was a kohen, could I one day play my kinnor there? What did the music of the Temple sound like? A melody rose in my heart. I sang through it once. As I returned to the beginning, an arm wrapped around my shoulder, and Yonaton's voice joined with mine, picking out deeper tones in the melody.

Shimon stretched an arm around my other shoulder. His voice was raw, and his harmony just awful. Still, there was something sweet about singing with this man who had carried me to safety as a child and had just now saved my life once again.

Uriel watched the three of us singing together and managed a sad smile. He lowered his head, and rocked his body in time to our music until he ascended in prophecy.

By the time Uriel stirred, Yonaton and I had built a fire and warmed our stale bread. Curious as I was to question my master, he had not eaten since the previous night, and my first duty was to him. I handed the prophet a piece of toasted bread and bit my tongue to restrain myself from asking about the vision.

"Thank you, Lev," Uriel said. "But you should not continue to serve me this way."

"Why not, Master?"

"The kohanim serve the Holy One, not man."

"But I want to serve you."

Uriel shook his head. "The laws of the kohanim are many and complex. Sadly, we have no proper time for your education. I will serve myself, and Shimon is here if I need assistance."

Yonaton popped up at this. "And me."

Uriel again shook his head. "Yesterday you could not go back to your family because of these soldiers, but they will tell their tale to no one now. You may safely return home."

"I want to stay."

"Lev's uncle handed him into my care. Your parents made no such choice. They are expecting you."

"When I told my parents that the soldiers were looking for you, my father told me I had to come. My mother packed me food. They wouldn't want me to leave you. Not if I can help."

"There is actually a way you can help. Very well, you may remain as long as you are needed."

No one spoke as the prophet ate. When he swallowed his last bite, Shimon asked, "What did you see?"

"We must contact Ovadia. He is still loyal, and in his position, he'll know how to advise us."

"Ovadia? How are we supposed to reach him? He's in Shomron, the heart of the Kingdom, right under the eye of Queen Izevel. We need to get you to safety. Wouldn't you be better served leaving the Kingdom?"

"No. You forget that King Ethbaal has the largest fleet on the seas. There's no kingdom with whom he does not trade, no end to his reach. The people have not yet accepted Queen Izevel's reign here, but once I leave the land, no one has reason to shelter me. I'd be given over immediately."

"And Yehudah?"

"Indeed, I would be safe there. But that is where Queen Izevel will expect me to go. She'll concentrate her power on the border." Uriel stood up and leaned upon his staff. "In any case, I have no intention of fleeing. Do not concern yourself with my safety. My last days will be here in the Kingdom, serving the Holy One in any way that I still can."

"Excellent. So we'll resist. But don't throw your life away going to Shomron."

"I didn't say we need to go to Shomron, we just need to contact Ovadia. It will be less dangerous for him to come to us."

"But how can we contact him without going to Shomron?"

Uriel turned to Yonaton and me. "The boys. The only soldiers that we know can connect us with the boys lie right here. You and I are hunted; they are not. Hopefully none of the Queen's other lackeys know the connection between us."

"So what do we do now?"

"We can't remain here the night; it's too well known as a gathering place. We need to find a place to hide until Lev and Yonaton return."

Hillel said: In a place where there are no men, strive to be a man.

Pirkei Avot 2:6

17

The Steward's Wife

Unable to help with the bodies, I returned to the cave to retrieve Balaam and the rest of our gear while the others buried the fallen prophets. I ran my fingers over the strings of my kinnor, a little surprised to find that it was still in tune. I was without it just one night, but it felt like greeting an old friend.

"Where to now, Master?" I asked when I returned.

"West. There's a cave not far from the King's Road where Shimon and I can hide."

"Are we taking the soldiers' horses?" Yonaton asked. Between his run the day before and the horse falling on him that morning, he was struggling to walk.

Uriel shook his head. "They'll draw too much attention. But your legs have earned a rest, Yonaton. You may ride Balaam today."

It was not yet midday when we started our journey, cutting across rolling hills like those around Levonah. By late afternoon we reached our destination—a cave in a hillside just over the ridge from the King's Road. The cave was chiseled by hand like the caves at Emek HaAsefa. A towering carob tree hid the entrance from view.

It had not rained since my return from Jericho, but a cold north wind blew and I craved a hot meal. Yonaton, who managed to sleep much of the afternoon while riding Balaam, offered, "I'll go look for—"

"No fire tonight," Uriel interrupted.

I surveyed the broad valley that we had just crossed. Were there more soldiers out there hunting us?

I rose before the sun after an uneasy night. Shimon sat in the mouth of the cave, illuminated by flickering firelight. "I was about to wake you to eat," he said. "The Holy One must truly love you. See what leapt right into my hands this morning?" A fat grouse dripped grease off its breast onto the smoking coals.

Shimon cut off a wing with his dagger and handed it me. "I envy you."

"Why?"

"You are walking toward danger, but at least your fate is in your hands. I…we…get to sit here and wait, praying that we're not discovered and hoping you're successful, knowing little and doing less."

I chewed the meat, keeping my mouth full so that I wouldn't have to respond. Hadn't Uriel, who now slept after taking the first watch, warned us against making a fire?

When we finished eating, we descended to where Balaam was tied up for the night. "You should ride," I told Yonaton. "I'll lead Balaam."

"I can walk."

"You can limp. Balaam can handle your weight, but both of us will be too much for him in the hills. When we reach the road, we'll ride together."

Yonaton shook his head but climbed on.

"Be safe," Shimon said, his hand drifting down toward something inside of his cloak.

"What do you have there?" I asked.

Shimon pulled back his cloak, revealing the hilt of a sword. "It's the one Yonaton handed me during the battle, from the soldier that he killed."

"You kept it?"

"I was blessed to save us with it once. Perhaps I'll be so blessed again." Shimon watched us as we set off, ducking back into the cave only when we reached the ridge.

Yonaton shot a glance behind him. "Shame he's not coming with us."

I said nothing, just led Balaam on the path that Uriel had pointed out to us the day before. A figure on the far ridge caught my attention—a soldier on horseback. He sat on one of the hillsides overlooking the road, but he wasn't facing the road; he was looking out over the valley where our path crossed. He noticed us at the same time, nudging his horse forward and rising in the saddle.

My pulse raced. There was no reason to panic—we were just two boys with a donkey. I lifted my hand, hissing out of the corner of my mouth, "Quick, wave."

Yonaton glanced around until he, too, saw the soldier and threw a friendly wave. The soldier waved back, then returned to his post on the hilltop.

Yonaton asked, "Was that an Israelite soldier or one of the Queen's?"

"I don't know, but there weren't any Israelite soldiers posted this far away before the wedding."

"You think he's watching the road?"

"He was facing the valley, so he could be watching both or—"

"Or he's keeping an eye out for anyone avoiding the road," Yonaton finished.

"If that's the case, we'll draw less attention on the road. We can cut over this hillside. It will be quicker, but I think it's too steep for Balaam to carry you."

Yonaton threw his leg over the donkey and lowered himself to the ground. "I can walk."

We saw no more soldiers as we made our way up, over, and onto the road. Both of us then climbed onto Balaam for the ride toward Shomron.

We entered Shomron just before the closing of the gates, and headed up the main road to Ovadia's street. Before long, Yonaton was glancing back over his shoulder, casting his eyes back and forth between the sides of the narrow alleyway.

"Did we miss it?" I asked.

"No. Well…you know, I'm not so sure. This is the street. I know it. Let's go back to the crossroad."

We passed the length of street two more times before Yonaton let out a loud "Ha!" and called a halt in front of a heavy wooden gate covered in fresh pitch.

"I don't remember any gate," I said softly.

"There wasn't one," Yonaton replied, "That's what confused me. But this is it. I'm certain. See, there's Ovadia's seal on the lintel."

The footstool carved into the lintel was indeed the same symbol that he used to seal his messages—I had delivered enough of them before the wedding to remember. I tried the gate, but it was locked.

Yonaton picked up a mallet hanging from the door post and pounded out three solid blows. No one answered. We stared at each other. We'd invested all

our energy in reaching Shomron; we hadn't even thought about what to do if Ovadia was away.

Yonaton swung the mallet once more, knocking louder. We heard a door open, then quickly close again. The gate swung silently outward on its hinges, and Ovadia stepped into the alley, fastening the gate behind him. "Hello, boys. A bit late for a visit, isn't it?" He shifted from foot to foot as his eyes darted up and down the dark street.

I opened my mouth to respond, but Ovadia cut me off. "Well, then, very good of you to let me know you're back. Come look for me at the palace in the morning, perhaps we can find work for you again. I recently heard Dov say he could use more musicians for all the banquets. Until tomorrow, then." Ovadia turned back to the gate.

I leaned in and breathed at his back, "Master Uriel sent us."

Ovadia whipped around, his eyes shooting up the street again. "Did anyone see you? Were you followed?"

"I don't think so."

Ovadia swept Yonaton, Balaam, and me quickly into the courtyard. He closed and bolted the heavy wooden gate, securing it without a sound. He tied Balaam to a post near a watering trough and tossed him a pile of straw. Then he hustled us through the main entrance.

Lamps burned in the main room where drawn shutters blocked the moonlight. Batya tucked a loose strand of hair under her scarf as her husband dropped us onto stools beside the hearth table.

Ovadia dropped onto a stool opposite me. "Uriel is still alive?"

I nodded.

"Is he safe?"

I nodded again.

"Where is he?" I opened my mouth to answer, but Ovadia interjected, "How did you get here?"

"He is safe," I replied. "He sent us to you for help."

Ovadia popped up and redoubled his pacing. "Help? So many need help. She's got eyes everywhere, you know!"

Batya offered us two hot loaves of flat bread, and would not allow Ovadia to question us while we ate. The new gate was not the only change in Ovadia's house. Heavy blankets covered shuttered windows, a strange sight on a windless night. A new oven had been constructed inside the house, just opposite the oven in the courtyard. I squeezed the warm bread in my hand—had they been baking at night?

Ovadia managed to hold himself back until the bread was gone, then leaned in close to us. "Where is he?"

I swallowed my last bite. "In a cave a day's journey from here."

"Well hidden?"

I nodded. "There's a tree blocking the entrance; I never would have known it was there."

"It must be one of Gidon's caves."

"Gidon's caves?"

"Built before Gidon's rebellion against the Midianites hundreds of years ago. Some, like those at Emek HaAsefa, were strongholds, others hiding places. Uriel has shown me several; no one knows them as well as he does. I've never heard of the one you speak of."

"That doesn't matter, we can guide you back."

"Me, leave Shomron to get a prophet? That's just what she's waiting for, an excuse to take off my head."

I stared at Ovadia—he was our only hope. We couldn't return to Uriel alone. What would we do, then? Sit in the cave until we starved?

"Of course, you have no idea what's been happening here." He pulled his stool closer to us and lowered his voice. "The Queen has declared war on the prophets."

"We know. We've buried the dead."

Ovadia motioned for me to continue. I recounted the events of the last three days. When I finished, Ovadia met his wife's eyes with a groan. "It is worse than we feared. We hoped that her power was limited to Shomron. Further into the hills, the people still love and fear the prophets. I thought they would protect them."

"The people love the prophets," Yonaton said, speaking up for the first time, "but they fear the sword."

Ovadia nodded. "Yet there are worse things than the sword, Yonaton. May you be blessed not to know them." He rose and faced Batya. "It seems that the fate of these boys is bound up with ours, yes?"

Batya gathered the remains of our meal. "You thought these boys were a tool in your hand. Yet, you see now, we are all tools in the hands of the Holy One."

I wondered what she meant, but was distracted by the sight of her collecting breadcrumbs from the table. During the wedding, I never saw her clean. "Where are your servants?"

A soft tear ran down her cheek. "They're attending to our land."

Attending to their land? Surely enough men attended Ovadia's land that he didn't need the house servants there as well? Perhaps for the harvest, but now? And even so, why should Batya weep over this?

I thought about everything I had seen since arriving: the gate blocking access to the house; a new oven, built inside the house instead of in the courtyard where it belonged; windows sealed on a still evening; hot bread past nightfall; and the servants gone. My eye fell on a waist high pile in the corner of the room, covered with a woolen blanket.

I rose from my stool. All eyes watched me go, yet neither Ovadia nor Batya hindered me. Lifting the edge of the blanket, I peeked beneath, discovering a stack of freshly baked loaves of breads.

Ovadia took the edge of the blanket from my hand. "Your eyes are starting to open, Lev. That is good. You will need them in the days ahead. All our servants, as you must have guessed, are gone. Our hired workers were dismissed even before the wedding; that was one reason I relied on you boys so much. Now even our slaves have been sent away to work our land in the Yezreel Valley. No one can know what we're doing."

A lump rose in my throat. "How many are there?"

"Thirty prophets and disciples. Hidden in a cave outside the city."

Batya gasped and clasped her hand over her mouth.

"As you said, Batya, they were sent by the Holy One. We must trust them." She nodded without removing her hand.

Yonaton stirred. "But why us?"

Ovadia raised his eyebrows. "Uriel sent you."

"Not now—during the wedding. You said you dismissed your workers and depended on us instead."

"Ah, yes. Even then I wondered if you would ask. Did it not seem strange to you that the King's steward, with all the servants at my disposal, was relying on two unknown boys to do my errands?"

"You told us that everyone was busy with preparations."

"Indeed they were—like bees in the hive. But I still saw to the most important details myself, and as you know, I often needed help. I directed dozens of slaves and servants, but always kept them at a distance."

"But why us?" Yonaton asked again.

Ovadia shifted his focus from Yonaton to me. I felt the challenge in his gaze to figure out this puzzle as I had about the bread. Ovadia dismissed his hired workers and relied instead on two country boys, both plucked from serving the prophets. The answer was suddenly clear. "We were safe."

"You were safe," Ovadia agreed. "From the time of the engagement, the King was constantly on the lookout for anyone who could be disloyal."

"But you were not disloyal then," Yonaton said, "Were you?"

"No, I have always served my King loyally."

"Until now," I added with a grin.

"Even now. This is the Queen's war. Her soldiers are after the prophets;

the Israelite soldiers haven't been brought into the hunt. The King is doing his best to ignore the Queen's attacks, neither helping nor hindering her."

"But if you're not disloyal," Yonaton asked, "why dismiss your servants?"

"The very innocence of the question is what made you so valuable."

"Why?"

"I'm known to have relations with the prophets. I'm foreign born. I'm a natural target."

"For who?"

"For anyone hoping to advance by setting me up for a fall. It makes no difference whether the accusations are true or not. I directed hundreds of servants, but I never let them get too close and never let them deliver my messages."

"Then why us?"

"As Lev said, you were safe. Uriel told me that neither of you had ever left home until you came to play for the prophets. You knew nothing of what was happening here in Shomron, and you were hardly looking to make names for yourselves in the court. But that was before. Then I had nothing to hide. I feared only lies."

"What changed?" Yonaton asked.

"I don't know. Something happened when the King went to Jericho a week and a half ago. He came back white-faced and silent. He told me nothing, just summoned the Queen to the throne room. Whatever she heard sent her into a rage, and she called in Yambalya. She emerged determined to kill the prophets and their disciples."

"And no one knows why?" Yonaton asked.

Ovadia shook his head. "The King is keeping his hands clean of the blood of the prophets, but there is someone else that he commanded me to find. I expect it is connected to him."

"Eliyahu," I said.

"Yes." Ovadia's eyes narrowed on me. "How do you know about Eliyahu? Did Uriel have a vision of what happened in Jericho?"

"He didn't need to. I was there."

"You were in Jericho?"

"Yes."

"Then do you know why we're hunting him? Did he confront the King?"

"He did."

"Over the Baal?"

"Yes."

"You see, Batya, I knew it. The Queen is proud. Eliyahu standing against the King must have prompted her to act before she was ready."

"Ready for what?" Yonaton asked.

"It was clear at the wedding that she intended to draw the people after the Baal—Yambalya wouldn't have pushed the guests to bow down except on her orders. Her influence has only grown stronger since then. Much stronger. But not enough to strike against the prophets. In her rage, she acted rashly. If we can reach Uriel, the resistance will have the leader it lacks. Under him, the surviving prophets can rouse the people to throw off Izevel's yoke."

"And the King's?" Yonaton asked.

Ovadia shook his head. "The King is more dedicated to the people than he is to the Queen. Even rebuilding Jericho and marrying Izevel were, in his mind, done for them. If the people rise against the Queen, I believe the King won't stand in their way."

Ovadia turned to me. "To think that I brought you into my home because you were some innocent boy who knew nothing of the Kingdom or the Court! You're finding yourself in the middle of too many events for it to all be chance. There is more to you than you are sharing, Lev, more perhaps than you know yourself."

My hand went to the bulge in my tunic where my father's knife lay. Ovadia was correct that I was holding something back: I hadn't mentioned anything about my father.

Ovadia broke into a sudden smile. "Uriel would never have led the resistance on his own. He would have put off war as long as possible, allowing Izevel to grow stronger and stronger. But now that Eliyahu has forced his hand, he will have to lead us."

Ovadia stroked his trim beard. "Unless Eliyahu expects to lead—he started this fight. Lev, did it sound to you as though he was planning to lead the people against the Queen? Tell me exactly what he said."

"As the Holy One, the Lord of Israel, before whom I stand, lives…there will not be dew nor rain during these years except by my word."

Batya gasped.

Ovadia staggered. "He tried to stop the rains?"

I nodded.

"I've never heard of such a thing. Can he do that?"

"According to Master Uriel, the Holy One indeed gave him the key of rain. The heavens are sealed until Eliyahu relents."

"The Holy One gave him the key? That must be why the Queen summoned Yambalya. He would know if Eliyahu spoke the truth—the dark priest has wisdom."

Ovadia's brow tightening. "What you said didn't sound like prophecy though. It sounded more like an oath. Or…"

"...a curse," I finished.

Silence fell over the room.

I asked Ovadia, "You said Eliyahu wasn't one of the prophets. He is now. I saw him receiving prophecy after he left Hiel's house. Was he not known as a prophet before?"

"I do not know. In his youth, he was among the last disciples of Achia, Uriel's master. I do not know if he ever achieved prophecy before. I have known him only at the court. He has always been respectful of the King there. Did anything happen in Jericho before he spoke?"

I shifted uncomfortably on my stool. "The King told Hiel that he blamed himself for Seguv's death."

"As he should. To hire a man to rebuild a cursed city.... Of course, Hiel himself is also responsible for agreeing to do it. Did he say anything else?"

"The King thought it strange that the curse of Joshua would work."

"Why did he think that strange? Few prophets were as great as Joshua."

"Because Moshe said that if the people worshipped other gods, there would be no rain."

"What does that have to do with Joshua?"

"The King said that the people have turned after the Baal, yet he could never remember having so much rain. He wondered why the curse of Joshua would work when the curse of his master Moshe failed."

"What! Eliyahu invoked the curse of Moshe?"

I remembered Uriel saying that Moshe's words were not quite a curse, but they certainly seemed like it to me. "Yes."

All eyes were on Ovadia as he paced the room. "I had it all wrong. This is not a battle—it is a siege."

Yonaton looked confused, "But the battle has already begun."

"By the Queen, yes. But Eliyahu brought a drought. It may take years for its effects to be fully felt." He turned to Batya. "This changes everything—our plan will not work. We need to think of something else."

"But this should make our resistance even stronger!" Batya exclaimed.

Ovadia shook his head. "It cannot be done."

"Batya is right." I said. "The Holy One gave Eliyahu the key of rain! What better weapon could we have? As you said, the Queen acted too soon—the people are still more loyal to the prophets than they are to the Baal. Why change the plan now?"

Ovadia shook his head. "Because the Holy One did not give Eliyahu the key of rain to fight Izevel. The drought's wrath will fall on all those who have turned to the Baal—and on all those who have been loyal as well."

"But isn't the Queen the cause of their turning away?" Batya asked.

"It does not matter. Either way, Izevel will be the last to feel the lack of rain. The poorest will suffer first."

I couldn't understand why Ovadia was suddenly losing resolve. "But won't that rouse them against the Queen and the Baal?"

"Perhaps. But the Queen will tell them that this is not just a temporary stop to the rains, it is a drought, brought on by Eliyahu, a prophet. She will claim that he's a tyrant, that she has come to rescue the nation from his grip. In their misery, the people could turn against the prophets themselves."

Tears rolled down Batya's cheeks. "Then what do we do? Nothing?"

"We have thirty prophets already hidden. We'll hide as many more as we can."

"But how will we feed them? We have enough barley for the hidden ones only until the new moon. What will you do then, sell land to buy grain? And you're being watched. How long can we keep this up before someone discovers what we're doing?"

"I don't know. But when it is known that a drought is coming, at least buying a store of grain will not appear suspicious. We must continue hiding the prophets—I see now that any battle will not succeed."

"But why not?" Batya cried.

"Didn't you hear the boy? Eliyahu evoked the curse of Moshe. There will never again be a prophet of Moshe's strength."

"But shouldn't that make victory even easier?" I asked, but even as the words left my mouth, I remembered what Uriel had told me when I returned from Jericho. The forces of light and the forces of darkness had to exist in balance. The more powerful Eliyahu's curse, the more powerful the counteracting forces would be.

As if answering my thoughts, Ovadia said, "If this war is won, it will not be by ordinary men like me, nor even by the prophets of today. If we send the prophets out of the cave now, we send them to their deaths. We just have to do what we can, help as many as we can, for as long as we have bread. If we fail, we fail."

Ovadia sighed. "We'll need to find a way to get Uriel and Shimon here without being detected."

"Bring them here?" The words leapt out of my mouth.

"Yes, here. There's nowhere else I can feed them."

I shook my head. "Master Uriel doesn't want to hide. He would support your original plan."

"We can save his life!"

"He said he will spend his last days serving the Holy One in any way he can. I don't think he'll go meekly into a cave."

"Shimon won't either," Yonaton added. "He'd rather fight."

Ovadia stared into my eyes. "Listen to me—it is crucial that Uriel survive."

"He won't want it. He says he doesn't have long to live anyway."

"Uriel must live. In the struggle between Eliyahu and Izevel, he may prove pivotal."

"If Eliyahu fails?"

"No, if Eliyahu succeeds. It may take the wrath of Eliyahu to defeat Izevel. But it will require one like your master to rebuild the nation—and there is none other like him."

"Why?" Yonaton asked.

But I thought I knew. "Master Uriel believes that we must turn to the Holy One from love, not fear."

"That's part of it," Ovadia said. "But Uriel is not the only prophet dedicated to the path of love."

"Then why?"

"You're too young to understand what Uriel has been through. Tell him whatever you must, but get him to me."

"And what about Shimon?" Yonaton asked.

"Shimon is loyal to Uriel. If he thinks that his help is needed to save Uriel, I expect he will do what he must. But once Uriel is hidden, Shimon may do as he pleases."

"Even if he agrees to come, how will we get him here? You said you can't travel."

"No, I cannot. The Queen distrusts me because I will not bow to her abominations. This is not yet required, but refusal is enough to draw her wrath. The King leans on me for many things, so I am safe at present. But I am watched. If I go to Uriel it will mean the death of us both."

"But what can we do without you?" We were counting on Ovadia's authority to get him past the soldiers.

"You saw the Queen's soldiers on the road?"

I nodded.

"Perhaps we can risk it anyway. There are many ways into Shomron. It is not the people we have to fear—they are not yet corrupt enough to hunt a prophet—it is only the foreigners. There are many paths that they may not know. No one knows these mountains as Uriel does. It was he who first showed me the cave."

I shook my head. "They have lookouts on the hilltops. They're watching

157

the valleys as well as the roads."

Ovadia groaned. "You see, Batya, a craftsman can have the finest tools, but he's an oaf without a plan." He drummed his fingers on the table. "Perhaps at night?"

To reach Shomron in the dark, on footpaths, would take three nights at least. That meant finding hiding places during the days on top of the hardship traveling at night. "Even if we could make it, we'd never get into the city. The Queen's soldiers watch the gates."

"The cave is not in the city. He will not have to pass the gates."

I didn't like the plan, but what choice did we have? "All right. If we can convince Master Uriel, we'll try at night."

"No, you won't." Batya stood, hands on her hips. "You'll go during the day."

This was too much. Hadn't she been listening? "The valleys are watched."

"You won't walk the valleys. You'll take the King's Road."

Ovadia gaped at his wife. "How will they do that?"

"With the crowd returning from the festival."

The edges of her husband's lips curved up in a smile. "Brilliant."

I stared back and forth between them. "What's brilliant?"

"The annual festival of the Calf is in five days," Ovadia explained. "The King will be there, along with all the nobility of Shomron."

"But if the King is there," Yonaton said, "there are sure to be soldiers as well."

"The King's guard will escort him, but he moves much faster than his subjects. Besides, those are Israelite soldiers—the Queen's guard won't dare attack while they're around. Once the King rides past, Uriel and Shimon can mingle in with the crowd."

"He won't agree."

"I told you, Lev, your master must reach that cave. And I have known him far longer than you have. I do not believe that he wants to die."

"If you know my master so well, then you must know how much he hates the Golden Calf. He hasn't even set foot in Beit El for sixty years. Even if he agrees to hide, he won't do it by pretending to be a Calf worshiper."

"It's the only plan we have. The Holy One has chosen you to serve your master. Now you must save him. Whatever you need to do, you do. Swear to me that you will get Uriel here alive!"

"He's my master. I'm not his."

"I am offering to save his life. Now swear."

Ovadia's eyes locked on mine. "All right, I swear," I said, wondering how I would stand up to a prophet when I couldn't even stand up to Ovadia.

Rabbi Yannai said: We cannot grasp the tranquility of the wicked, nor can we understand the suffering of the righteous.

Pirkei Avot 4:19

18

Shimon's Tale

"Yonaton?" I said the next day, once we were on the road.

"What is it?"

"Ovadia said that Master Uriel must get to Shomron—at any cost. But what about Shimon?"

"What about him?"

"Do you think he's safe to travel with?"

"Safe? I can't think of a better person to travel with. When was the last time you shattered your enemy's sword?"

"Yesterday morning he lit a fire."

"He built it to roast us a grouse."

"I know, but Master Uriel told us not to. And Shimon complained about waiting in the cave. It sounds crazy, but I wonder if he wants to be found."

"You think he wants to die?"

"Not to die, to fight."

"The way he fights, I don't blame him."

"But that's not the way he fights—three days ago he ran from battle."

"You heard what Master Uriel said. He received a spirit from the Holy One. Like prophecy."

"Exactly, a spirit like prophecy, which he's pursued for years, and which he lost as soon as the battle ended. You saw the look in his eyes when he told Master Uriel about it. It was hungry."

"You don't trust him."

"Ovadia made me swear to bring Master Uriel to Dotan. Master Uriel might listen to me, but will Shimon?"

"If Master Uriel agrees, Shimon will come along to make sure he's safe."

"That's what I'm afraid of. The plan is to sneak past the guards, not confront them. If Shimon won't enter the cave, we're better off without him on the road."

"Tell him that. Tell him that if he's not willing to hide, he shouldn't make the journey."

"He thinks he's protecting Master Uriel."

"Tell him you'll do that."

"He won't listen to me. He knows I couldn't kill the soldier. He thinks I'm a coward."

"He's glad you didn't kill the soldier—the last thing he'd want is for a kohen to kill. You heard what Master Uriel said, that kohanim are forbidden contact with the dead. Think of the debt he owes your father. He wants to protect you."

"Exactly, which means he's not going to listen to me."

"Listen, I think you're worrying about nothing. You ought to be more concerned about convincing Master Uriel. Will he agree to act like a Calf worshiper and then retreat to a cave?"

"I doubt it, but we have to try. Perhaps we shouldn't tell him about hiding? Whether the plan is to fight or hide, he still needs to get to the cave. Let Ovadia convince him to stay put once we're there."

Yonaton snorted. "He's a prophet; don't be a fool. But if you can convince Master Uriel, I'll work on Shimon. Twice he's told me how I impressed him at the battle. I think he'll listen to me."

"So you think it's better to bring him along?"

"Shimon's not stupid—he won't fight unless he has to. And if we have to fight, there's no one I'd rather have on my side."

"You succeeded?" Uriel asked when we returned that evening.

"Yes, Master."

"Where are we to go?"

"The cave of Dotan, Master."

Uriel nodded. "A choice with wisdom. How many are already assembled there?"

"Thirty."

"There will be more."

"Dotan?" Shimon said. "That's north of Shomron. Did Ovadia say how we are to get there?"

I swallowed. "Yes."

Uriel fixed me with a piercing stare, seeing through me as he so often did. "Are we to join the pilgrims returning from Beit El?"

"Ovadia says it's the best way. Hopefully no one will—"

Uriel cut me off. "Very well. So we will do."

I sighed in relief. That part at least was easier than I feared.

Shimon turned to Uriel. "We will be considered among those who bowed to the Calf!"

Uriel shook his head. "I will walk hooded and cloaked. You may do the same. No one will recognize us. If any do, they will understand that we are seeking the cover of the crowd. As Lev said, it is the best way."

"I agree, Master Uriel, that we must reach Dotan," Shimon said, "but perhaps you should seek vision before you decide how. The Holy One may grant us guidance whether this path is really the—"

"It is not the time for vision."

"But why not? Couldn't—"

"I never use prophecy to question my heart. This is true now more than ever. We are being carried by a powerful stream of events—ascending now could make me deaf to the voice of my own heart."

"Which is what?"

"We were told to seek Ovadia—we must heed his advice. Traveling with those returning from Beit El is the safest way to get to Dotan. The only difficulty is the delay. It is essential that we get to Dotan quickly. Even now they may be forming plans to resist Izevel. They will need our guidance."

I sucked in my breath.

The sound drew Uriel's attention. "Is there more, Lev?"

There was no need for Uriel to know the next part until we reached Dotan, but Yonaton was right—Uriel would know if I was hiding anything. "They are not seeking guidance, Master."

"Then the resistance has already begun? All the more so, they will need leadership."

"No, Master, they seek no leader."

THE LAMP OF DARKNESS

"No leader? What, then?"

"There is to be no resistance."

"No resistance?"

"No, Master."

"Then why assemble in Dotan? To hide?"

"Yes, Master."

The prophet shook his head. "I am too old to bury myself in a cave. There is no point in dying hidden. Even being struck down by the sword is better than that; then the people might see the brutality of their so-called Queen and rise up against her."

Shimon stepped between the prophet and me. "Then what shall we do, Master?"

"You were right—I must seek vision. Lev, your kinnor." Uriel lowered himself to the ground.

I hesitated. I had taken two oaths: one to serve Uriel, one to bring Uriel to Dotan. All that day I wondered what I would do should those two oaths conflict. Was Uriel set on resistance even if his death would only be a symbol? What if Ovadia was right? What if my master would prove pivotal once the war was over? "No, Master."

Uriel raised an eyebrow.

"You said it yourself, Master, now is not the time for vision. There must be others resisting Izevel, but the Holy One did not send us to them. We were sent to Ovadia—we should heed his advice."

"Perhaps you are correct, Lev, and I should heed Ovadia's word without seeking further guidance. And perhaps you are wrong. You boys have traveled far today—I have demanded enough words for now. To sleep. Let us each seek the counsel of our dreams."

Riding Balaam, it took most of the day to travel from Shomron, but my dreams returned me there in an instant.

"We killed their prophets and still they resist!" Izevel's said.

"It takes time, my Queen," Yambalya replied, "to uproot a people's connection to their god."

"It is Eliyahu. And this drought."

"The people know nothing of Eliyahu, my Queen, nor do they yet realize there's a drought. Once they do, they will have all the more reason to turn against their prophets."

"Or perhaps they will see Eliyahu as stronger than Baal? What of the hunt? You claimed that your servants have never failed."

"They are Baal's servants, not mine. And they will succeed. I told you, I have seen Eliyahu's future in the stars."

"Yet, for now, they still resist."

"Yes, my Queen, but I have a plan."

She leaned forward. "A plan? What will you do?"

"If her Majesty will be guided by me, then before the moon wanes, half the stubborn ones in Shomron will bend their knees before Baal."

Pale light filled the cave when I woke the next morning. Shimon and Yonaton still slept beside me, but Uriel's mat lay empty. My eyes scanned the back of the cave—Balaam's saddlebags were gone. I got up quickly and pulled my tunic over my head.

Yonaton stirred. "Where are you going?"

"Master Uriel's gone."

Yonaton sat up. "His sleeping mat is still here."

"The saddlebags are missing."

"So?"

"So Master Uriel would take them only if he intended to travel."

"Without us?" Comprehension filled Yonaton's eyes, and he rose to his feet.

Uriel had taken the saddlebags and left without waking us, without even taking his cloak, which Yonaton used as a sleeping mat. Had he decided to journey alone so as not to endanger us? And if my master were headed for a place of safety, would he have left so many of his possessions behind? Uriel said last night that it was better to be struck down than hide. Was he riding now toward a final meeting with Izevel's soldiers? Would he even raise his staff to defend himself this time?

We ran down toward the spring where we left Balaam the night before. From a distance, we saw Uriel tying the saddlebags into place. We were not too late.

"Master," I called, "Don't go!"

Uriel stopped his work. "Lower your voice, Lev. If you are seen with me—"

"Master, Ovadia can protect you."

"I have given much thought to Ovadia's plan, Lev."

"Ovadia made me swear to bring you to Dotan."

Uriel lifted an eyebrow at this. "Ovadia is very devoted." He placed his hand on my shoulder. "As are you."

"It's not just that, Master. The people need you alive."

"I can do little for the people hidden in a cave, Lev."

"But this war will not last forever."

"Not forever, no. But Eliyahu has not attacked with iron chariots. He brought a drought—it may be years until its end."

"You must live. Ovadia says you can save the people."

"Where is the salvation in hiding?"

"When it's over. Ovadia said it might take an Eliyahu to defeat Izevel, but we will need you to heal the people."

"Ovadia is mistaken. He has wisdom, but is still young. He has not seen what I have."

"Which is what, Master?"

"The Holy One always creates the remedy before bringing the malady, though it remains hidden until its proper time. The nation will not be rebuilt by an old man crawling out of a hole. My time has passed."

Yonaton said, "My father taught me that the prophets never lose faith. How can you give up your life? Master?"

Uriel started at the word "master." I had been calling Uriel " master " since returning to him months earlier, but this was the first time that Yonaton had. Uriel peered into Yonaton's eyes. "Give up my life? Certainly not. My life may be the only thing I have left to offer the people, but I will not hand it over needlessly."

"But Master," Yonaton said, "you saddled Balaam and left your sleeping mat behind."

"That is because I must travel a road that he cannot follow." Uriel took Balaam's lead rope and placed it in Yonaton's hand. "And neither can you. I cannot be your master, Yonaton, not now. There are two pieces of bread and a skin of water in the saddlebag. It should be enough to get you home."

Yonaton's eyes dropped to the rope in his hand. "But I want to come with you."

"You have a strong heart. I promised you could stay with us as long as you could help. You have done much, but you can do no more. You are not yet of age and your family is waiting. Your path lies with them now.

"Take Balaam for me. He has been my faithful companion, but he can no longer accompany me."

The significance of his words hit me. "Does that mean we're going to Dotan, Master?"

"Yes, to the cave."

"But you said that Ovadia was mistaken?"

"Indeed, I believe so. But you were correct last night—I was told to seek Ovadia. There is a power at work beyond my own. I must follow the direction I was given."

Uriel shot a glance toward the sun breaking over the horizon, then back at Yonaton. "Tonight is Shabbat. You must leave now to be home before sunset."

I embraced my friend, knowing that it might be for the last time.

"The Cave of Dotan," Yonaton whispered as he tightened his hold around me. "When I'm of age, I'll find you."

"Don't," I replied. "Stay and help your family. There's nothing you can do for us now."

Yonaton released me and pulled the old donkey toward the road. As he had brought no belongings, there was no need for him to return to the cave. I stood watching until he was out of sight. It was only after he disappeared that it occurred to me—I would now have to deal with Shimon on my own.

That evening, before sunset, Shimon and I built the fire high so that it would keep burning into Shabbat. Reclining after we ate, Shimon said to me, "We're following you now."

"We're following Ovadia," I responded, "just as the Holy One instructed Master Uriel."

"The Holy One sent us to Ovadia, but we're following his guidance because of you."

I wouldn't admit it, but Shimon was right. "You think I'm leading us astray?"

"What I think doesn't matter; the decision has been made. I will help in any way I can."

Shimon's sword leaned against the wall of the cave. "Then perhaps you should leave the sword behind," I said.

"Why?"

"It's too easily recognized."

"It will be out of sight. Until needed."

I knew Shimon would refuse, just as I had refused to leave my knife behind during the wedding. If Yonaton was with me, perhaps together we could have pressed him. But how could I persuade him on my own that his eagerness to fight was a danger to all of our lives?

Shimon answered my unspoken thoughts. "Even if your plan is to sneak past the Queen's soldiers, it's best to be prepared." I leaned in to argue, but he wasn't done. "Had your father been so prepared, you might be dining with him now in Yehudah, rather than hiding in this cave."

"What do you mean?" My gaze jumped from Shimon to my master. "You said that my father was murdered for preaching against the Golden Calf?"

"He was," Uriel said. "It was during the Civil War. King Ahav's father, Omri, was locked in struggle for control of the northern kingdom with Tivni. They fought with arms, yes, but mainly the battle was over the hearts of the people. Omri considered the people's reactions to every step that he took, and many of them admired your father. Sending soldiers to his house would have driven many into the arms of Tivni."

"But then why kill him at all? Did he support Tivni?"

"Your father supported neither, but both saw him as an opponent."

"Because he was against the Calf?"

Uriel shook his head. "Because he was for real kingship. He dreamed of a reunification of the two kingdoms. To him, only a descendant of David had the right to rule. Omri aimed to catch your father in an act of rebellion so he could be rid of him without upsetting the people."

"My father rebelled?"

"It was only the appearance of rebellion that mattered to Omri. He knew that Yochanan traveled to Jerusalem to serve in the Temple for each of the three pilgrimage festivals. The roads were well guarded, but your father would lead anyone that he could convince to join him through the mountain passes. Everyone knew that the penalty for crossing was death. If Omri caught your father crossing, he could be rid of him without upsetting the people."

"And my mother?"

"Your father sought my counsel the week before he died. We agreed that it was best for you to be raised in the Kingdom of Yehudah, with his brethren. This is why both you and your mother were with him at the border when the King's soldiers fell upon him."

Shimon fidgeted. "I'm sorry, Lev. I shouldn't have spoken."

"I want to know. Please, tell me."

Shimon stared into the burning coals rather than face me as he spoke. "I was sixteen, making my third journey to Jerusalem with your father. I walked up front near your parents and heard their last conversation."

"What was it about?"

"You."

Something stirred inside me. I knew suddenly that this was the story that had haunted my dreams since age two. Yet, now that I was about to hear the truth, a strange thing happened. There was no longer any need for my memories to remain hidden away. As Shimon spoke, images unfolded in my mind. My mind returned to a crisp autumn day ten years before.

"Lev's cold," Mother said, tightening the shawl that bound me to her back.

"This isn't a place to stop," Father replied, his sharp eyes scanning the mountains on either side of the narrow path. He was older than she was, with the sides of his beard fully gray.

"How much farther?"

"See that ridge up ahead? Once we pass there we'll be out of the territory of Ephraim and into the territory of Binyamin. Then we'll be in the Kingdom of Yehudah."

"And then we'll be safe, Yochanan?"

"Omri's soldiers aren't supposed to cross the border. Still, I never feel safe until I get back on the road." Father gazed into her teary eyes. "I'm sorry, Sarah, I don't mean to scare you."

"It's not that. I was just thinking that I might never return."

He peeked over his shoulder at the twenty men following him through the mountain pass. "You're going to be all right?"

I grabbed at Mother's ear. She took my hand in hers and drew it to her mouth to kiss it. "I just need to remember that I'm doing this for him."

Father continued to scan the surrounding hillsides. His eyes fell upon a lone soldier mounted on horseback. At first he laughed, for there was nothing a single soldier could do against twenty men. The soldier grinned back at my father, raised a ram's horn to his lips, and blew three short, soft blasts.

I stared at Shimon across the fire. "Soft blasts?"

"Yes, soft. It was the softness that alarmed your father. Blasts like that could never be heard all the way in Mitzpah, where the soldiers were stationed. As soon as he heard the blasts, he knew it was a trap."

Father turned back to his followers and screamed "Run!" He grabbed Mother's hand and pulled her along behind him, dragging her toward the safety of the border.

One of the men following behind screamed, "No, this way," and ran back into the Kingdom of Israel. The other followers hesitated, then followed their new leader, separating themselves from my family and the border.

Five soldiers broke into the gap between the two groups. The officer turned to two of his soldiers and said, "The two of you, pursue the large group, but don't catch them. It's enough that the dread of King Omri fall upon them." Two soldiers chased after the group fleeing back into Israel. One soldier banged his sword onto his shield, creating a racket, yet kept his horse at a relaxed trot. The officer addressed the remaining two soldiers. "You follow me," he said, kicking his horse after us.

Father still ran, moving as fast as he could while pulling us behind him. Turning back, he saw that the three soldiers would overtake him before the border. Pushing Mother ahead of him, he yelled, "You run! It's me they're after. Save yourself and Lev. Get him to my brother's family."

"Yochanan!"

"Run, Sarah! If I can follow, I will." He waited until my mother, with me on her back, began running again toward the border, then walked toward the approaching soldiers.

The soldiers pulled up their horses, surrounding him. "Why do you pursue me, Yoav?" Father asked the officer.

"But he must have known why," I insisted.

"Of course he knew," Shimon replied. "But your mother was still running for the border with you on her back. The longer he could keep them talking, the greater chance she would have to reach safety."

"Where were you?"

"Hidden. I couldn't decide which group to follow, and I found myself stuck in the middle. Just before the horses arrived, I ducked behind a boulder."

I felt anger that he did not stand by my father's side. Then I remembered he was only sixteen, not much older than me. Hadn't I also run away from Uriel when the Queen's soldiers came to take his life?

"You know what this is about, Yochanan," Yoav said. "I've warned you myself against defying the King's orders."

"You've already won, Yoav. You've scared away all those following me. Now it's just me, my wife, and my son, and we're leaving Israel, going to join my brethren in Yehudah." As he spoke, he watched my mother pass safely over the border into the Kingdom of Yehudah.

"Oh? Never to return?" Yoav sneered.

"I vow, if you let me go, I will never return."

"You lie!" Yoav thrust with his sword, and Father dove onto the ground to avoid it. He rose to his feet clutching his knife in his hand. He lunged at Yoav, driving the knife into his leg, just above the knee. Yoav screamed in pain and brought down the hilt of the sword on top of Father's head, knocking him to the ground. "You never know when to quit. The rest of your tribe fled to Yehudah long ago. They knew it was over for them here. You refused to go, always defying us. Now your time has come to an end."

"I'm leaving, I swear. You don't need to kill me."

"Did my father intend to return?" I asked Uriel.

"He was moving you and your mother to a safer place, but he intended to keep going back and forth himself. Though now that he was caught, I believe he would have given up on his mission in exchange for his life. I never knew him to break a vow."

"I'm not going to kill you," Yoav said. "I'm going to let my soldiers kill you. I'm going to make sure the Kingdom of Israel never has to suffer you or your seed ever again." Though mother had already crossed the border, he kicked his horse after her."

"You did nothing?" I screamed at Shimon. "This whole time?"

"While Yoav was there, I didn't dare. I would have been throwing away my life. Only once he rode off did I step out from behind the boulder. I hurled a rock at one of the soldiers, striking him in the ear and knocking him to the ground.

"But now I was exposed. The other rider turned on me. I was unarmed, so I kept the boulder between myself and the soldier, forcing him to dismount to get at me. The only thing I had to fend off his attack was my sleeping mat, but reed doesn't hold up for long against iron. That's how I got these." Shimon pointed to his face and pulled back his sleeves to show more scars on his arms.

"Yochanan had already taken many blows, but somehow managed to come to my aid. When I saw him approaching, I screamed as loud as I could. The soldier thought I was yelling out of fear, but I did it to cover your father's footsteps. I'll never forget the look of surprise on the soldier's face when your father planted that knife in his back.

"Yochanan said to me, 'Come...Sarah and Lev.' I seized the soldier's sword and mounted his horse, pulling your father up behind me."

Shimon's bottom lip trembled.

"Go on," Uriel whispered. "He should know this part as well."

"We had not ridden far when Uriel appeared before us on the trail. He held you screaming in his arms."

I turned to my master. "You were there?"

"I also traveled to Jerusalem for the festivals, but I knew my way. I did not need your father's guidance." Uriel's eyes never left the fire. "I was ahead on the path when the ram's horn sounded. I turned back when I heard it. After that, I followed the sound of your cries."

"Will you continue the tale?" Shimon asked.

"No, you should. Now that you've started, he needs to hear it all."

Shimon nodded. "Your father slipped off the horse and took you in his arms—he could barely hold you, he had already lost so much blood. We heard hoofbeats and Yoav appeared, bearing down on us with his sword drawn. Uriel stepped in front of your father, and Yoav pulled back to avoid trampling him.

"Stand aside!" Yoav screamed.

"I'm going where he's going," Uriel replied. "Won't you kill me as well?"

"King Omri grants you passage, but I have my duty."

"And I have mine," Uriel said, still standing between Yoav and my father. "I have two messages, one for you and one for your master."

Yoav's eyes jumped from Uriel to my father to Shimon, who still sat on horseback, sword drawn. Outnumbered, Yoav sheathed his sword. "Very well, prophet. Give me my master's first."

"In two years' time Omri will be victorious. Should he turn away from the path of Yeravaum, opening the road and removing idolatry from the land, then his will be an everlasting kingdom. Otherwise, his will be destroyed as the kingdoms of Yeravaum and Bassa."

Yoav's face was set like stone. "And the message for me?"

"Ride home to your wife, for the child comes."

"But it is not yet time!" He took a deep breath and straightened on his horse. "It is no matter. The child will come with or without me. I cannot leave my post."

"The child you will never know, and your wife is already beyond your help. I am offering you a chance to say goodbye."

"Goodbye?"

"Yes, goodbye. As you judged, so are you judged. You struck down Yochanan's wife and son. The lives of your wife and unborn son will be lost in turn."

"A son?" Yoav looked down on me, crying helplessly in Father's arms. "But Yochanan's son lives!"

"Yes, he lives, but not from your mercy—you left him to die!"

"What if I have mercy on him now?"

"That is not mercy, it is desperation. You think only of yourself, not the child."

"Then she will die? And my son?"

"So it will be."

"And what of me? Will my life be lost for Yochanan's?"

"Your future is in your own hands. You are a man of strength. Turn your strength inward, conquer your anger, and live."

"And if I don't?"

"Then your greatest act of valor will be your last. King Tivni will die by your sword, but you will fall as well."

"Quill," Father said, his voice weak. Uriel gave father a quill and a scrap of parchment from Balaam's saddlebag. Father dipped the quill into the pool of blood at his feet and wrote. "Take," he said, handing the scrap of parchment back to Uriel.

Uriel received the scrap and turned back to Yoav. "Yochanan is dying. Let me take his son to his brethren in Yehudah."

Yoav turned at the sound of approaching horses. The two soldiers that he had sent after Father's followers came to a stop behind him. Yoav straightened himself, and the tone of authority returned to his voice. "I have my duty. King Omri allows you to pass, but no one else."

"Does your duty include killing children, or may he return to his family in Israel?"

Yoav eyed the two soldiers behind him, then turned back to the prophet. "King Omri is just. He does not desire the blood of children. He may return."

Uriel carried me back to Father. "It is time to say goodbye to your child, Yochanan HaKohen."

Father lay his strong hands upon my head. Our eyes met as he blessed me for the last time. He kissed me on the forehead, leaving a small, red mark. While he did this, Uriel tucked the parchment into my garments.

"Take him. Don't let him see me die."

"Shimon, take the child," Uriel said. He dropped his voice so that Shimon had to bend down on the horse to hear him. "Take him to his uncle in Levonah, Menachem son of Yitzchak."

Shimon placed me on the horse in front of him. I screamed, reaching out for Father. "Hold him tighter," Uriel said. "Now ride. He will calm down once we're out of sight."

"Wait!" Father called, holding out his knife. "Take this. It is his birthright."

Uriel passed the knife up to Shimon. Shimon kicked the horse and rode off.

Yoav turned to his two soldiers. "I'm going to follow him, make sure he doesn't make another try for the border. Wait here until Yochanan dies."

"And Uriel?" one of the soldiers asked.

"King Omri grants the prophets leave to go where they will." Yoav kicked his horse to pursue Shimon, but as soon as he was out of sight of the others, he turned his horse and galloped toward Mitzpah.

I felt no sympathy for my parents' murderer. "He got what he deserved."

"What he deserved?" Uriel said. "Perhaps. But could any of us survive in a world where we receive what we deserve?"

"Wouldn't that be justice?"

"Yes, it would. The Holy One created the world with justice, then saw that with justice alone, the world would be destroyed."

"So Yoav lived because there is no justice?"

"There is justice, but the Holy One give us mercy as well."

My fists clenched. "He killed my parents."

"Indeed, and I cursed him for it."

"So where was your mercy then?"

Shimon flinched at the question. This was not the way to address my master, but at the moment I didn't care.

"You must understand," Uriel said, "we are all containers for the light of the Holy One. As we expand mercy in ourselves, it expands in the world. So too the opposite. As we judge, judgment increases in the world, and we are often the first to pay its price." Uriel dropped his hands and turned back to the fire.

During Shimon's tale, I had been focused on myself, hardly noticing the prophet's tears. I assumed that Uriel cried for my father, his lost friend. But in the silence that followed, I began to understand.

Ovadia said two nights earlier that it was essential to rescue Uriel. Not because of what he could do, but because of what he had been through—because of what he had become. Had this been the transformation? Had Uriel shifted from a stance of strict judgment to one of mercy? Was this the reason that he, alone among the prophets, could heal a nation shattered by Eliyahu's judgment?

I remembered Uriel's words from earlier that week. "A curse brings suffering to all. It falls upon the guilty and the innocent alike. Even the one who called down the curse is not spared its destruction."

Back at Shiloh, I was shocked when Zim told me that Uriel's son served the Golden Calf that his father despised. Didn't Zim say he left his father's path ten years ago, exactly when I lost my parents?

"Master?" I trembled. "When you cursed Yoav, were you judged as well?"

A sob shook Uriel's chest. "Indeed."

Shimon's mouth hung open—he must not have known this part of the story.

"At the same time that Yoav's wife died, my wife left the world as well. By then, I had reached Jerusalem and did not know until I returned weeks later. My son was forced to bury his mother alone."

Shimon asked, "Is that why he left the Way and turned toward the Calf?"

"So he says. As you know, I spent my life traveling among the people. I was often away, and he resented it. He said that burying his mother alone was the final act that pushed him to leave my path. But even he doesn't know the full truth: that it was my curse that drove him from me.

"Three families destroyed on a single day!"

Hillel said: Do not believe in yourself until the day you die.

Pirkei Avot 2:5

19

The Final Journey

The full moon hung in the western sky when we set out from the cave three days later. We stopped well before dawn hiding a stone's throw from the road in a clump of bushes. I lay down, and soon fell asleep.

A rumbling woke me. I opened my eyes to see it was full daylight.

"What's that noise?"

"Horses," Uriel replied. "Thirty at least, from the sound of it, being driven hard. The King and his escort."

"Ovadia will be with them?"

"I expect so. You may go back to sleep; we still have a long wait."

I sat up and pulled on my tunic, knowing I wouldn't be able to fall back asleep. The rumbling grew louder until the horses thundered past.

Other horsemen followed the King's escort, riding past in ones and twos. Next came those on donkeys, ambling past in small groups. It was midday when the first walkers appeared. Before long, the road was thick with travelers.

"It is time."

I crept out of the bushes and sat beneath a tree on the roadside. When a gap in the crowd left the road in front of me empty, I ran one hand over the strings of my kinnor.

Uriel and Shimon appeared beside me, and we all took to the road, walking quickly until we mingled in with the back of the group in front of us. Occasionally we saw soldiers stationed on hilltops next to the road, but they would not be able to pick us out in this crowd returning from Beit El.

The numbers of travelers on the road thinned as the day wore on, as men turned off toward their homes. In the late afternoon, we rounded a bend and saw a cluster of men stopped ahead, just before the shade of a large carob tree.

"What's going on up there?" Shimon asked.

Uriel stood to his full height. "Soldiers."

"Israelite or foreigners?"

"Foreigners."

"A roadblock. Should we turn off?"

Uriel pointed toward the sides of the road. "They have soldiers stationed along the hillsides. They will be watching for anyone trying to avoid them. We are better off walking through."

At first I didn't spot them—they were not like the lookouts sitting mounted on the hilltops. These watchers were further down, in the shadows, where they could see without being seen.

Shimon's body tensed as he studied the soldiers bordering the roadside. His hand slipped under his cloak to the hilt of his sword.

I inched closer to him and whispered, "Remember, Master Uriel must reach Dotan."

Shimon released the hilt and placed his hand on my shoulder instead. "I know the plan."

We drew closer to the roadblock. Uriel said, "There's a priest of the Baal as well. Under the tree."

I craned my neck to see. Sure enough, I saw a man in violet robes in the shade of the carob tree. Soldiers forced the travelers to pass under the tree one at a time. A man in a gray cloak stepped under the tree, dropped to his knees and pressed his forehead to the ground.

"Clever," Uriel said.

"What's clever, Master?"

"Izevel is most powerful in Shomron, but many are opposed to her, even there. So she waited until all the men of the city left for the festival, then placed a Baal on their path home. Now she can see who will bow and who will resist."

"We must get through, Master."

"I will not bow before the Baal."

"Even to save your life?" Yet, I knew Uriel placed too little value on his life. "Even to save my life?"

"Some things are more precious than life, Lev."

Shimon's hand returned to the hilt of his sword. "You see, Lev, I was right to prepare for battle."

"There are three soldiers ahead and at least five more on the hillsides—you can't fight them all!"

"Samson killed a thousand in a single battle. You heard Master Uriel, Lev. The spirit I received was the same as Samson's."

"You don't know if you'll merit that power again."

"No, I don't. But even if I don't, I won't be fighting alone."

"There's not much Uriel or I could do against all these soldiers."

"It's not just the three of us. It's easy to scare the people one at a time, but in their arrogance they've become reckless. The crowd is moving through too slowly. There are fifty men waiting and more coming up behind us. If we resist, we will draw support—especially if it's known that we are led by a prophet."

I wanted to believe him, but I remembered the fear on the faces of farmers at the wedding. "But these men aren't armed. They will run at the first sight of blood."

Uriel shook his head. "It matters not if they are armed. Izevel is seeking to strengthen her support, not to spark a rebellion. Her soldiers will not fight so many, even if they could."

My mind raced. If all the men rallied around Uriel, we might get through the roadblock, but the soldiers were sure to learn there was a prophet in their midst. They could follow us and bring others to their aid. Any violence would mean abandoning the plan, and I had sworn to deliver my master safely to Dotan.

We were close enough now to see the statue, a larger version of the one now resting in my uncle's house. It stood on a wooden pedestal beneath the tree. Another farmer stepped forward, and he too bowed before the Baal. A thought occurred to me. "Master, if Izevel is afraid of a rebellion, then her soldiers cannot be killing all those who refuse to bow, can they?"

Uriel shook his head. "No, Lev, you must be correct. There are still too many in Israel, even in Shomron, that would refuse."

"So what happens to them? Are they allowed to pass?"

"Let us watch. There are fifty or more who still stand before us—I would expect at least ten to refuse."

One after another the soldiers waved the men forward. Some bowed quickly, falling to their knees and touching their foreheads to the ground. Others hesitated, then bent at the waist, like the men in Jericho bowing before the King. Yet, each and every one of them humbled himself in some way before passing through.

Hardly ten men now stood between us and the tree. The crowd waiting to pass only grew longer as more men arrived. Shimon's eyes darted back and forth between Uriel and the soldiers. "If we're going to fight, we need to warn the men. Are we agreed?"

Shimon was right. If we were going to act, it must be now. I trusted Uriel's instincts—there was no sign that the soldiers were killing those who refused to bow. If they were, where were the bodies? But no one refused, so I couldn't know for sure. My vow to Ovadia turned over in my mind. There was only one chance to prevent the violence that would ruin our plan.

"I'll go."

"What?" Shimon started.

"I'll go to the head of the line. I'll refuse to bow. If they let me through, you follow with Uriel. If they…if not, then fight."

"Wait, Lev, I don't think—"

But I didn't wait to hear what Shimon thought. My small size allowed me to slip easily to the front. A soldier put out his arm, blocking me from going until the man under the tree passed. Like all the others, he too bowed down before the Baal.

The soldier's arm dropped, and I stepped forward.

My eyes were on the priest, but my thoughts were on the soldiers.

The priest approached. "Bow. Then go on."

I stood silent and still, holding my arms tight so they wouldn't tremble.

The priest insisted, "You bow. Do it now, then go."

I didn't move.

The priest moved closer. "You not bow? Baal angry. Curse the rain."

One of the soldiers turned to watch me now. But still I didn't move.

The priest leaned in and spoke in a whisper. "Don't bow. Just pick up and go." A copper piece dropped from his hand onto the ground before the statue.

I almost laughed. Uriel was right; not all the men ahead of us wanted to bow. That's why they were only allowed through one at a time. Most men, seeing those ahead of them bow, would bow as well. Any who refused just had to pick a piece of copper off the ground. Those behind—who were not watching closely enough to see the precious metal—would think they were bowing from the waist.

"Pick up. You keep copper."

Hardly anyone among the men returning from the festival of the Golden Calf would refuse to pick up the copper. But what about those who refused to give even the impression of bowing? Was that the real point of the roadblock? To find the prophets and disciples hidden among the commoners?

What about Shimon and Uriel? Would they pick up the copper to save their lives?

One of the soldiers stepped in toward me—I had delayed for too long. I could pick up the metal and get past the Baal, but needed to do it in a way that Shimon and Uriel would realize I wasn't bowing. I stepped to the side, then bent down and picked up the copper. Anyone watching closely would see that I wasn't even facing the Baal. Yet, it was enough—the priest waved me through.

Once out of the shade of the carob tree, I turned around to watch. Neither the soldiers nor the priest paid me any mind—to them, I was just a boy waiting for his father to pass through.

Easy as it was to pass through the roadblock, would Shimon still refuse? I caught Shimon's eye and gave him the slightest of nods, the most communication I could risk with the soldiers so close. But Shimon just glared back, his eyes hard.

Three more men passed through the roadblock, two dropping quickly to the ground, the third bending to pick up the offered metal. Shimon drifted ahead of Uriel, placing several men between them.

The soldier on the far side of the road looked up as Shimon approached—his scars distinguished him from the crowd even without the fresh wounds. Did the soldiers know that four Tzidonian soldiers had been killed the previous week? Could they be on the lookout for their killers?

Shimon stepped up to the priest.

"You bow. Then go on."

Shimon's voice was calm, yet pitched to carry. "The people of Israel do not bow to the Baal."

A murmur rose from the edge of the waiting pack. One of the soldiers left his post at the side of the road and stepped under the tree. His hand rested on the hilt of his sword. Black jagged lines decorated his neck before disappearing beneath his tunic. I'd heard rumors of the coastal people's tattoos, but had never seen them before.

Shimon met the soldier's gaze.

The priest waived the soldier back. He retreated, but kept his eyes on Shimon. The priest leaned close and whispered, dropping a piece of copper to the ground. Shimon looked down at the metal but did not move.

I wanted to scream at him to take it. I bit my lower lip until I tasted blood. How stupid I had been. An old man and a boy would have passed through easily. Shimon had no desire to hide. He had accompanied us only to help Uriel reach safety. Yet, his scars and stubbornness made him our greatest danger.

Once Uriel had agreed to join the crowd returning from Beit El, the time had come to part ways. I should have confronted him, even without Yonaton. What would happen to my master if Shimon refused?

The soldier stepped forward once more, this time loosening his sword in its sheath. The priest again waved him away, but the soldier retreated just halfway. The priest pulled another piece of metal from his pocket, this time silver. He didn't just drop the silver on the ground; he rolled it to where Shimon could pick it up without even bending in the Baal's direction.

Shimon locked eyes with the soldier, whose sword was now half drawn. Then he broke eye contact and bent down to pick up the silver.

As Shimon bent over, his cloak parted in front. The hilt of his sword peeked out between the fabric, revealing the cedar tree emblem engraved on the handle. The priest was no longer watching, but the tattooed soldier was.

The soldier leapt forward, drawing his sword. Shimon grabbed for his own weapon, but in his bent over position his enemy was faster. The tattooed soldier struck and Shimon fell limp to the ground.

My teeth sliced my lip—I must not scream. Shimon was beyond my help. I must save my master.

The priest ran forward and slapped the soldier's face, pointing wildly at the crowd of men waiting to get through the roadblock. But he was no longer in charge.

The tattooed soldier called to the other soldiers. They were eight in all, with the tattooed appearing to be their leader. He pointed to Shimon's body, and another soldier ran forward, grabbed Shimon's arms, and dragged him to the side of the road.

The soldiers may have been heavily outnumbered, but they were the only ones armed. They bunched together under the carob tree, backs to the trunk, ready to defend themselves.

Though shock and anger flashed across the faces of the Israelite men, their fear proved stronger. There was no outcry from the crowd, and no one advanced to attack.

Seeing themselves unchallenged, the soldiers broke their defensive position. The tattooed soldier pushed the priest back toward the Baal. Then he screamed at the man in front of the line, "Come. You bow now!"

The man dropped to the ground, turning his head to avoid looking at the blood. Another man bowed, then ran back toward the open road. Uriel now approached.

The prophet stepped up to the priest.

"You bow. Then go on."

Uriel's face held none of Shimon's defiance—it was radiant, his eyes distant.

The priest stepped closer to whisper in Uriel's ear and dropped a copper to the ground.

The smile on Uriel's face stretched as he bent his head forward. He was bending down to pick up the copper! But I was wrong; Uriel merely brought his chin to his chest and held it there.

At first I didn't understand what my master was doing. I could barely contain the urge to scream, "Take it! Take it!"

Then I understood.

The prophet would neither bow nor pick up the copper. He wouldn't fight or resist. He was offering the back of his neck to the sword. Uriel would give up his life quietly, a martyr before a mass of witnesses. His death would be a symbol of the brutality of the Baal and the Queen. Just as he wanted.

Why hadn't I let Shimon fight? He was already armed and surrounded by fifty men. The priest's reaction showed that the soldiers were there mainly to scare the people, not to kill.

And what if Shimon received the Divine spirit again—then nothing could have stood before him. But now he lay dead on the side of the road because he had listened to me, while Uriel stood with his neck exposed, awaiting a similar fate.

The tattooed soldier had still not sheathed his sword. Another group of travelers reached the roadblock, making more than sixty men who now stood watching.

I reached under my tunic and gripped the handle of my father's knife. If I fought, would I receive the same spirit Shimon had? If I was determined to succeed, would the Holy One give me the strength to battle these soldiers?

The tattooed soldier advanced toward Uriel. The priest stepped between them, pointing back toward the side of the road. The soldier pushed him out of the way.

I loosened my blade in its sheath, my fingers whitening on the hilt. If I was going to act, the time was now.

As I drew the blade from under my tunic, Zim's voice rose in my heart. "Remember, if you believe it, it's true."

The soldier raised his sword above Uriel.

I sheathed my knife and ran forward screaming, "Grandfather, Grandfather!"

The soldier's arm stopped.

I grabbed Uriel's hand, placing myself between my master and the sword.

"He's not right in the head," I begged the soldier, loud enough for all the Israelite men to hear.

A shadow of doubt dimmed the tattooed soldier's eyes.

"He'd bow to your sandal if you wanted him to, but we'd never get him up off the ground."

"He bow." The soldier swept his arm across the waiting crowd. "They all bow."

"He's just an old man," I insisted.

Murmurs of protest rose from the waiting men. They watched Shimon die, but were now starting to rouse themselves. A tall farmer at the front of the line shoved his chest against the arm of the soldier holding him back. "Let the old man go through!"

I turned to the priest. "Could my grandfather have one of those pieces of copper? It would mean so much to him."

The priest stepped forward, pushing the tattooed soldier back. "Go," he said. "Don't bow, just go." The priest thrust a piece of copper into my hand and pushed the two of us through.

Uriel allowed me to guide him out of the shade of the carob tree, past the remaining soldiers. The radiance departed from his face. He said nothing as we fled, just walked on in silence.

As the roadblock shrank into the distance behind us, the reality of our situation settled in. My success had sealed our fate: we were heading into hiding. We would live in the darkness of the cave until redemption came.

I thought about Eliyahu—more hunted than any of us. I had never seen drought myself, but the elders of Levonah spoke of the terrible suffering it brought. How many dry seasons would it take for the people to stand up to the tyranny of Queen Izevel?

The nearly full moon rose above the horizon just as we reached the hills ringing Shomron. Still silent, my master pointed toward a small path that turned off the road. We pressed on through fields and clumps of trees until we came to an orchard on a terraced hillside.

Uriel climbed the hillside until we came to an old olive tree at the base of a cliff. Uriel stepped behind it, disappearing from view. I followed, slipping sideways through a crack in the cliff wall.

I crept forward in the darkness, my fingers brushing the stone walls that squeezed steadily inward. Then the walls opened and the echo of my footsteps told me we had entered a large cavern.

A flame emerged in the distance. A man with a short, gray beard beckoned to us to follow. We walked along a passageway, every now and then passing openings in the darkness. I had never been in so intricate a cave before, with so many caverns and passageways. Was this another one of those caves carved out in the time of Gidon?

The Final Journey

We stepped into an empty cavern, and Uriel had to duck to avoid striking his head on the cavern roof. Our guide placed his lamp in a niche in the wall, then bowed to Uriel and stepped back into the darkness.

I surveyed the chamber in the weak light: my new home. The events of the past week had uprooted everything I knew. There would be no sunshine in the cave, no Yonaton, no Dahlia. Yet I was still alive, which was more than could be said for Shimon or Tzadok.

Drained from the journey, I laid out my sleeping mat. Uriel knelt down in front of the lamp, contemplating it with unblinking eyes.

Despite my exhaustion, I asked, "What do you see, Master?"

"All things above are reflected below. So it is with the lamp of darkness, reflected in the flame."

"You see darkness in the flame?"

"Look closely at the center. Darkness surrounds the wick, consuming it, yet giving off no light."

I moved closer, examining the flame.

"That is the shadow of the lamp of darkness. Beneath the darkness is a thin layer of sapphire, the color of the Throne of Glory, on which the Holy One sits. The darkness appears greater than the blue, but does not dim its brilliance."

"It's the other way around. The darkness makes the blue seem even brighter."

"Indeed. So it is with our world. No amount of darkness can destroy the light, no matter how deep the darkness grows."

Uriel sighed. "The order of the world has flipped. Once, light dwelled above and shadows filled the caves. Now darkness will reign over the land and light will retreat underground."

My master turned away from the lamp to face me, the fire reflected in his bright eyes. "It appears, Lev, son of Yochanan HaKohen, that we have the time to begin your education after all."

Did you enjoy
The Lamp of Darkness?

Connect with us to stay up to date with all of our projects, including a special sneak peak at Book 2,

The Key of Rain

Find out more at
TheAgeofProphecy.com/young-readers

Also, we love hearing from our readers. Send author Dave Mason a personal email at **Dave@TheAgeofProphecy.com** to tell him a bit about who you are, what your passions are, and what you enjoyed most about The Lamp of Darkness. All emails get a reply.

Glossary

Ahav: Also known as Ahab.

Am Yisrael: The nation of Israel.

Avdei Canaanim: Non-Israelite slaves (plural).

Avadim Ivrim: Israelite slaves (plural).

Binyamin: Also known as Benjamin.

Bnei Nevi'im: Literally the children of the prophets, figuratively their students.

Dvekut: Cleaving to the Divine.

Eliyahu: Also known as Elijah.

Emek HaAsefa: Literally, the valley of gathering. A fictional location.

Eved: Slave.

Eved Canaani: A non-Israelite slave.

Eved Ivri: An Israelite slave.

Halil: A straight flute.

Hevron: Also known as Hebron.

Ish Elokim: A man of G-d.

Izevel: Also known as Jezebel or Isabel.

Kohanim: Priests (plural).

Kohen: A Priest.

Kinnor: An instrument that most resembles an ancient lyre.

Labneh: A sour, spreadable cheese.

Malkosh: The late rains.

Matnat Ro'im: The shepherd's gift.

Navi: Prophet.

Navi'im: Prophets.

Navua: Prophecy.

Nefesh: The lowest level of the soul.

Neshama: A higher level of the soul.

Nevel: An instrument that most resembles an ancient harp.

Nigun: A melody, usually without words.

Niggunim: Plural of Nigun.

Pesach: Passover.

Shalom: Peace, also used as a greeting.

Shavuot: Also known as Pentecost or the Feast of Weeks.

Shomron: Also known as Samaria.

Sukkah: The temporary huts built during the festival of Sukkot.

Sukkot: The Festival of Booths when we build and live in temporary huts.

Tefillah: Prayer.

Tikun: Fixing.

Totafot: Also known as Tefillin or Phylacteries.

Yericho: Also known as Jericho.

Yerushalayim: Also known as Jerusalem.

Yisrael: Also known as Israel.

Yoreh: The early rains.

Yovel: The fiftieth year, called Jubilee year in English.

About the Authors

Dave Mason

Mike Feuer

Dave and Mike have led bizarrely parallel lives. Born just four days apart, they both grew up in secular, Jewish, suburban communities, then found their way to Colorado College. Despite having friends, interests, and even one class in common, they remained complete strangers. Dave then backpacked through over a dozen countries including Syria, China, and Cuba, while Mike lived in the woods for two years, immersed in wilderness therapy with at-risk youth.

Later, both turned their attention to the environment. Dave went to NYU Law and subsequently became a litigator for the Natural Resources Defense Council (NRDC). Mike studied desert agriculture and water resource management, but ultimately found his calling as a teacher.

Fifteen years after first becoming classmates, the two finally met as part of a core group formed to create a new kind of Torah study institution in Jerusalem, called Sulam Yaakov. There, they became study partners, close friends, and both became ordained as Orthodox Rabbis. Dave was blown away by his studies about the inner workings of prophecy, and was surprised at how little exposure he had to this crucial part of his tradition. He decided to create The Age of Prophecy to bring this world to light for others like himself.

Mike joined the project initially as a research assistant, bringing an expertise in the terrain, history, and stories of the Bible to the book. His deep involvement earned him contributing author status, though Mike prefers the term creative co-conspirator.

Professionally, Dave is a businessman, social entrepreneur, and business strategist. He and his wife Chana live in the eclectic Nachlaot neighborhood of Jerusalem, where they homeschool their son, Aryeh Lev.

Mike lives with his family outside of Jerusalem, at the edge of the Judean wilderness.